THE SECRET GUESTS

B. W. BLACK

ISIS
LARGE
PRINT

First published in Great Britain 2020
by
Penguin Books
Penguin Random House UK

First Isis Edition
published 2021
by arrangement with
Penguin Random House UK

A catalogue record for this book is available
from the British Library.

ISBN 978–1–78541–936–2

Published by
Ulverscroft Limited
Anstey, Leicestershire

Set by Words & Graphics Ltd.
Anstey, Leicestershire
Printed and bound in Great Britain by
TJ Books Ltd., Padstow, Cornwall

This book is printed on acid-free paper

To C.M.
. . . and his father

The young girl stood in the darkness before the tall window and watched with excitement and fascination the bombs falling on the city. The sky in the east, where the docks were, flared and flashed in all sorts of colours, yellow and blue and pink and mauve, and big clouds of smoke, red-rimmed, billowed up. It was as if Guy Fawkes Night had come early. Or no: it seemed a sort of theatrical event, like the last act of an opera, the whole performance conducted by the sweeping batons of the searchlights.

Indeed, she saw herself as a figure on a stage, standing there, with the enormous, shadowed room behind her and the sky in the distance on fire.

Then something came flying swiftly out of the dark and banged against the pane in front of her, making her jump. After the first shock she stepped nearer to the window and saw the bird on the gravel outside, lying on its back with its wings tucked against its sides with unnatural neatness. It was twitching, and its eyes were open: she could see them shining like little black beads in the glare from the sky. What kind of bird was it? Not an owl — could there be owls here in the middle of the city? — but it might be a starling, or even a small crow.

1

She knew it was going to die, and even as she watched, the twitching stopped, and the wings went slack.

She imagined people over at the docks, workers, sailors, firemen, people in the streets and even in their homes, dying like that, with their arms pressed tight against their sides and staring into the flaming sky, and then their eyes dimming and their arms going limp.

The door opened behind her.

"What are you doing?" her sister asked sharply.

The girl didn't turn from the window. "Nothing," she said.

Her sister came forward swiftly and pulled the heavy curtains shut, making the rings rattle on the rail high above. "Don't you know there's a blackout?"

Her sister was four years older than she was, and terribly bossy.

"The lights weren't on."

"It doesn't matter — the rule is to keep the curtains drawn at all times after dark."

The little girl sighed. Her name was Margaret. She was ten.

"A bird flew into the window and was killed," she said. "It's outside, on the ground, if you want to see it."

"You shouldn't be here, standing at the window. If a bomb fell there would be a blast and the glass would shatter and you would be killed."

"Would they drop bombs on us, here?"

This was a possibility she hadn't thought of before. She was curious to know what it would be like, to be blown up. But the Palace was so big it wouldn't collapse, surely. Only the roof would be damaged, and chimney pots knocked over.

"They drop bombs everywhere," her sister said. "Now come along — Mummy and Daddy are waiting for us."

She led the way out of the room. They went along a broad corridor where there were chandeliers, and rows of gilt chairs facing each other on either side, and big ornate mirrors on the walls, impassive as sentries.

As they walked, Margaret studied her sister with interest. "You're shaking," she said.

"What?"

"Are you frightened of the bombs?"

Her sister would not look at her. "Of course I'm not frightened."

They came to a pair of broad double doors, with two footmen in livery standing to attention, one on either side.

"I wonder why the bird flew into the window," Margaret said thoughtfully. "Maybe it was frightened, too, of all the noise and the lights."

The footmen stepped forward smartly, each one opening his side of the double doors to allow the girls through.

The large, high-ceilinged drawing room had faded gold wallpaper and a dark-yellow carpet. There was a chandelier, too. Big blurred paintings, portraits, mostly, in varied shades of black and brown and red, leaned out a little way from the walls, as if the people in them were listening intently to everything that went on in the room. There was an enormous marble fireplace, with an

3

absurdly small coal fire smoking in the grate: in wartime it was the duty of everyone to use fuel sparingly.

The girls' father, tall and lean and wearing a three-piece suit of grey tweed, stood by the mantelpiece with a glass of sherry in one hand and a cigarette in the other. Their mother, in a green silk dress, her hair a layered helmet of marcelled waves, sat on a chintz sofa; she also had a cigarette and a glass, though hers had gin in it.

"Hello there, you two!" their father said cheerily. A cluster of bombs landed somewhere not far off, shaking the windows in their frames, and he added, "Frightful racket, what?"

He had a slight stammer, which got worse when he was excited or upset.

After fifteen minutes the sirens sounded the all-clear. Margaret and her father had seated themselves at a small round table with curlicued legs and lion's-paw feet. They were playing draughts. Her mother, still reclining on the sofa, was flicking through a copy of *Punch*. The older sister was sitting in an armchair with a book open on her lap. It was plain she was only pretending to read. Margaret glanced at her now and then with narrowed eyes; her sister, she could see, was still afraid, even though the bombing had stopped.

Their father made a move on the board. "Aha!" he exclaimed in triumph. "See, you'll have to king me!"

Margaret laughed disparagingly. "Then you'll be a king twice over."

4

"That's r-right!" her father said, flushing a little at the difficulty of getting the word out; he was ashamed of his stammer, or "speech impediment", as her mother encouraged her to call it, though in fact it was rarely referred to, and never in her father's hearing. She felt embarrassed for him. She didn't know any other grown-up who had a stammer.

"Lilibet, my dear," the woman on the sofa said to her older daughter, where she sat clutching her book on her knees, "are you sure you both have everything packed and ready? Miss Nashe will be here very shortly."

"Yes," the girl replied, "everything is ready."

She kept her eyes fixed on the book. Margaret looked across at her again. The atmosphere in the room had become tense.

"You shall have to be brave, both of you," their mother said, in a lightened tone. "It will only be for a little while, and then we shall all be together again."

"Why can't we just go to Scotland, and you could come with us?" Margaret asked.

"Because your father and I must stay here, to be with the people and share in their — in their —"

"In their what?" the younger girl demanded.

"Their bravery," her father said. "And to show Mr Hitler we're not afraid of him and his bombs, and that we shall never give in to his b-bullying." He turned to his elder daughter. "Isn't that so, Lilibet?"

"Yes, Daddy," the girl in the armchair said. Her father began to move a draught, changed his mind and sat thinking. Margaret again gave her sister a narrow look, and, unseen by their parents, made a simpering face and stuck out her tongue.

"I can't see how it's being brave to send us off to Ireland," she said. "That seems more like running away to me."

Her mother and father exchanged a glance.

"I sometimes think," the King said, smiling across the draught-board at his younger daughter, "that we should set you on to Mr Hitler, my dear. I'm sure you would frighten him half to death, just by looking at him!"

Outside, the sirens started up again. The girl in the armchair lifted her eyes from her book to the curtained windows and turned another page.

CHAPTER
ONE

Detective Garda Strafford stood at the foot of the steps of the Kildare Street Club and glanced for the third or fourth time up the road in the direction of Government Buildings. The minister was ten minutes late — deliberately so, Strafford was sure: self-important men never passed up an opportunity, however trivial, to demonstrate their importance.

It was a warm October lunchtime, the sun was hanging about the sky somewhere, and the air was suffused with a pale-gold haze. Strafford, congenitally thin, wore a three-piece suit of dark tweed that hung loosely on his tall, skeletal frame, a dark-green shirt and a dark tie. In his right hand he held a soft felt hat, and a gabardine trench coat was draped over his left arm. His hair was so pale it was almost colourless, and a lock of it at the front had a tendency to droop over his eyes, so that he had to keep pushing it back into place with a quick gesture of his hand and four extended stiff fingers.

He looked up the street again.

Strange to think of a war going on in Europe while everything here was dreamily at peace, or at least looked to be. The Irish Republic, having declared itself neutral in the conflict, and intending to stay that way, didn't even call the war "the war", referring to it instead as the "Emergency". The pub wits had a lot of jokes about that.

The minister of external affairs, Daniel Hegarty — Dan the Man, as he liked to be known among the party faithful and, more importantly, among the public, especially at election time — the person on whom Strafford was impatiently waiting, had the reputation of being halfway civilised. In his youth he had studied for a time at Heidelberg, and was said to have dined once with W. B. Yeats and Lady Gregory at the Russell Hotel. This side of things he played down, however. It was a mainstay of his political strategy to pretend to be a simple countryman, though he was nobody's fool, as everybody knew.

A large, shiny black car drew up to the kerb. The black-suited driver hopped out smartly and opened the rear door, and the minister himself emerged, putting on his hat.

He was in his early forties, though he looked older. In shape he resembled a slightly compressed and elongated Guinness barrel. The impression was emphasised by a voluminous long black winter overcoat, the great girth of which was compressed a little at what would have been the waist, if the man had had a waist, by a broad belt tightly buckled. His head was remarkably large, much too much so for his features, which were crowded together in the middle of a face as wide and round as a dinner plate. He wore rimless spectacles and sported a small black moustache, like a smudged, sooty thumbprint applied to the groove under his nose, which was a godsend to his opponents, whose nickname for him was "Adolf". His little washed-blue eyes were deep-set in folds of fat, and his mouth, which made Strafford think of the valve of a football, was drawn down sharply at the corners. It was said his bark was worse than his bite — though there were quite a few people in politics who could show you the tooth marks he had left on various tender parts of their anatomy — and that when he was with his cronies he liked to relax over a bottle of porter or a glass of whiskey. He had even been known to crack the odd joke and, at the end of the hooley on the last night of the annual party conference, to sing a rebel song, in an unexpectedly light baritone voice.

"Are you Strafford?" he demanded. He had a strong Cork accent. "What age are you? You look like you should still be in shorts."

He shook hands perfunctorily with the detective. His hand was moist and warm and surprisingly small, almost dainty, and for a moment Strafford entertained the notion that within the folds of that enormous overcoat there was concealed a tiny woman, a female assistant, even a wife or daughter, whom the minister bore along in front of him everywhere he went to perform his handshakes. Strafford often came up with such droll notions. It made him think he must be fundamentally frivolous, surely a serious weakness in a policeman, though he didn't know what he could do about it.

The two men climbed the steps, passing between the polished stone pillars on either side, and Strafford drew open the door with its big square glass panel and stood back to let the minister enter ahead of him. Should he mention the legend that the glass had been put into the door during the War of Independence so that if there was a raid the gunmen could be seen coming up the steps? Of course not, no, he thought, remembering in time that in those days the minister himself had been a gunman. Strafford had considered pointing out, too, further along the outside wall, the frieze with the carved stone monkeys playing billiards, a striking curiosity — whose idea had they been? But he doubted that Dan the Man would be interested in such fanciful details.

Unlike Strafford, Minister Hegarty took himself very seriously indeed.

From the open doorway a waft of thick warm air came out to meet them, heavy with the odours of cigar smoke, overcooked beef, old wine and old men. The Kildare Street Club represented the unofficial headquarters of Anglo-Irish Protestant Ireland. Strafford could see from the way the minister darted glances here and there, attempting to square his unsquarably fat and sloping shoulders, that he was not only unfamiliar with the place but was intimidated by it, too.

The minister removed his hat and struggled out of his overcoat. He wore a tightly buttoned double-breasted suit of navy-blue serge, a white shirt with a high, stiff collar, and a dark-blue tie with a tiny knot that looked as if it hadn't been undone since he was a young man. From the moment he'd stepped out of the car the minister had reminded Strafford of someone, and now he realised who it was. In that constricted suit and strangling tie, with his big head and a thin slick of shiny black hair stuck to his pale damp forehead, he was the dead spit of Oliver Hardy.

A stooped, white-haired old fellow in a dusty tailcoat materialised suddenly before them — he might have risen at that moment out of a concealed trapdoor in the floor — and the minister started back, clutching his overcoat and his hat possessively to his chest.

"I'm here to see —" he began.

"Yes, yes, Mr Hegarty," the doorman interrupted, reaching for the minister's things. "This way, please."

Hegarty threw the detective a wild look — how had the porter known who he was? — and Strafford smiled and nodded encouragingly. He knew his way around places like this. His father had been a country member of the club, though he had long ago let his membership lapse. When Strafford's father had come up for his regular weekend once a month he used to amuse himself by standing in the bay of the big window that gave on to Nassau Street, in his loudest check suit and matching waistcoat, with his hands clasped behind his back and his watch chain and silk pocket-handkerchief, the tokens of his class, prominently on show, glaring down at the passers-by.

The minister was at last induced to relax his hold on his overcoat and hat, and the elderly porter took them, and draped the coat over his arm and set the hat on top of it, and led the two men to the bar.

11

It occurred to Strafford that, in the same way that Hegarty looked the spit of Olly Hardy, perhaps he himself, in his turn, resembled a young Stan Laurel, pale and spindly as he was, with concave chest and narrow head and mild, distracted manner. He had to press his lips tightly together to stop himself grinning. His mother, long dead, used to say, when he was a boy, that he had an unnatural sense of humour, and he thought that on the whole she was right, although as he grew to manhood he had learned to keep it more or less in check. He had always been a solitary, and his private jokes were a kind of company for him, like, he supposed, a child's imaginary friends.

The bar was empty, save for the barman, in striped trousers and a black waistcoat. The minister ordered a Jameson.

"I suppose you're not able to have a drink, being on duty," he said to Strafford.

"Well, I'm not sure I am on duty, strictly speaking, Minister. I'll take a Bushmills."

Hegarty sniffed. Bushmills, of course: the Protestants' tipple.

The barman set the two tumblers of tawny liquor on the counter, pointing out which was which, then placed beside each one a glass of plain water.

Hegarty lifted the glass of Jameson. "*Sláinte,*" he said, with the hint of a challenge; he was known to be very hot on the language question, and had once even proposed a ten-year plan to make the speaking of Irish compulsory throughout the country. He wore a little circular gold pin in his lapel to proclaim himself a *Gaeilgeoir*.

Strafford, too, took up his glass. "*Sláinte*," he responded stoutly; social life was a minefield, in this still young nation.

They drank in silence for a while, facing the mirror and the ranked bottles behind the bar. Hegarty looked at his watch. "He should be here by now, shouldn't he?" he said testily. "I thought your crowd were always punctual."

Strafford knew exactly what was meant by "your crowd". He was one of the very few non-Catholics on the Garda Force, and, so far as he knew, the only Protestant at detective level. He had enjoyed rapid advancement — he had been on the force for only a couple of years when he was taken off the beat and promoted to the rank of detective — though he still wasn't entirely sure why he had joined in the first place. Maybe he had wanted to make a gesture of support for the new order. Protestants constituted only five per cent of the population of the Republic, and the majority of them had quietly withdrawn from public life after independence, leaving the running of the place to the new Catholic bourgeoisie.

Strafford was a son of the Anglo-Irish ascendancy — though as an individual he could not have been further from one of Yeats's hard-riding country gentlemen — and he had a slightly shamefaced sense of duty, towards what, exactly, he couldn't have said. At any rate, he had by now reconciled himself to his anomalous position as a Protestant member of an almost exclusively Catholic institution of state, and hardly thought about it except on those occasions when it was brought forcibly to his attention.

He and the minister had almost finished their drinks and still there was no sign of the official from the British embassy who was the reason for them being there. Strafford could hear the minister breathing down his nostrils, the sound of a man of consequence feeling slighted and having a hard time controlling his temper. Minister Hegarty was not accustomed to being kept waiting.

In the end, a good quarter of an hour elapsed before Richard Lascelles turned up. He was one of those languid-seeming Englishmen — Strafford knew the type well — deliberately affected but with a backbone of tempered steel and a ruthless light glinting behind a carefully maintained easygoing smile. He wore a British Warm overcoat and glossy, handmade brogues, and carried a bowler hat balanced on the upturned underside of his wrist with a thumb hooked over the brim; it looked like a trick that had cost him considerable time and effort to master, to what end it wasn't clear, except perhaps the small pleasure in so deftly performing something at once trivial and difficult.

Yes, Strafford decided, Lascelles, behind the suave exterior, would be a bit of a joker. That was something to keep in mind.

"Sorry I'm late," Lascelles said, jerking his arm and making the hat do a somersault and catching it in his

14

fingertips and setting it down on the bar; no end to his flashy adroitness. "Bit of a flap at the embassy." He shook hands with Hegarty, and cast a quizzical smile in Strafford's direction. "I was led to believe this was to be a private meeting?"

Hegarty introduced the detective. Lascelles smiled again, more warmly. It had only taken a closer look at Strafford's clothes and general demeanour for him to place the young man precisely as to class, caste and religion.

"You go along and see what he wants," Strafford's boss, Inspector Hackett, had told him. "You'll be able to talk to him in his own lingo."

The minister's department had objected to the detective being present, but the request for this meeting had come from the embassy via Hackett — the British knew and trusted him, insofar as they trusted anyone in this country — and it had been considered advisable that someone from the force should accompany the minister.

Strafford thought the whole business distinctly irregular, given the tensions with Britain over neutrality, and the British government's bullishness on the question of the Royal Navy's demand for access to Irish ports, which the Irish government had resolutely refused to grant. And why the Kildare Street Club, of all places? But, then, most things were irregular, these days, with Britain's cities under nightly attack by German bombers and the United Kingdom braced for an invasion.

"So," Hegarty said, "what can I do for you, Mr Lascelles?"

Lascelles had been offered a drink but had declined. Now he said, "Why don't we go up and have that lunch? The chop is not bad here, and they have a cracking fine cellar."

Hegarty and the detective drank the last of their whiskey, which they had been carefully nursing, and the three men climbed the stairs to the first-floor dining room. Here, three big, light-filled windows looked out across Nassau Street to the railings of Trinity College and the cricket ground beyond. A match, surely one of the last of the season, was in progress, the tiny figures in white moving over the grass in seeming slow-motion, like the celebrants of an archaic religious ritual, which, it occurred to Strafford, in a way they were.

In the room a dozen or so men were at lunch, some in pairs but most of them alone; there were no women in today, though a couple of years previously it had been agreed, against some strong opposition, that members might invite ladies into the club for luncheon or dinner. In one corner a table set for three stood in conspicuous isolation: Hegarty's people had called ahead to make sure no one would be seated within eavesdropping range. Although the embassy had not disclosed the nature of the business to be discussed, it was clear that it would be a matter of some significance, and it wouldn't do if word of it were to be put about.

Hegarty and the Englishman both chose oxtail soup, and all three asked for grilled sole to follow. Lascelles suggested a glass of red wine, since they would have a bottle of white with the fish. "The house claret is excellent," he said.

A bottle of the claret was duly ordered, though Strafford took none, saying he would wait a while; as a rule he hardly drank at all — in the bar he had asked for the whiskey only to make a point, and he was feeling the effects of it now.

While they waited for the soup to arrive, Lascelles nodded towards the window and the distant cricketers. "Can't help wishing I was out there," he said wistfully, then turned back hastily to the two men at the table and added, "No reflection on you, gentlemen, of course."

"So, Mr Lascelles." Hegarty's rimless glasses flashed with reflected light from the window. "Will we get down to brass tacks? You have something to ask of me, I suspect."

Lascelles directed his gaze once more towards the cricket match, leaning with one elbow on the arm of his chair and rubbing a fingertip slowly back and forth across his chin just under his lower lip.

"Well, the thing is, Minister," he said, and hesitated, obviously choosing his words with care, "we — the embassy, that is — we've been instructed by our masters in London to approach your government with a somewhat delicate request."

"What kind of request?" Hegarty made no attempt to suppress the edge of hostility in his voice.

Lascelles took no notice: he hadn't been long in his post but already he had plenty of experience in dealing with Irish officialdom. "It concerns a couple of children," he said.

Hegarty stared. "Children?"

"That's right. Two young girls, to be precise."

CHAPTER
TWO

The soup was brought then, and the plain green salad Strafford had ordered so as not to be conspicuous while the other two were consuming their first course. Nevertheless Hegarty threw a disdainful glance at the somewhat wilted lettuce. No doubt considered Strafford was being ostentatiously abstemious, or so Strafford thought; there was no middle way, with a man like Hegarty. What must Yeats and Lady G. have made of him?

The cricketers had stopped for a break, and were heading towards the pavilion, Strafford saw. He disdained sports of all kinds, except tennis, which he liked for its fluid elegance — not that he had been any good at it, but he had admired, and in some cases envied, the few talented players who had passed through his school.

"The girls are aged fourteen and ten," Lascelles was saying, vigorously sprinkling salt on his soup. "They must be got out of London straight away. We've been rather at a loss as to what to do with them, since the Blitz started. But it's imperative they be lodged somewhere safe, somewhere we can be sure of them."

Hegarty, his soup spoon suspended in mid-air, was watching Lascelles with the keenest attention. "And may I ask who they are, these 'girls'?"

Lascelles, too, stopped eating, and smiled at him again, showing his teeth. He was handsome, in a refined yet somewhat brutal way, with a narrow forehead and high cheekbones and dark, oddly glittering eyes. His skin had a leathery quality, as if he had spent many years in an equatorial climate. Diplomats were a strange breed, in Strafford's experience: their frequent uprootings and re-postings to various quarters of the world gave them, behind their studiedly bland demeanour, a slightly nervous quality, as if they expected a courier to come bustling in at any moment with orders for them to pack up and be gone within the hour.

Hegarty was still waiting for an answer to his question. Lascelles glanced to the side with his lips pursed. "Let's just say, Minister," he replied, "that the girls are from a good family — a frightfully good family."

"I see," Hegarty said, and returned his spoon to his soup. He was smiling slyly, which had the effect of making the features of his face contract, so that they seemed to become even more closely crowded together. "Your king and queen, I hear," he said, in a conversational tone, keeping his eyes hooded, "insist that they'll stay put in London for as long as the nightly bombing lasts, in order to" — he looked up, with lifted eyebrows — "to share in the sufferings of the common people."

20

"Yes, indeed. Their Majesties are adamant, they will not be moved."

"Very noble of them, I'm sure," Hegarty remarked, with a dry little sniff. "And their family will remain with them?"

"That is the implication, yes," Lascelles said, measuring his words. "But of course in times like these there are many things that are better kept from the public. It's a question of morale, you see."

"Oh, yes?" Hegarty said, with a throaty chuckle.

Strafford was fascinated, sitting between the minister and the diplomat, to watch the progress of the haggle they were engaged in, even though the terms of whatever deal they might eventually make had not yet been set out for consideration.

Two girls, from a family at the pinnacle of British society: he had a pretty fair idea of who they would be. This meeting had become extremely interesting.

Hegarty finished his soup, pushed the plate aside, and applied his napkin to his little moist red mouth and coughed into a tiny fist; for all his bulk, various parts of him were made in miniature, as if their growth had been arrested, the last vestiges, as it were, of the child that, however implausible it seemed today, he must once have been. Slowly he picked up his glass and drained the last remaining drop of wine.

"Ireland is neutral in this war, Mr Lascelles," he said pointedly. "As you are well aware."

"Of course. Yet I also know — in fact, I believe we both know — where Ireland's best interests lie."

The waiter, a grizzled bruiser in a striped waistcoat, came to the table. He had brought the wine list, and Lascelles took it from him and studied it, frowning, and palping his lower lip between a finger and thumb. Hegarty caught Strafford's eye and, without the slightest change of expression, winked.

Lascelles looked up at the waiter. "The hock, Dudley," he said.

"Very good, Mr Lascelles," the waiter growled. The skin on his cheeks and chin was red and mottled and in places peeling in grey flakes. He had the look of a retired prize-fighter, to Strafford's eye. The staff in a place like this were always an interesting lot, and it was frustrating that he could never hit on a way of finding out their backgrounds without seeming to patronise or giving outright offence. Dudley was the most un-Dudley-like person imaginable. Yet that was his name, unless Lascelles had invented it, which he might well have done, as his idea of a joke. Hard-eyed types like him enjoyed making sport of those to whom they might have referred as the lower orders.

"Our best interests, you say," Hegarty said, gazing out thoughtfully in the direction of the cricketers. "And what might they be, would you think?"

The mist was thickening over the pitch, and the sun was having a harder task than ever in striking through it.

"As a matter of fact, I believe our interests, yours and ours, coincide, in this case," Lascelles responded softly, glancing to right and left, making doubly sure there was no possibility of his being overheard.

22

"The British shot my father twenty years ago, in the War of Independence," Hegarty said, maintaining a mild, even a friendly, manner. "Did you know that, Mr Lascelles?"

Lascelles drank the last of the wine in his glass, then set the glass on the tablecloth and turned it round and round slowly on its base, keeping his gaze fixed on it. "Yes, I knew that," he said smoothly. "But from what I hear, in that same bit of unpleasantness your father managed to shoot his fair share of our chaps. Indeed" — he smiled again, again showing his teeth — "if I'm not mistaken, you bore arms yourself, as a young fellow, in — what was it? The West Cork Brigade?" He looked to the window. "Oh, well bowled, sir!" he exclaimed.

Lascelles poured another glass of wine for himself and the minister — Strafford put a hand over his empty glass. In attending to the course of these exchanges between the two men, he had increasingly the sense of being slowly drained of all pigment, so that presently he would have become perfectly transparent. Indeed, as far as the pair at the table with him were concerned, it seemed he was already invisible, a figure made of glass, so thoroughly were they ignoring him. He didn't mind: as far as social intercourse went, he was, and was content to be, one of life's born bystanders, most frequently the observer, seldom the agent.

Dudley the Unlikely came with their fish, assisted by a rawknuckled, red-haired young man — a boy, really — who had the look of a frightened bull-calf. The wine was produced, and Dudley uncorked it with a show of brusque expertise of which plainly he was proud. He poured a measure into Lascelles's glass and waited, with one forearm behind his back. Lascelles tasted the wine, swilling it about in his mouth, filling one cheek and then the other before swallowing, then nodded to the waiter.

"So, Mr Lascelles," Hegarty said, when Dudley and his helper had departed, "you'd like to separate these two girls from their frightfully good family and send them over to us for a while for safe-keeping?"

Lascelles had cut up portions of the fish and potatoes into individual bite-sized cubes. He must have spent at least some of his young days in America, Strafford decided, for this, he knew, was the way in which American children were taught to eat. Just as with the club staff, you could never know, in the case of these embassy types, where they came from, or what their antecedents were. This one looked and sounded like your typical Eton and Oxford man, but he could have been from anywhere. Was Lascelles even an English name? Though Strafford seemed to remember that the King's private secretary was called something like it — in fact, it came to him now, not something like it but the same: Tommy Lascelles. He wondered if this one might be a relation; there couldn't be many families by that name.

"That was the general idea, yes," Lascelles said, still deftly dissecting his food. "As you point out, Minister, Ireland is neutral, and I'm glad to say is a very peaceable place" — he paused for a second — "nowadays. Therefore ideal for our purpose. We

24

thought at first Canada would be best, but the Jerries' submarines are becoming worryingly effective all over the North Atlantic. Australia? Much too far away. South Africa? Well. So we wondered — that is, London wondered — if indeed you over here might agree to take in the poor waifs and give them shelter for the duration." He took a sip of his wine and pursed his lips appreciatively. "Quite decent, isn't it, this hock?"

Hegarty held his face bent over his plate — like a sheep over a patch of grass, Strafford thought — mashing the potatoes into the fish juices and inserting forkfuls of the resulting mush into his mouth, the process accompanied by small, surely unconscious, mumbling slurps of appreciation.

"And tell me now, Mr Lascelles," Hegarty said, still with his eyes lowered, his jaws working, "what would be" — he paused a moment, then resumed — "well, not to put too fine a point on it, what would be in it for us?"

Lascelles was engrossed in separating and measuring out and cutting up his lunch. However, despite his Yankee way with the grub, he had to be a public-school man, Strafford decided: only a person who had been to one of England's more exclusive educational establishments would consume the watery sole and sodden spuds with such unforced indifference — though even he had given up on the marrowfat peas, which were not green in colour but an unhealthy-looking dusty shade of grey. Ireland, for all its neutrality, was having to put up with some of the privations of wartime.

Despite appearances to the contrary, Lascelles had been listening. He put down his knife and fork, took another swig of wine and, dabbing his mouth with his napkin, drew his chair closer to the table and leaned forward confidentially.

"Your country, I'm told, is in need of coal," he said quietly, speaking out of the corner of his mouth. "Now coal, Mr Hegarty, is something Britain has a great deal of — it's one of our few inexhaustible assets in these perilous times."

"I don't doubt it," Hegarty said, narrowing his already heavy-lidded little eyes. "The Yorkshire dales, the Welsh valleys . . ." He let his voice trail off dreamily. Ireland had only its turf.

"Quite so," Lascelles said, nodding. "Now, HMG, in the form of the Foreign Office, suggests the possibility of a fortnightly shipment to Dublin port of — well, let's just say, for the moment, X tons of the stuff, as a gift from a former oppressor" — he put on a twinkly smile — "to a former oppressed."

"A gift?" Hegarty said, turning his lower lip inside-out and showing its shiny purple lining, in what looked to be at once a smile and a sneer.

"An inducement, then," Lascelles lightly conceded. He turned suddenly to Strafford, as if he had just remembered he was there, and addressed him directly. "And you, young man, how are you finding the sole?"

"Very good," Strafford answered, in his most studiedly toneless and unemphatic fashion.

In fact, he had given up on the fish, which as well as being insipid was no more than lukewarm. Lascelles

26

was still eating his with unflagging dispatch, forking the individual portions from the plate to his mouth with practised rapidity. Strafford speculated as to what age he might be. In his forties, he supposed, like Hegarty, but, unlike Hegarty, seeming younger than his years, with those big white teeth and that sun-tanned skin, which in the folds under his eyes and beside his ears had a markedly blackish cast. Yes, the colonies, definitely.

Hegarty meanwhile was looking out of the window and sucking at what must be a scrap of the fish wedged between his molars.

"It's a lot you're asking," he said, addressing Lascelles. "If the German legation was to get wind of the kind of deal you're suggesting, we'd all be in hot water."

"But how would they 'get wind' of it?" Lascelles laughingly enquired.

"What if they were to be recognised?"

"The feeling is that their presence in the wilds of — their presence in rural Ireland would seem so unlikely that it simply wouldn't occur to people that it could be them. They've been coached to go by false names — Ellen and Mary. I'm sure they'll treat it as a sort of game, and throw themselves into the spirit of the thing."

"It's risky."

"From our point of view, leaving them in London would be a far greater risk. It has all been weighed in the balance. We can send the girls in by plane one dark night, or on an unmarked naval vessel, and no one will be the wiser."

"Aye, except every clerk and cleaner at the British embassy, for a start," Hegarty said drily. For a while, he worked again at that morsel trapped between his back teeth. "And tell me," he said, "what are we supposed to do with these lassies, if we were to agree to take them?"

The Englishman closed his eyes briefly and made a smoothing-out gesture with his left hand.

"We've spoken to the Duke of Edenmore," he murmured, "and he's willing to offer accommodation. His place is Clonmillis Hall, near Clonmillis, in County Tipperary —" He broke off. "D'you know, until I was posted here I never realised that Tipperary was a real place? I thought it was just a made-up name in the old song." He chuckled, shaking his head. Then he turned serious again. "The duke is some sort of relative of the — of the girls' family. The Clonmillis estate is large, quite isolated and safe. There couldn't be a better place for the poor dears, in the estimation of our people."

Hegarty cast a restless glance about the room. It was apparent he wished to bring the meeting to a close. "All I can do is put your request to — to our people," he said.

"Excellent!" Lascelles gave the edge of the table a happy little slap with the tips of the fingers of both hands. "I'll await word, then." He turned solemn again. "But I must emphasise, it's a matter of the utmost urgency."

"I understand that," Hegarty said, with a touch of irritation. "All the same, we'll have to go into the various aspects of the business. There's the question of security, and confidentiality, and — and all the rest of it." The lunch was at an end. He cast about again uncertainly. He looked all the more like Oliver Hardy, in those moments in the films when the fat man begins to realise that something might be about to go seriously wrong. "Who do I ask for the bill, in this place?"

"Oh, don't bother with that, it goes on the embassy account," Lascelles said, with an expansive gesture. "Will you have some coffee, before you go?"

"Would they run to a cup of tea, do you think?"

"I'm sure they would, Minister, I'm sure they would. And what about you, Mr Stafford — will you have coffee or tea?"

"It's Strafford," Strafford said, and smiled. "With an r. Don't worry, everybody gets it wrong."

CHAPTER
THREE

As far as looks were concerned, Celia Nashe was the classic English rose, but her father, who had served for some years on the Palestine Police Force, always said that of the two of them, she was the tougher by far. She had what advertising copywriters would describe as a peaches-and-cream complexion, short fair-to-blonde hair that had never needed a perm, and the kind of smile any airman would count himself lucky to have for a last memory as his shot-to-pieces Spitfire headed screaming nose-down into the drink. She had been one of the very few women members of the Special Branch — her father had high-up contacts there — but as the possibility of war turned into certainty, she had succeeded in wangling a transfer to MI5. This had been done due to her own merits, but also with the application of a serious amount of pull, by her father again but also, and more significantly, by an uncle on her mother's side, who was a brigadier in the Household Cavalry.

Whatever she might have expected of the Service, the reality was, she had to admit, a distinct let-down. From the start she had been assured by her male colleagues, and in no uncertain terms, that "bloody women" were the last thing that was needed or wanted about the place; that she was being brought in only because it was wartime and men were required elsewhere; and that she shouldn't imagine she would ever become a fully operative agent. She would be kept in reserve until some easy task presented itself.

The commission she was being sent on now struck her as not so much soft as distinctly rum. Her masters had given her little background information on it. She was to leave London for somewhere not very far away — Scotland, she assumed, or Wales even, though she hoped not the latter — and was to bring enough clothes and things with her for what might turn out to be a longish stay. Her job would be to look after "a couple of gels", Manling, her direct superior, had informed her portentously, and actually tapped a forefinger to the side of his nose.

"May I ask who they are, these girls, sir?" she had enquired.

"No, you may not, my dear young lady," Manling had told her, with a supercilious laugh. "You'll find out soon enough. You will be taken tomorrow night to pick them up, then the three of you will be driven to the coast to catch a boat."

Not Scotland, then, but not Wales, either, which was something.

"A boat to where?"

Manling had only shaken his head in pretend regret. She could see how much it gratified him to keep her in the dark. He was fat and middle-aged, with a bad case of dandruff, and busily roving hands — he had tried it on with her more than once, and each time had been politely but firmly rebuffed — and loved the cloak-and-dagger aspect of the secret world in which he moved.

But then, all of those she worked with were like that, to a man, if men they could be called — overgrown schoolboys, more like, from what she had seen of them. She only hoped they knew what they were doing. She had heard rumoured accounts of more than one operation having gone disastrously awry because the mandarins in control had been foolishly adventurous. They were too cavalier when it came to the lives of men in the field. After one total cock-up, in which three experienced agents had perished, she had overheard Manling's boss, who was even more pompous than Manling, remark, almost with amusement, "Well, that was hardly one of our finer moments, eh?"

Women, of course, would do a better job of it, but women were never going to get to the top, not unless, as in the Great War, enough of the menfolk got themselves killed. But the likes of Manling — she often smiled to herself at the aptness of his name — were never going to risk their necks in action. Desk-men, the lot of them, though they affected the swagger of battle-hardened warriors recently returned from highly secret and extremely hazardous offensives.

She had been issued with a Browning automatic — "Sign here, and don't bloody point it in my direction" — a dandy little weapon, as she first thought, and was taken for an afternoon to a shooting range in Surrey to learn how to fire it. In fact, the gun was not so little, and was surprisingly heavy. The lesson in the use of it was rudimentary, since no one imagined for a moment she would ever be called upon to fire off a round in anger. The corporal in charge had complimented her on how quickly she had got the hang of the thing and told her what a good shot she was, then ruined it by asking her to go to the pictures with him.

On the night she was to leave London a great gleaming black beast of a car, more like a battleship than a motor, its headlights painted over and with only small bright crosses showing in the middle of each lamp, had picked her up just before ten o'clock from her flat on the Finchley Road, and headed for what she'd assumed to be the city centre — because of the blackout it was hard to know exactly in which direction they were going. Then a bombing raid had come on, though the worst of it was concentrated at the docks. Her driver, a civilian, or dressed at least in civilian clothes, had greeted her curtly and after that had uttered not a word more. She had wanted to sit in the front seat, beside him, but he had as good as bundled her unceremoniously into the back.

It all became steadily more and more unreal. As they drove along through the darkness she could barely make out the driver's form in front of her, and she began to think of him as an automaton, and that they would continue on like this all night, the big car whispering along and the buildings looming around her and then falling away behind, and over in the east the bombs raining down and the sky filled with flames and roiling clouds of smoke and the vivid tracery of anti-aircraft fire.

At last the raid ended, though the docks went on blazing, and would continue so until dawn and after.

The night was overcast, but then the moon came out briefly and she saw they were on the Mall, with the long low grey bulk of Buckingham Palace straight ahead. She supposed they were on the way to the safe house she had heard the Service kept somewhere down near Victoria station. However, when they seemed about to pass by the Palace and head south, the driver, to her surprise and sudden consternation, pulled around to a side gate, which opened ponderously before them, and they arrived in a small, cobbled courtyard.

The King and Queen — she had nearly fainted: the King and Queen! — had received her in a yellow drawing room.

"Didn't anyone tell you the nature of the t-task you are being entrusted with, my dear?" the King kindly enquired.

"Well, I knew I was to accompany two young girls on a trip abroad, but not who the girls were or where we would be going."

Plainly the royal couple were displeased to hear how little she had been told, and Celia could see it was a struggle for them not to show it.

"Well," His Majesty went on, turning back to Celia, "ours not to r-reason why, in times such as these, eh? I'm sure you'll do a splendid job. Certainly we wish you the b-best of luck!"

34

They went on to chat for some minutes, but afterwards she could recall very little of what they had talked about — the Queen had mostly kept silent, smiling vaguely into the middle distance. It was all overwhelming at first but then quite, well, ordinary. The royal couple might have been a rather grand aunt and uncle whom she had never met before but who were as lukewarm and distantly polite as rich relations tended always to be.

Then the girls appeared, in their travelling coats and sensible shoes, and were introduced to her. She remembered to curtsy: they might be children, but they were also princesses. The older one seemed ill at ease and avoided meeting her eye directly, whether out of haughtiness or because she was shy it was hard to decide. The younger one, she saw straight off, was as sharp as a tack, and coolly looked her up and down with a measuring and, unless she imagined it, even a sceptical eye. Such cheek, even if she was a royal highness!

They had identical handbags, surprisingly cheap-looking things made of pink-tinted leather the sight of which for some reason touched her, and made her feel maternal and protective. Like everyone else, she was becoming used to the war, but sometimes, as now, it was brought home to her that hundreds of people, even thousands, including children not much different from these two, were being slaughtered on the streets, in their homes, in makeshift bomb shelters, every night in the great industrial cities up and down the country. In the worrying uneventfulness of the early months, the months of the so-called Phoney War, everyone had speculated on what total warfare on the home front would be like. Now everyone knew.

She left the gilded room and waited discreetly in the hall while the parents were saying goodbye to their daughters. Her hands were shaking still. To think she had just been in the presence of royalty, of the King of England and his Queen, who were entrusting their daughters, the older of whom was the first in line to the throne, the Heir Presumptive, to her care! The prospect made her feel dizzy all over again.

Then the girls came out, looking brave, but pale, too, even the younger one, whose lip trembled as she fought to hold back tears.

They were led along dim, draughty corridors and down a broad set of stairs, with the girls going ahead of her — after all, they were familiar with the place — and then she was outside in the darkness again. She almost had to pinch herself to make sure she was awake and that the past quarter of an hour hadn't been a dream.

Two Palace servants, anonymous men in shirtsleeves and long black aprons, were packing the princesses' numerous items of luggage into the boot of the car. The bags were of pigskin, with gleaming brass buckles, and made her own scuffed suitcase and Gladstone bag look pitifully shabby. The driver had been by the gate having a smoke, but at the appearance of the party had dropped his cigarette hurriedly and trodden on it, and made an awkward bow to the two girls. Then he got behind the wheel and they were off.

But to where?

CHAPTER
FOUR

It was a long and trying journey. The girls, who had spoken hardly a word to Celia, soon fell asleep, huddled against each other under a fawn-coloured woollen blanket. Celia sat beside them, looking out of the window at the nightscape flowing past. Once they got away from the city the sky cleared and a partial moon came out again, and by its ghostly glimmer she could see for miles across the flatness of the countryside. They passed through Reading, and then across the Berkshire Downs, skirted Bath and Bristol and followed the Avon all the way to the coast, where at last they came to a halt.

They were at an anonymous little fishing village, with not a sign of life anywhere and not a single light showing. At the pier a navy vessel of some kind was waiting for them. All its markings were painted over. A corvette, Celia thought it might be, though she knew very little about boats. The girls had to be woken — the younger one had been muttering in her sleep and grinding her teeth — and were helped on board by what were obviously navy personnel, though they were dressed as ordinary sailors, in thick jumpers and dungarees and caps with shiny peaks.

The quarters belowdecks were cramped, and smelt of machine oil and male sweat. The girls were put in the forward cabin, where there were twin bunks. Celia was given a sort of cubbyhole behind the bulkhead, with nowhere to sleep except a battered old armchair with loose springs that stuck into her in various places and would turn out to allow her no more than brief intervals of agitated, nightmarish dozing.

The captain was dismayingly young — he could hardly have been more than twenty-five. He was handsome and diffident, and spoke deferentially to Celia and apologised for the general squalor and discomfort on board.

"The powers-that-be thought an old tub like this would attract less attention, heaven knows why," he said. "Once we're clear of the estuary the crossing will be quick, hardly more than a few hours, if the weather holds."

"But where are we going?" Celia asked, annoyed with herself for sounding so querulous; she was tired and edgy after the long drive.

The young man ducked his head in another show of apology. "Didn't they tell you?" It seemed to be the refrain of the entire evening. "Ireland. We'll be heading straight across towards Waterford, and will let you off just up the coast from there. A car will be waiting for you —"

"You mean we have another journey ahead of us, on the other side?"

Once again she had tried hard not to sound whiny.

"I'm afraid so."

"How far will we have to go?"

She had never been to Ireland and knew next to nothing of the place; she might as well have been told she was bound for a benighted colony on the shores of Africa.

"That I don't know," the young man said. "My orders are to get you over and see you into the motor. After that —" He shrugged, showing friendly sympathy by way of a deliberately clownish downturned smile.

She thanked him, and he gave her an awkward salute and went off to the bridge. She settled herself in the armchair as best she could.

Was it for this she had begged her uncle the brigadier to get her into the Security Service?

After a time she fell into a sort of sleep, but woke with a start of alarm, unable for the first few seconds to understand where she was or what was happening. The little ship was rolling heavily in a long, slow swell. She sat with her hands braced on the arms of the chair, listening to, or feeling, rather, the uneven beat of the propeller, which sent successive rapid shocks throughout the ship, making its steel plates shiver and rattle. She must check the girls.

When she opened the door to their cabin, having turned the brass knob with great care to keep it from making a noise and waking them, she felt a chill of fright settle on her heart. A night-light in the ceiling shed a faint bluish glow in the cramped space, by which she saw that one of the bunks was empty, the rough navy-issue blanket thrown back. She bent over the second bunk. The older girl was there, asleep, with one arm thrown diagonally across her face, as if to fend off a blow. There was a strong smell of vomit.

Celia hurried into the corridor again, and halted, looking wildly about her. Which way should she go?

She realised that she was praying, muttering, Dear God, please! over and over in her head. To the left the corridor ended abruptly at a doorway, all mahogany and brass; to the right, a short set of metal steps led up into the darkness of the night. She remembered that this was the way the captain had gone when he had left her earlier. Her shoes clattered on the steps, making a terrifying racket — it might have been the sound, greatly amplified, of her own heart rattling madly in its cage.

The boat hit a particularly strong swell and the deck yawed under her. She almost lost her balance, and would have fallen had there not been a metal handrail for her to hold on to. The moon had set, but there was a livid glow in the sky astern, which she knew was not the dawn.

When she saw the tiny figure outlined against that distant patch of febrile radiance she thought at first she must be imagining it. But she was not.

"There you are!" she cried, seizing the child by the shoulders and drawing her tightly against herself.

The thought came into her head with a kind of crazy inconsequence: what was she to call them — how was she to address them? It would seem ridiculous to speak to a child as "Your Royal Highness". But no one had told her — no one had told her anything, really, except that the princesses were never to be referred to as such, and were not to be known by their real names. How was she to cope, being left in such ignorance? It wasn't fair. It was, as her mother would say, with thudding, angry emphasis, just — not — fair!

"I was looking at the bombing," the little girl said, struggling to extricate herself from Celia's close, relieved embrace.

Celia looked towards the fiery sky in the distance. Later she would learn that the target of the raid had been the naval yards at Pembroke. "You shouldn't have come up here!" she almost yelled. "You could have fallen over the rail and —"

The child broke free and stepped back, her chin lowered and her fists clenched at her sides. "I know what to do on boats!" she exclaimed, in an ominously low, truculent voice. "My father has a yacht the size of — the size of —" Her imagination failed her. "It's about twenty times the size of this pathetic barge of a thing, and when I'm on board her I'm allowed to be on deck and see everything that's going on."

"You should have stayed in your cabin. Why did you leave?"

"She kept being sick."

"Your sister?"

"It was disgusting, the sounds she made — you should have heard."

For a moment neither spoke, then Celia bowed her head contritely, as if she felt a fool for having carried on so. "Forgive me," she said, "I shouldn't have grabbed you. But I was frightened —"

"Everybody is frightened," the child announced scornfully.

"But I like watching places that are being bombed."

"Oh, my dear," Celia said, with a catch in her voice. "My dear — my dear, sweet Margaret, you mustn't say such things, especially when you know very well they aren't true."

The little girl laughed, but less harshly this time, though with the same level of disdain. "Is that what you're going to call me? I mean, are you going to call me by my real name?"

"No, no, I'm sorry, I meant —"

"Daddy told me I'm to say my name is Mary. He said it would be a sort of game, but I know it's not. Do you think we'll be in danger, over there" — she jerked her head in the direction of the dark horizon in the west — "since we have to pretend to be someone else?"

"You won't be in danger, I promise," Celia said. "That's why I'm with you, to keep you safe and out of harm's way."

CHAPTER
FIVE

William Fitzherbert, Duke of Edenmore, MC, DSO, stood at the window of the first-floor drawing room of Clonmillis Hall and watched with surprise and no little dismay the motor-car approaching up the grass-lined drive. Somehow signals must have crossed, for the party had not been expected until the afternoon. Mrs O'Hanlon, he knew, would be greatly put out. The prospect of his housekeeper in one of her moods filled him with the deepest dread. He was afraid of the woman, he freely admitted it to himself, but the place couldn't function without her.

The car was a maroon-coloured Bentley, long, low-slung and sleek — just the thing, the old man reflected wryly, to pass unnoticed on the back roads of Tipperary. What had they been thinking, the bright boys in Whitehall, or wherever it was the Security Service was based, these days? The operation was supposed to be strictly hush-hush, wasn't it? He had taken part himself in a few undercover ventures in the last show, but he imagined, or at least he hoped, that in this latest round of knocking the Germans' socks off the Service would have smartened itself up and would go about its business in a more professional manner.

The sight of a maroon Bentley bumping along the drive did not inspire his confidence. If only he had been asked he could have sent Hynes to meet them somewhere in the battered old Humber, which would have caused no comment. Everyone in the county knew the old Humber by sight.

Meanwhile, in the offendingly ostentatious car, the atmosphere, which early on had been tense, had by now gone slack, thanks to boredom and travel weariness. It hadn't been all that much of a drive from Waterford, but it had seemed long, after the trip from London and then the sea journey. Lascelles was driving, for his was the Bentley, one of the few luxuries he had allowed himself in compensation for having been posted to this godforsaken excuse for a country. He had wound down his window, but the air inside still held the sweet-sour stink of vomit: the older of the princesses had been seasick, and her breath was bad.

The detective, seated beside him in the passenger seat, hadn't uttered a single complete sentence since they had set out from Ballymacbackward, or whatever the place over on the south-east coast was called, where the navy vessel had docked. Strafford had been standing at the pier, waiting, a lone figure in a trench coat and slouch hat, skinny and motionless. In the dark before dawn he had been driven down from Dublin in a Defence Forces military car and abandoned to his own devices on the deserted quayside.

The little ship, blunt and broad as a trawler, had been late, due to rough weather off the Pembroke coast;

44

it was just as well, since Lascelles, too, had been delayed, not by the weather but by another kind of storm, namely a squabble, yet another, with his current girl in Dublin, the fledgling actress Isabel Galloway — she was not yet nineteen, as he had recently discovered, to his surprise and some alarm — who, he was coming to think, was more trouble than she was worth, being less than half his age and exhaustingly wilful.

Strafford's clothes, when he got into the car, had given off a cold breath of damp salt air. He looked, to Lascelles, ridiculously young, worryingly so, as young almost as his girl Isabel, and too young, surely, for an operation as sensitive and onerous as this one.

After exchanging murmured greetings and shaking hands they had sat side by side in silence for half an hour, staring through the windscreen into the darkness, smoking — or rather, Lascelles smoked, since Strafford was not a smoker and, so it would turn out, not much of a drinker either — until the cruiser, showing no lights, loomed up suddenly beyond the pier, like Leviathan rising out of the deep.

The transfer of the sleepy girls and their female attendant had been carried out in silence, speedily. Then, a mile outside the village, a pair of cars pulled out of a gateway and fell in with them, one in front and the other behind. There were four men in each, wearing hats and sitting stiffly upright, like shop-window dummies. Lascelles had been alerted that there would be a Special Branch escort. The cars, their headlights dimmed, maintained a steady speed, keeping a discreet

45

distance, and would accompany them as far as their destination.

They were crossing into Tipperary when the dawn came up, setting a misty light the colour of dishwater creeping across the slopes of a range of mountains the name of which was the Knockmealdowns, as Lascelles surprised himself by remembering; well, it would be a hard name to forget.

Now, as the Bentley progressed up the drive, the girls in the back seat looked out of the windows with listless eyes at the acres of parkland through which they were progressing. They sat on either side of their — what was the young woman, anyway? Their chaperone? Their bodyguard? Both, Lascelles supposed. She, too, had little to say for herself. What was her name? Damn: they had told him but now he couldn't remember. How was he going to introduce her to the lord of the manor?

He sighed. He had been in line for the post of second secretary at the Paris embassy, before the balloon had gone up. Paris! A lost world, or lost to him, anyway.

She was decidedly pretty, all the same, the blonde Miss Whoever, a fact at odds with the sternness of her manner — she carried herself like a lately commissioned young army officer impatient at having been released on early leave and itching to get back to the front.

Celia! He recollected her first name, at least. But what was her second?

Halfway up the drive — it must be at least a mile long, Lascelles calculated — a young man appeared, walking along in the opposite direction. He wore corduroy trousers, a sleeveless leather jerkin over a woollen jumper, and a flat tweed cap; a shotgun, broken at the breech, was cradled in the crook of his left arm. He did not give the car so much as a glance, but kept his eyes lowered, and did not slow his pace.

When they had passed him by, the younger girl turned quickly and craned her neck to look after him through the back window. A mass of shiny black curls tumbled out from under his cap all around the rim. He reminded her of one of the gillies at Balmoral; one in particular, similarly dark and unsmiling, a gypsy-looking fellow, with just the same kind of curls.

Lascelles swung the car in a wide right-hand half-circle on the gravel — he loved to play with this wonderful big machine, delighting in the way she shimmied her rear end on a hard turn, like a demure girl dancing the jitterbug — and drew to a stop at the foot of the front steps. He kept the engine running, for the pleasure of listening to its exquisitely calibrated purr, but also to give himself a moment to take a quick visual recce of the Hall. Moss between the flags of the steps, a rusted handrail leading up to the weathered front door, a granite lintel pockmarked by the centuries. General air of seediness, of a house not quite gone to ruin but well started on the way. Edenmore was down on his economic luck: that much was clear.

Hadn't anyone vetted the place before choosing it as a refuge for the royal evacuees?

Maybe, he reflected, that was the point, to hide the girls most improbably in a dilapidated pile in the back of beyond.

In the seat behind him the girl who had been sick stirred herself lethargically. The young woman was telling her and her sister to remember to take all their things with them from the car. Strafford was pressing the dents out of his hat. Lascelles had noticed that the detective had hardly bothered to look at the house — probably knew a dozen places like it: Strafford was a bona-fide descendant of sixteenth-century Protestant settlers. But, if so, what the hell was he doing in Paddyland's pretend police force, which was hardly more than a gang of pensioned-off gunmen pressed into blue-serge uniforms and told to behave themselves?

"Hang on here a minute," Lascelles said. "I'll just let them know we've arrived."

He got out of the car and trotted up the steps, and was reaching for the knocker when the door before him began to fall in backwards slowly from the top. What the hell — ? He felt like Buster Keaton, standing there with his mouth open and his hand lifted, as the door subsided in a slow swoon on to its back in the hall.

A fellow in dungarees and a collarless shirt, letting the door down gently with both hands, looked up at him, mouth fallen open. Each of them was as startled as the other. Then, behind the workman, the duke appeared, scowling in choleric displeasure. "For God's sake, McLaverty," he snapped, "you were supposed to finish an hour ago! Get that door out of the way at once!"

McLaverty, who was young, red-haired, pink-faced and freckled, took hold of the door and dragged it back into the hall — it might have been a steamrollered corpse gone stiff with rigor mortis — and lifted it on to its side and leaned it against the wall. Various tools were scattered about the stone-tiled floor, and a wooden workhorse stood foursquare on its sturdy legs in the attitude of a recalcitrant donkey. There was a smell of wood shavings and dry rot.

"Sorry, sorry," the duke said to Lascelles, picking his way through the clutter on the floor. "Edenmore. How do you do? Forgive the mess. Hinges nearly rusted through, thought I'd better get them fixed before you came — that didn't work out quite as planned, obviously. Which are you? Lascelles, or the other fellow, the detective?"

Lascelles did the trick with his bowler hat, balancing it on the underside of his forearm and then flipping it over into his hand, making the duke blink and then frown. "Richard Lascelles, sir. From the embassy. We spoke on the telephone."

"Yes, of course." They shook hands in a brusque, awkward fashion. "And Their Royal Highnesses —" he broke off, and quickly corrected himself "— the young ladies."

The girls, with Celia and Strafford behind them, were mounting the steps. They walked with slow, deliberate tread, as they had been trained to do since they were toddlers. In their buttoned-up coats, neat hats and brown leather gloves, their pink handbags looped over their wrists, they had a quaint, grave, antique look to them; they might have been, Strafford thought, a pair of infantas out of one of Velazquez's court portraits.

Now from the depths of the house emerged a low-sized, squat, almost square-shaped woman in an oatmeal-coloured dress and a black cardigan. Her hair was a mass of dense grey curls, like twists of steel wool, piled up at the back, and in the front clustering on her forehead. She had a tiny face that might once have been pretty, and cold blue eyes and a pursed mouth. This was Mrs O'Hanlon, the duke's housekeeper. By rights she was Bean Ó Hanlüain, but the duke, in spite of his fear of her, had flatly refused to address her by the Gaelic version of her name. She advanced at a queenly pace, and as she came on, the duke, not seeing her, took a step backwards and collided with her, almost treading on her toes. Strafford, now arrived at the threshold, saw a red-haired young man scrambling to gather up the tools of his trade.

Lascelles introduced the girls. He gave their names as Ellen and Mary, and the duke stared at him blankly for a second in bafflement.

"Ah, I see," he said then, his brow clearing, "Ellen and Mary. I see." He looked down at the girls and produced a sort of parody of a smile, awful to behold, showing a set of ill-fitting, discoloured dentures. "Welcome to Clonmillis —" He stopped. "My dears, you're very welcome."

He seized the housekeeper by the upper part of one of her arms and drew her forward, thrusting her in front of him, making of her a sort of human shield. Mrs O'Hanlon began to execute a curtsy but Lascelles, warningly, gave his head a quick shake.

50

Celia Nashe — yes, Nashe, Lascelles thought, that was her name! — was peering into the shadows of the hallway with misgiving. The antlered bust of a large animal, a deer it must be, or an elk — had she not read somewhere that there were elks in Ireland? — was mounted on the right-hand wall, contemplating itself with a glazed stare in a gilt-framed, fly-blown mirror on the opposite side.

Beneath the mirror stood a massive dark mahogany table on which was set a tall Chinese vase with a chipped base, containing a bunch of dried chrysanthemums. Strafford, who had passed his childhood in the midst of such forbidding and soulless surroundings, felt sorry for the young woman, who no doubt was thinking, as was he, of the weeks, perhaps months, that lay ahead, as the damp of autumn gave way to the iron chill of winter.

So far neither of the girls had spoken a word, and now, with the one who was to be called Ellen in the lead, they detached themselves from the scrum of people in the crowded doorway and walked forward into the hall, stopped, and turned back calmly to face the others. McLaverty was down on one knee, gathering up wood shavings and stuffing them into a gunny sack. The girls did not even glance at him as he knelt there, the suppliant commoner. Indeed, they had the air of ignoring everything, well-schooled as they already were in the subtle art of not noticing anything except those objects and instances to which their attention was specifically drawn.

"Yes, yes," the duke said, "yes, let's all go inside," He looked about for the housekeeper, who had got herself behind him again. "Mrs O'Hanlon, some tea, perhaps?"

He led the way, and the others followed. Strafford and Celia Nashe drew up the rear. Strafford touched a finger lightly to the young woman's elbow. "It will be all right," he murmured.

She gave him a hard, cold stare.

Silly of him, of course, he thought, with amused chagrin, to seem to put himself on a par with her by attempting to offer her comfort. He had no doubt that in her estimation he occupied a position very low down on the scale of importance, somewhere between herself, at the top, and, say, the red-haired young carpenter at the bottom.

Mrs O'Hanlon was enquiring of the girls if their journey from England had been a pleasant one.

"She was sick," the younger one said, indicating her sister, with vindictive satisfaction.

CHAPTER
SIX

They all trooped into the morning room. Everything had been thrown into disarray not only by the fact of the girls being who they were, but also, more prosaically, by their having turned up earlier than expected. No one seemed to know quite how to behave, given the general sense of agitation and contingency that the arrival of royalty had created — no one, that was, except the royal pair themselves, who appeared perfectly self-possessed, despite the faint aroma of vomit still clinging to one.

The duke cast a yearning glance towards the cluster of bottles standing on a sideboard next to the fireplace, ranked neatly according to size and dusted off weekly by the hand of Mrs O'Hanlon herself. It was probably too early to offer sherry, and anyway he wasn't sure to whom he might offer it. Lascelles, yes, but what about the detective, and the girls' governess, or whatever her title was?

He could hardly have declined to give shelter to the princesses — he was a distant cousin to the previous queen, the girls' grandmother — but it was going to be damnably tricky, having them here. The house wasn't suitable, really, for the accommodation of children.

Pamela, his wife, had died twenty years before, without issue, and after she was gone he had sunk back into a state of more or less contented bachelorhood.

Mrs O'Hanlon appeared, stopping in the doorway, her hands clasped under her bosom. She had expressed a few less than subtle complaints about the burden that would be placed on her time and her energies by the girls' presence. If they hadn't been who they were she would probably have found a way to circumvent their coming. But she had seemed somewhat mollified by learning that she was the only person other than the duke himself who had been informed officially of the young guests' true identities.

The duke turned to the girls, with another startling flash of yellowed dentures.

"I imagine you'll want to inspect your billets," he said, with a strained attempt at cheeriness. "Mrs O'Hanlon, would you show the girls to their quarters?"

"Will that be before or after I send for the tea?" she enquired, with heavy sarcasm.

"Tea?" the duke said vaguely, then made an impatient gesture.

"Yes, yes, show them to their room first. They'll need to unpack their things, and so on."

The housekeeper stepped aside, and the girls walked past her and out. In their coats and hats and gloves they seemed perfectly scaled-down versions of two grown-up women, neatly groomed and self-possessed.

Celia Nashe followed them — it was clear to her from the housekeeper's frosty look that this alarmingly formidable woman had already taken against her.

The duke, always glad to be relieved of the presence of females, rubbed his hands together in a vigorous washing motion and made for the bottles. He didn't care how early it was, he was going to have a tot of something.

He was startled when Richard Lascelles — evidently in need of a more serious bracer — declined the offer of sherry and asked if he might have a Bushmills whiskey instead. The detective politely declined anything at all.

"Sit down, sit down," the duke said to both men, busying himself with bottles and glasses. He hadn't intended his invitation to apply universally, but when he turned he saw that not only Lascelles but the detective, too, had taken him at his word: the former was sprawled in an armchair by the fireplace, as if he belonged there, while the latter was seated on a sofa facing the windows. As an old army man, the duke wasn't at all certain that the policeman, who, even though a civilian, was surely to be considered "other ranks", had the right to make himself at home in such an easy fashion. He let it pass: all kinds of rules would have to go by the board in these disordered times.

He handed the whiskey to Lascelles and, with a modest glass of sherry for himself, he went and stood in front of the fire, with his back to the flames, or to the smoke, rather, for the turf was wet and wouldn't burn with anything more than a sullen glow.

"The mainland's taking a fearful bashing," he said, addressing Lascelles. "Will the people stand up to it, do you think?"

Lascelles had taken a sip of his drink, and was holding the glass before him, contemplating the rich, peat-brown liquor with an expression of deep appreciation. One good thing, he told himself, was that it wasn't a dry house, as he had rather feared it might be, even though this was Ireland: one could never be sure, either with Protestants or the aristocracy, though usually they were one and the same, of what the protocols would be. Although it was a thing he preferred to keep dark, his own people were Scots Presbyterians, on his mother's side, so he knew about such matters. There were relations up there still whom occasionally he was compelled to visit. A couple of years ago there had been a Christmas spent at a granite mansion near Auchendinny in Midlothian, the horrors of which would remain stamped on his memory for ever.

"Will they stand up to it?" He gave a shrug. "All a question of morale. Winnie is very hot on morale, you know. It's the key word, at the moment."

"Winnie?" the duke said sharply.

"Mr Churchill."

"Oh, is that what people call him?" He knew very well that it was, but he rather disapproved of the casual manner in which Lascelles had spoken of the prime minister. These younger fellows were markedly lacking in the proper respect for those in authority. War had a deplorably loosening effect on the social norms. He thought darkly of young McLaverty and his lackadaisically slipshod workmanship. Ireland wasn't even in the fight, unlike last time, but standards were falling here just as badly as they appeared to be doing across the water, or probably even more so, come to think of it. In the old days it had been different. In fact, nothing had been the same since 1922 when the country, or twenty-six counties out of its thirty-two, had won its so-called independence.

"Our people are related," Lascelles said.

The duke, at a loss, peered at him from under grizzled eyebrows. "Eh?"

"The Churchills, and my family. Cousins, of some kind, from way back, time of the first Duke of Marlborough."

"Ah. I see." The duke cleared his throat. He wondered if he might mention his own even loftier family link — his cousin Queen Mary had once stayed here at the Hall — but it didn't do to appear competitive in such matters. Anyway, he assumed this Lascelles fellow would already know of the connection; it would be a poor reflection on him and on the embassy if that kind of thing had not been thoroughly gone into. But if he did know, he might show a little more deference. He was altogether too much the modern uppity type. "Well, if anyone can save the day, it will be Mr Churchill," the duke said, with conclusive force.

His glass was empty — he had poured only a small measure — and so, too, he noticed, was Lascelles's tumbler. Should he offer him a refill? He didn't want the notion to get about that the place was awash with drink at all hours of the day. Well, he would risk it.

He took the glass from Lascelles and went again to the sideboard.

"What's the thinking among your chaps at the embassy?" he asked. "How long will it take to pull the rug from under that man Hitler's jackboots?"

Lascelles took his replenished glass with murmured thanks. "Not sure it's going to be so easy. If the Germans cross the Channel, well —" He sipped his drink with relish. "They say," he went on, "there's a plane on permanent standby to fly the PM and his key ministers to Canada, in the event of an invasion."

The duke had returned to his place in front of the fire. "Defeatist talk," he said, so brusquely that it made his lips flap. "We beat them into a cocked hat last time out."

"This round is rather different, I'm afraid." Lascelles turned to Strafford, who had been sitting with his fingers steepled under his chin, attending to the two men's exchanges with what seemed only the mildest interest. In fact, he was regretting having refused the offer of a drink, not that he craved alcohol but he would have felt more at ease with a glass to hold: he always found it hard, in the presence of others, to know what to do with his hands — one had altogether too many loose extremities, or so it seemed to him.

"I wonder, old chap," Lascelles said to him, "if you'd excuse us for a minute or three? The duke and I have some matters to discuss."

"Of course," Strafford said, and rose and crossed the room and went out and closed the door soundlessly behind himself.

"Peculiar feller," the duke said darkly. "I'd almost forgotten he was there."

"One of yours, I believe."

"Eh? Oh, yes — Church of Ireland, I should think. What's he doing on the Garda Force?"

Lascelles gave no answer, except to show those fearsome teeth of his; he had about him something of the old Africa hand — of the big-game hunter, or the like. The duke wasn't at all sure he approved of him. What sort of diplomats were they turning out, these days?

Pretty well everything, as far as he could see, was going to the dogs. It was hard to believe it could have been this bad during the last war. He had fought at Passchendaele, and when he was invalided out, with a gassed lung and a sliver of shrapnel in his left knee, everything on the home front had seemed much as it had been before he had gone off to war. The chaps who had died in that battle — so many! — would hardly recognise the world of today, the world they thought they had been fighting for.

Lascelles lit a cigarette, and produced from his breast pocket a small leather-bound notebook and a silver propelling pencil. "Now then," he said, in a suddenly brisk and businesslike voice. "As to terms."

The duke coughed again, and his manner turned distinctly sheepish. The word "terms" sounded, to his ear, altogether too crassly commercial a note — as if he were in trade! "There'll be expenses, yes," he conceded gruffly. "Bound to be."

"Hinges, and suchlike?" Lascelles said, with unsmiling facetiousness.

A flush of resentment darkened the old man's brow. "We aren't equipped for long-term guests here, you know," he snapped. "Arrangements should have been put in place. These girls —" He distracted himself by taking a sip of sherry. After a moment he spoke again, more temperately this time. "We've got out of the way of luxuries, I'm afraid. Their Royal Highnesses will have to put up with things as they are. This is not the Home Counties, remember — this is Ireland."

Lascelles flicked his cigarette against the edge of the ashtray. "You must not — the entire establishment must not — refer to the girls in those terms," he said severely. "They are not Their Royal Highnesses — forget they're royal. I take it, by the way, that the servants aren't in on the secret?"

"Well, they haven't been told the true identity of our guests, if that's what you mean," the duke answered cautiously. Who could say what they knew or didn't know downstairs? "I had to tell Mrs O'Hanlon, of course, but I'm pretty sure I can count on her to be discreet."

"We'll need a bit more than discretion," Lascelles said.

"Oh, she'll keep it under wraps," the duke said. He chuckled. "She considers herself a cut above the rest of the servants." Anyway, he was thinking, it didn't matter: the secret would get out sooner or later.

Lascelles had not been listening. He glared at the fireplace. "This damned country is overrun with wild

60

men who think the War of Independence is still going on. It's not safe."

"Then why send the girls here?" the duke put in quickly. Of course it wasn't safe — how could anyone have imagined it would be?

Lascelles frowned, in a mixture of irritation and disgruntlement, and expelled a stream of cigarette smoke. "I argued against it. But the government was adamant, and so, to my surprise, was the Palace. If they wanted somewhere neutral, why not Sweden, or even Switzerland? They have relatives in every realm and principality of Europe. But, no, it had to be here. So we're stuck with it." He opened the notebook and set it on his knee, holding the silver pencil poised. "Anyway, the embassy has been authorised to look after any costs arising — reasonable costs, that is. Of course, accounts will have to be strictly kept, and receipts rendered."

The duke's already flushed forehead now turned brick-red. How dare this jumped-up ex-colonial address him in such a manner? A movement outside the window distracted his attention. One of the maids was in the garden, hanging sheets on the clothesline. As the old man looked, the corner of one of the sheets broke free and dipped into a muddy puddle and the maid snatched it up and began rubbing energetically at the stain, having spat on it first.

"Receipts," he said resignedly. "I'll speak to Mrs O'Hanlon. She looks after that kind of thing."

CHAPTER
SEVEN

Mrs O'Hanlon, who did indeed oversee most, if not all, of the practical matters of life at Clonmillis Hall, had led Celia Nashe and the girls up two flights of stairs, the second one dingier than the first, and along a series of winding passageways, into what seemed a separate wing of the house. The girls were to share a bedroom; this was not because there weren't plenty of rooms available to them, but it had been thought they should be put in together to keep each other company. It was a large, gaunt chamber with a high ceiling and a single broad sash window looking down on to a strip of lawn beyond which lay the wood. Two narrow beds stood side by side, separated by an oak chest of drawers on top of which there was a jug and two enamel basins. There were also an enormous mahogany wardrobe, with a mirror in the door, a couple of spindly, straight-backed chairs, and an uninvitingly lumpy-looking sofa with a carved wooden scroll along the back. The girls' bags had been brought up, and stood together in a neat squadron in front of the wardrobe.

"Well, this is nice!" Celia Nashe said brightly, looking about. "Isn't it nice, girls?"

Ellen and Mary, as they had now become, stood in their overcoats and hats, also side by side, like their suitcases, and gazed back at her in silence. Despite their unyielding attitude, which bordered on downright rudeness, Celia felt a qualm of sympathy for them, which she knew better than to let show. They would all have to take the situation as they found it. Yet, like Richard Lascelles, she wondered if the girls' parents knew the kind of place they had dispatched their children to — had they ever stayed at Clonmillis Hall? Had they ever even visited it?

For her part, she wouldn't have consigned her pet dog to such a looming mausoleum.

But then, as everyone knew, the royals were different from the rest of us. They lived in a world run according to rules of which ordinary people had no experience and the demands of which they could hardly begin to imagine.

The beds, she was surprised to note, had not been made up. Mrs O'Hanlon caught her look, and her already tight expression turned a notch tighter.

"We weren't expecting the — the young ladies until after lunch," she said. "I had not been consulted, so I can't say what happened for you all to arrive so early."

Mary sat on the side of one of the bare beds and bounced up and down a couple of times, and made a face. She was holding her handbag on her lap. Her hat was a tam o' shanter, and under her coat she was wearing a tartan skirt decorated with a giant safetypin. Celia, who was single and childless, nevertheless knew at least something of children — her brother had a couple of daughters, who were about the same age as these two — and she could see that the little one was getting ready for a major bout of the sulks. No doubt she was missing her parents, although patently she had no intention of letting on that this was the case.

Mrs O'Hanlon had stopped by the window and was looking down into the garden. She clicked her tongue. "That girl," she muttered. Then she turned to Celia.

"We've put you in the Blue Room," she said. "It's just along the corridor."

"May we begin to unpack now?" the older girl, Ellen, enquired. She had unbuttoned her coat but had not taken it off. The day had clouded over and the air in the high-ceilinged room was distinctly chilly; the autumn had been clement so far but the coming winter's damp had begun to encroach.

Mary stood up from the bed and went to the window and looked out to see what or who had caught Mrs O'Hanlon's disapproving attention. She saw the maid in the garden, struggling with the heavy wet bed linen. From this part of the house, if Mary put her face close to the glass and looked down sideways at an angle, she could see the duke, too, in the morning room, standing with his back to the window. As she watched, the maid, a plump young woman with dark hair gathered inside a white linen bonnet, took up the laundry basket and walked with it under her arm towards a door that stood open on what seemed to be a scullery. As she came level with the window, which was open some inches at the bottom, she slowed her pace, and from the way she held herself, crouching down a little, it was clear to

Mary that she was trying to hear what was being said inside. Then she went on into the scullery.

Ellen had lifted one of her suitcases on to the sofa and was unpacking it.

"Let me help you," Celia said, going to her.

Mrs O'Hanlon moved towards the door. "I'll leave you to it, then," she said.

No one paid her any heed — Celia was kneeling before the suitcase, from which Ellen was removing a pale-blue frock — and Mary noted with interest the vengeful look the older woman threw at the younger one as she was going out at the doorway. Those two were not going to get on, that was clear to see. Mary made it her business to watch people and note how they behaved. She thought she would make a good detective, probably a better one than the shiver-shanks in the trench coat who had been assigned to them — she wasn't even supposed to know he was a policeman.

Behind her, her sister spoke to Celia, in the bossy tone she adopted when she was addressing a servant: "Really, Miss Nashe, I can do the unpacking myself, thank you. I'm sure you have your own things to attend to."

Celia, Mary could see, was startled to be spoken to in this imperious fashion. Well, she would have to get used to it. Mary had already thought up a nickname — Miss Nasty — for their frosty-faced overseer.

"Of course, if you're sure," Celia, still on her knees, said to Ellen. "And, please, do call me Celia" — she glanced at Mary, over at the window — "will you, both of you?"

65

Ellen pretended not to hear. She was cross, which meant she was uncertain as to exactly how she should behave in these particular circumstances.

Celia rose to her feet, smoothing down the front of her skirt. She cast a vague and somewhat unsteady little smile in Mary's direction, and left the room.

She would say one thing for her sister, Mary reflected. Uncertain or not, she knew how to put people in their place, with only the slightest hardening of the voice.

"You had better unpack too," Ellen said to her, without turning. "I expected we would have personal maids, but it seems they don't run to that kind of thing in Ireland."

Mary could hear, in an adjoining room — the Blue Room — Mrs O'Hanlon and Celia conversing in chilly tones.

"If you should need anything," Mrs O'Hanlon was saying, "anything at all, you only have to ask. I'm the one to come to."

"Thank you, Mrs . . ." Celia had apparently forgotten the housekeeper's name.

Mrs O'Hanlon let some moments of heavy silence pass — Mary could imagine the glitter in her pale-blue eyes — and then said, with heavy emphasis, "The name is O'Hanlon."

"Of course, of course!" Celia exclaimed, in an embarrassed rush. "So sorry, Mrs O'Hanlon. Thank you."

The housekeeper left the room, and Mary heard her going down the passageway. She waited a moment, then stepped out quietly and went along close by the wall until she came to the Blue Room. The door stood ajar. Inside, Celia had set her Gladstone bag on top of a low chest of drawers beside her bed, and she drew from it what it took Mary a moment to recognise as a holster, made of shiny dark-brown leather, with a flap held shut by a metal snap fastener. Celia clicked open the snap and lifted the flap and drew out a pistol, blue-black and burnished. She checked it over for a moment, then slid it back into the holster and opened one of the drawers in the chest and put gun and holster into it, and pushed it shut.

Mary wasn't surprised at all, only excited, by what she had seen: she had been certain someone would have a gun.

So there was danger.

She heard a person below starting to come up the stairs, and she ran back and ducked into what she supposed she would have to get used to thinking of as her room, hers and her sister's. Ellen had interrupted her unpacking, and was standing before the window, looking out at the cloudy morning. Why was she so still, and why did she have her hand to her face? Was she crying? When she became aware of Mary behind her she went back to her suitcase, but kept her face turned away.

Mary lay down on the bed that she had chosen to be hers. She was still wearing her overcoat. She folded her hands on her breast — she lay stiff and motionless, practising being a corpse — and gazed up at the ceiling. She liked the look of the soft shadows congregated in the corners; there was something secret and pleasantly melancholy about them. It was the same with all ceilings, even in the brightest rooms. She often wished she could float up out of her body, float up and stay up there, like a spider, suspended in that permanent, dreamy twilight.

The person climbing the stairs had reached the top, and she heard a man's tread in the passage, and turned her head in time to see the detective going past the doorway.

She thought again of Celia Nashe's gun. She would creep in some day when Celia wasn't there and take it out of its holster and hold it in her hand. She wanted to know what it felt like to hold a gun. This one would be different from the shotguns her father had, which he shot birds with. They were more like tools than weapons. Miss Nashe's gun was another matter altogether.

There was the distant sound of hammering. That would be the young man with the freckles — McLaverty, he was called — still at work repairing the front door. How was it she could remember his name but had forgotten the detective's? Life was full of such odd contradictions. She thought of the young man they had passed by on the drive. She wondered what his name was. He really did look like Jamie McDonald, the gillie at Balmoral. Only he was more handsome than Jamie.

CHAPTER
EIGHT

Strafford had been wandering about the house quite happily, sticking to the ground floor at first — the library had been a not unexpected disappointment: musty, leather-bound copies of *Hudibras* and Scott's *Ivanhoe*, and other titles in that vein — and then venturing more tentatively into the upper regions. He was aware of a sense of mild despondency; it was the only word he could think of to characterise his mood, even though the feeling wasn't entirely negative. Indeed there was a certain pleasure in it, the pale pleasure that nostalgia usually afforded him. Everything he encountered was familiar to him from his childhood, especially the smells — of dust, of drains, of Cardinal floor polish on red stone tiles, of a myriad prehistoric overcooked dinners — so that he felt as if he were asleep and dream-walking through a place he had known well, long ago, in waking life.

When he had climbed to the second floor he passed by the partly open door of the girls' room, but he did not look in and did not stop. He found it slightly uncanny to be in their presence; they still seemed to him figures from some famous old painting that had come magically alive.

He looked down from a landing window and glimpsed the maroon Bentley starting up and heading off down the drive. *Lascelles fugit*, he thought sardonically, recalling his even more sardonic Latin teacher at the Quaker school in Waterford.

Along the corridor another door was open, and he could see Celia Nashe moving about inside the room.

He hesitated. As a child he had spent a less than happy week in hospital when his appendix had been removed, and he had been tended by a nurse whose name was Nashe. Nurse Nashe was a chilly and alarming person, with remarkably large hands and a distinct, mouse-coloured moustache, whose first words to him, as she was putting him to bed in the middle of the morning on the day of his admission, were that she would "stand no nonsense" from him. On the journey down, the present Miss Nashe had maintained a similarly stern and glacial attitude towards him, which she seemed bent on keeping up. It was clear she was determined to show herself the cool, detached professional, which he had no reason to think she was not.

He took it she was not the girls' governess — she hadn't the look of a governess, though he wasn't sure what governesses looked like — but an agent of the British intelligence services. His boss, Hackett, had assured him that he had been given little hard information about her from the embassy, or about anything else to do with the operation, for that matter. Strafford supposed she was concerned that as a woman she would not be taken sufficiently seriously in her role, whatever it was exactly, in such a delicate and potentially perilous mission. Still, they were in the thing together, himself and her, whether they liked it or not, and would have to get on with each other as best they could. It didn't matter to him if she was to be higher than him in authority here. He would make sure to let her know that: he had no desire to get into squabbles with her over seniority, of all things.

He tapped a knuckle lightly on the open door, and the young woman gave a start, and glanced at him over her shoulder.

"Oh, come in, Detective," she said; she sounded less than welcoming.

He wondered if she would continue to address him in this formal fashion for the duration of their time at Clonmillis. If so, how was he to address her? No doubt she had a title, too, but it seemed she had no intention of telling him what it was. He had a notion that MI5 officers were known as commanders. Perhaps he would try it out on her, just to see how she would respond. Then he changed his mind. More often than not even his mildest jokes fell flat.

She was engaged in unpacking the last of her things. In an open drawer he saw a neat pile of folded silk stockings, along with some other unidentifiable, intimate things, and, being a well-bred young man, he quickly averted his eyes, though not before he had spotted, almost hidden by the clothing, what was unmistakably a holster, under the flap of which was visible the glint of a gun.

He shouldn't have been surprised, but he was, in a way. He would have expected her to be equipped with something far more subtle — poison in a signet ring, perhaps, a sword in a shooting-stick, or even a magic umbrella, like Mary Poppins.

Celia asked what had become of Lascelles. He told her the Englishman had departed for Dublin just a minute ago — the Bentley's rear wheels had thrown up what might have been a derisory shower of gravel as it bounded away from the house — and her face betrayed for a second a flicker of hurt surprise. He had himself thought it less than polite of Lascelles to go off without bothering to bid either of them goodbye. Miss Nashe's fleeting expression, unless he was wrong about it, suggested she had already taken something of a fancy to Richard Lascelles — he would be her type, all right.

"You're settling in, I see," he said, folding his arms and leaning one shoulder against the door frame.

"Well, trying to," she answered, with a prim little rueful smile. "I didn't expect the house to be quite so huge."

He thought he detected a faint tremor in her hands. Travel fever, he supposed — she and the girls had come a long way. Or was she beset by anxiety? He supposed he should be, too.

A lighted cigarette, lipstick-stained at one end, was balanced on the edge of an ashtray on top of the chest of drawers and sending up a thin, wavering line of smoke.

"You'll find it's not so big, when you get used to it," he said. "These old houses are deceptive."

At once, inwardly, he chided himself: he should have learned by now not to claim such casual intimacy with big and venerable houses. She would think he was trying to impress her.

"What about the — the girls?" he asked. How on earth, really, was he going to refer to them? "Do you think they'll get used to the place? It is rather daunting."

She was fitting a pale-pink cardigan on to a wooden hanger from the wardrobe.

"I can see they're homesick already," she said. "But they'll be all right. Ellen will keep the little one's spirits up."

"Do you think so? I rather feel it might be the other way round."

"I'm sure a lot of that is just show. Ten-year-olds are always full of swagger, until something goes awry."

"Then let's hope nothing does — go awry, I mean."

She did not return his smile, but frowned and picked up the cigarette and drew on it deeply. She had not been a smoker for long, he could see, and did it as if performing some small, difficult and delicate chore, holding the cigarette at an unpractised angle and not inhaling. His mother used to smoke like that when she was nervous or upset. He looked more closely at Miss Nashe. She was definitely not at ease. Perhaps she wasn't quite the ice maiden she was determined to seem. Anyway, he thought it unlikely he would be permitted to get close enough to her to take her true temperature.

She put the cardigan into the wardrobe and lifted a pair of shoes out of her suitcase.

"And you? What about you?" he asked, aware of venturing out once more upon perilous waters. "Will you be all right?"

She flashed him a sharp look — her eyes were a peculiarly luminous shade of grey — but then shrugged. "Yes, I'm perfectly fine," she said briskly, yet with a softening of her tone that he would not have expected: she was not entirely impervious, after all, to sympathy. She gazed unseeing before her. "I keep thinking of — oh, I don't know. The Babes in the Wood. The Princes, or in this case the Princesses, in the Tower. Ridiculous, of course. It's just this country, this place — it's not what I expected it to be."

He smiled again. "And what did you expect?"

For a moment she stood in the middle of the floor with the shoes in one hand and the half-smoked cigarette in the other. "Something a little less daunting, I suppose," she said. "A little more friendly. The Irish people one meets in England are always so jolly —" She broke off. "Does that sound terribly patronising? You're Irish, aren't you?"

"Yes, of course," He looked aside, frowning. He had surprised himself: why "of course"?

"You don't sound like — like other Irish people I've spoken to, over the years," the young woman said. She leaned down and placed the shoes on the floor of the wardrobe, side by side, their toes pointing outwards; they were black, not new but well-polished, with neat square heels. "I mean, your accent is different."

"Is it? I don't notice." This was not true — he did notice, always — but it had seemed the right thing to say.

Celia took a last quick puff at her cigarette and ground it out in the ashtray. "Pay no attention to me," she said, visibly cross with herself now. "I'm behaving like a ninny — which I'm not at all, really," She looked him directly in the eye. "I hope you'll believe that." It sounded less like a plea than a warning.

Well, he did believe it: there was a hardness to her deep down, despite the nice eyes and the pink cardigan. He did not forget, of course, that he found all Englishwomen more or less hard; it was something about the way they spoke, clipped and fast and always faintly, coldly amused. Or so it seemed to his Irish ear. If he didn't speak as she was used to Irish people speaking, maybe he heard differently, too.

"I don't think you're being a ninny at all," he said, making an attempt at gallantry.

"I'm sorry," she said, flushing a little, "but I have no head for names. Dreadful of me, I know. I already forgot the housekeeper's, and got glared at. Will you tell me yours, again?" He told her. "Strafford," she said, "yes, I should have remembered. It's quite unusual, isn't it? I mean, with an r."

Then it came to him suddenly, to his surprise, that he quite liked her, despite, or perhaps because of, her deliberately cold and distant manner. Yet he didn't seem to be attracted to her, particularly. Perhaps it was, rather, that he admired her, admired the look of her, the way she carried herself, trim and compact and

75

neatly folded as a brown-paper parcel. And she had a nice smile, grudging though it was. She could have been his sister, if he'd had a sister.

All the same, that unguarded show of agitation and uncertainty concerned him a little. He wouldn't have gone so far as to say he thought her nerve was in danger of failing her, but it had shown a distinct quaver. He recalled again Hackett pointedly assuring him, or warning him, more like, that this was Celia Nashe's operation, and that his position was strictly secondary. He was back-up, Hackett had said, strictly back-up — as well as, of course, Minister Dan Hegarty's eyes and ears at Clonmillis Hall, though no one had instructed him as to this, not in so many words. But was this Miss Nashe as tough as she wished to appear? He hoped she was.

The country had more than its share of former gunmen, as well as a few brand-new ones, who nursed an undying hatred of perfidious Albion. What if he was called on to act? He was a detective, not a secret agent. He wasn't even armed. When he had joined the force he had been given a gun — a revolver it was, a big, unwieldy beast of a thing, with a six-inch barrel and a braided lanyard attached to the butt — but he had no sooner taken possession of it than he put it away at the back of a drawer and tried to forget about it. Now he had begun to think he should have brought it with him. If Nurse Nashe was armed, shouldn't he be, also?

Nurse Nashe! He would have to be careful not to address her in that mocking fashion.

Yes, he should have brought the gun. There were still acts of violence being committed, especially in the countryside. Sometimes a gang of gunmen, disaffected IRA members hankering for the war that had ended nearly two decades previously, would take it into their heads to go out and shoot a policeman, and as often as not policemen in their turn shot them back, in retaliation. Summary executions had been carried out by the state. The times were parlous, as his father would say. What if a band of hotheads turned up here one dark night with tommy-guns and hand grenades? Was he supposed to fend them off with his posh accent?

All the same, the last thing he wanted was to have to shoot someone. It was not that he didn't have the stomach for it — he could think of quite a number of people he considered richly deserving of a well-aimed bullet — but he knew it would change everything. He would be a person who had killed someone, a person who, looked at now in the possibility of the deed, was someone he did not recognise: a stranger.

"You know there will be regular military patrols around the perimeter of the estate," he said. "You won't see them, but they'll be there. It will be all right, I'm certain of that." Another falsehood: he had no such certainty.

Celia gave a brief and unexpectedly steady, almost gay little laugh; she had regained her equilibrium. "Yes, I mustn't let my imagination run away with me," she said. "Who would want to harm two young girls?"

To this, again, he made no reply: if he were to respond with what he really thought, it would be no comfort to her. Ireland had been held in British overlordship for eight hundred years, more or less, depending on who was doing the counting, and although the larger part of the country was independent now, that it had been occupied for so long had a potent, abiding and visceral significance for a considerable portion of the population.

"You're right, of course," he said, opting yet again for the soothing untruth. "Who would think of hurting a couple of children?"

This she rewarded with a smile that transformed her face, making her good looks softer, less steely.

But if she really imagined there was no threat, did it not strike her as superfluous that there should be a troop of armed soldiers guarding the perimeter of the estate round the clock? From below there came the reverberant and peculiarly ominous sound of a gong being gently struck. The chimes, three of them in slow succession, seemed to bounce up the steps of the staircase, like weightless big burnished copper globes.

"That will be lunch, I should imagine," Strafford said, and smiled.

Oh, with what ease he could smile, he thought, especially when a smile was the last thing the circumstances warranted.

CHAPTER
NINE

It was indeed lunch that the gong had announced. It proved a hectic affair, unsurprisingly to Strafford, who knew well the tendency of the Anglo-Irish kitchen to come close to collapse when the daily rhythm of the household was even slightly disturbed.

For years this house had drifted along contentedly enough, like a great anchorless hulk in a torpid sea. The last people who had come to stay had been the duke's nephew, a Captain Danvers, and his red-haired wife. They were a flighty pair, in the estimation of all below stairs — the captain drank anything he could get his hands on, and was invariably blotto by bedtime, while Mrs D., as she was known, would flirt, at the very least, with anything in trousers. Since then, little had happened to make waves in the placid surface of life at the Hall. Now, suddenly, all was disrupted by a boarding party of exotic, mysterious and faintly frightening strangers.

The legend that had been put about among the servants, who would, naturally, spread it beyond the Hall, was that the two girls, evacuated until the nightly bombing raids on London should have eased, were the daughters of the duke's grand-niece — there was, of course, no such person — married to an officer high up in the military, who had been posted, along with his wife, to Cairo. Celia Nashe was supposedly the girls' governess, brought over to look after them in a bachelor household.

Accounting for Strafford's presence had required a little more ingenuity. In the end it had been decided that he would be presented as Miss Nashe's first cousin. The fact of consanguinity between the gentleman and the young lady was a neat way of preserving the decencies, tacitly demanded by Mrs O'Hanlon and, so it was imagined, by the rest of the staff also, especially the females.

The young man had come to stay in the country supposedly for the sake of his health, which was poor, as evidenced by the tubercular paleness of his complexion and the meagreness of his frame. Maggie the maid had been heard to observe that there wasn't a pick on him, which would not prevent her, as the days went on, from giving him the glad eye whenever the opportunity arose; Maggie, though no beauty, was said to be "wild", and in need of watching. It was she whom the duke had sighed irritably over, and whom Mrs O'Hanlon had clicked her tongue at, when from their different vantage points they had observed her spitting on the corner of the sheet and rubbing it vigorously prior to hanging it on the clothesline.

Strafford wondered how much was believed of these elaborate fictions; precious little, he guessed. Servants, in his experience, knew everything that went on in a household, upstairs and down. "Sure, don't we change

80

the beds?" a housemaid had once said to him, giving him a bold, laughing look. Strangely, however, they seemed hardly to value what they knew, perhaps operating on the principle that if they were in on a secret then it couldn't be much worth knowing, and probably wasn't much of a secret anyway.

Lunch had barely begun when Hynes, the butler and general factotum, an ancient party with unruly hair as white and fine as bog cotton and a distinct wobble in the region of the knees, caught his foot on the threshold of the dining room and let fall a platter of cabbage, which made a crash that to those at table seemed as loud and cataclysmic as the sounding of the Last Trump. Florence the parlour-maid, too, a tall, swan-necked, gauntly handsome young woman, was all thumbs, as she later confessed to Elsie the scullery-maid. Elsie was a bit simple, and had been known for so long as "Poor Elsie" that it had become silently hyphenated, as "Poor-Elsie", and had almost taken the place of her real name.

Meanwhile the duke surveyed the table with a dubious eye, as if he were not entirely sure that the people sitting around it were real or whether they might be merely the phantasmagorical products of his imagination — with the years, he had noted in himself an increasing tendency to wool-gather. By now he was gloomily convinced that agreeing to take in the princesses had been a mistake, even if it were to result in the fulfilment of his secret aim, which was to make enough of a profit on his act of magnanimity to have the roof of the Hall re-leaded. The repair was badly needed, though Lascelles's impudent talk of accounting and receipts and so forth had already put that plan in doubt. Receipts indeed!

After the initial flurry of travel and arrival, Strafford had become aware of a vague sense of desperation rising inside him, like seawater in the hold of a foundering ship. How on earth was he to cope with the barrenness of the coming days and weeks — months, possibly? His job here was not a job at all, except potentially. He was a policeman, and in normal circumstances would be called in only after a crime had been committed. What sort of work was it, if it was work at all, to be ordered to wait and watch in case something might happen? Did the job really require the presence of a secret agent and a full-time professional detective?

His gloom deepened when he discovered that he was not to lodge in the main house but in a sort of annex in the stable yard built of rough-cut stone, with tiny windows and a steep slate roof. There was something wrong with the scale of the place: it looked too cramped for a human being to inhabit — probably it was itself a converted stable — and he would not have been surprised, when he first approached it across the yard, to see a family of elves, the true occupants, in bootees and scarlet caps and bright green tunics, crowding at those little windows to get a gander at the towering invader as he came to commandeer their quarters.

Within, there were three rooms, a cramped living room and a claustrophobically narrow bedroom, and, at the back, a kitchen hardly bigger than a good-sized cupboard. Beyond the kitchen was attached an evil-smelling outhouse, with a sloping sheet of galvanised iron for a roof, a lavatory with a chipped wooden seat, and two ancient taps sticking out of a bare plaster wall above a badly pockmarked enamel sink. In the living room there was a table and a chair, a prolapsed chaise-longue, its straw innards hanging out underneath and partly resting on the floor, and a pot-bellied wood-burning stove, with a rusted chimney poking up through a hole in the ceiling. His bed was a metal-framed folding affair, from underneath which the off-white china ear of a chamber pot peeped coyly out, clear evidence that the lavatory was not to be depended on. When Florence the parlour-maid had first shown him into the place, he had set his suitcase on the floor at the foot of the bed and looked about with what must have been, to judge by the young woman's sympathetic eye, an expression of deep despair.

"You'll be grand, staying over there in style," Hackett had assured him. "They'll probably put you in the West Wing, in a big suite of rooms with marble fireplaces and a view of the lake."

There were no big rooms and no marble fireplaces, or not for him, anyway; there was not even a lake.

He trusted he would be allowed the run of the main house during the hours of daylight at least: if he had to spend the greater part of his time in banishment in this stone hovel he would be in serious peril of losing his reason.

There were horses in the stables, half a dozen of them; on his first appearance each had come to its half-door and put out its head and looked at him with that equine mixture of curiosity and glossy-eyed indifference that he always found uncanny and faintly worrying. He was not a rider, though there had always been horses about the place when he was young.

He had been a solitary child, furtive and, to those around him, unnervingly inscrutable. It occurred to him, later, that he must have been a disappointment to his parents, his mother especially, who, when she first came as a bride to Roslea, had aspired to be a *grande hôtesse*, and would have crowded the house with visitors, had they been available in the bleak corner of County Wexford where Roslea House stood, at the far end of a meandering drive, with a ridge of grass running along its centre, that was at least half as long again as the drive here at Clonmillis. His father, who treated his son with benevolent neglect, frustrated his wife's pretensions to grandeur since he lived for the farm and his livestock and detested social gatherings of all kinds, grand or otherwise.

"That fellow from the embassy went off fairly sharpish," the duke said now, breaking in on the young man's despondent rememberings. "Didn't seem the type who would care much for country life. That car he was driving . . ." His voice descended to a dark muttering, as he munched away at his food.

Mary, Strafford saw, was engaged in carefully separating a piece of broccoli from the other comestibles on her plate and pushing it to one side with her fork. Her sister, seated opposite her, held her spine so rigidly tensed that her back from the shoulders down formed a shallow, concave arc. Her dark hair was curled above her forehead and all the way round her head in a shape suggestive, to Strafford's eye, of a tiara, or even — ha! — a crown. Perhaps, he reflected, the effect was intentional.

"I'm sure there must be some lovely walks around here," Celia Nashe said suddenly, glancing up from her plate with a forced brightness. "Are the grounds very extensive?"

The duke looked at her, frowning, with one bushy eyebrow indignantly cocked. It was as if she had asked about the state of his bank balance. "Grounds?" he said, as if exclaiming at some impossibly extravagant notion. "Don't know about grounds. There are three thousand acres of land, give or take." He made a munching motion with his jaws. "Most of it is walkable, I suppose. Not sure if you'd find it lovely" — the word "lovely" was followed by a small, dismissive snort — "though there's some good shooting, and our little river, the Henny, still has a few salmon the poachers haven't managed to kill."

"Is there a library in the town?" Strafford asked.

This provoked from the duke a bilious stare. It was Celia Nashe who replied. "There's a Carnegie library, yes," she said. "I checked, before we came."

"That was clever of you," Strafford said. "How far is it from here? The town, I mean."

"Ten miles, on foot," the duke replied, with another faint snort, as if to suggest that for a true countryman ten miles would be a mere step or two down the road. He did his awful mirthless grin. "Eight, if you ride cross-country, though you don't look like a horseman to me. There's a bus. It stops at the gate."

Celia had turned her gaze to the window and the vague world beyond. Strafford studied her covertly. Her expression was that of one who, newly arrived in prison, is already forming a plan of escape.

He saw again, by the pale light from the window, how pretty she was. She would not be in the least interested in him, he knew — he had seen her take one look and dismiss him, certainly in the romance department — but Richard Lascelles was a different matter. It would be interesting to see what might happen if the diplomat were to return and stay for any time here at Clonmillis Hall. A spicy little *affaire*, of the kind that Lascelles was bound to specialise in, would at least have the effect of raising the emotional temperature of the house by a degree or two.

However, the matter with Celia just then, as Strafford might have realised if he had stopped to consider the thing seriously, was simply that she was furious with herself for having gone silly after he had appeared at her bedroom door earlier, and caught her off-guard by being sympathetic and asking her if she would be all right.

Of course, he would arrive at the precise moment when she was feeling anything but all right, when she was feeling thoroughly rotten, in fact, after that ghastly sea crossing and then the shock of landing up here at Castle Rackrent. What must he have thought of her, rattling on about the Babes in the Wood and the Princes in the Tower? She was supposed to be a professional, wasn't she? But as she had confessed to him — oh, why couldn't she have kept her mouth shut? — she hadn't been prepared for Ireland, and this awful ancient pile, and the people's accents that at first she had thought must be put on to make mock of her, they sounded to her ear so stagily "Oirish". And then there was the housekeeper — what was her name? Hanly, or Hanlon, something like that — who, the moment she had set eyes on Celia, had as good as declared all-out war.

How was she to cope with it all? This wasn't what she had been trained for, looking after two girls, both of them determined in their different but equally obstinate ways to cause her as much heartache as they possibly could.

Well, she would just have to put up with it. She was a professional, even if her masters had chosen to land her with an assignment that any chit of a recent entrant could have handled with perfect competence.

Eventually lunch came to an end, provoking an almost audible sigh of relief from all at the table. So grim had the occasion been that Strafford toyed wistfully with the thought of requesting if, in future, he might take his meals in his quarters in the stable yard, but knew it would be even more uncongenial and discomforting out there, on his own, in the damp and the cold.

Ellen and Mary requested to be excused, and went off to finish their unpacking, or so they said. The duke lit his pipe. Strafford was interested to see if Celia would follow suit and light up a cigarette, to demonstrate what a modern woman she was.

Outside, the autumn mist, more grey than gold, hung dense and unmoving over the silent fields.

"So tell me," the duke said, emitting a swirl of tobacco smoke, which surrounded his head like ectoplasm, "you're a sort of team, are you, you two?" Strafford and Celia Nashe looked at him blankly. "You're here to guard them, aren't you," the old man went on testily, "the princesses, or the girls, or whatever they're to be called?"

"I'm charged with looking after their security, yes," Celia said, choosing her words with tight-lipped care, letting the old boy know she did not appreciate being spoken to so dismissively. "I'm not sure 'guard' is the word I'd use — certainly not in their hearing."

The duke turned his bristling glare on Strafford. "And what about you?" he barked.

Strafford smiled. The old boy was, delightfully, a perfect parody of himself. "I'm with the Garda Force —"

"For heaven's sake, I'm well aware of that! What I want to know is, what are you going to be doing about the place? This is a working farm, you know."

Strafford did not reply, but fell to brooding again on this strange commission. The presence of royalty made Clonmillis Hall into a sort of extension of the British embassy, so that it was, like the embassy, a little part of England, cordoned off in the middle of what for centuries had been rebel territory. The Irish government would hardly have agreed to take the princesses if there had not been the offer of regular shipments of desperately needed coal. Strafford, as a product of his upbringing — his father despised public life and all who lived it — found the deal distasteful. At best it was a piece of cold, pragmatic statecraft, at worst an example of Britain's unscrupulousness and neutral Ireland's greed and shameless opportunism.

"I think I must defer to Miss Nashe in the matter of a security regime," he said to the duke, and added, in a lower tone, "if there is to be one." He glanced at the young woman seated opposite him, but she seemed determined not to meet his eye. "My understanding of the thing," he went on, "in so far as I do understand it, is that we're all to maintain a calm and relaxed appearance, so as not to upset the young ladies."

"But what are they going to do, those two?" the duke moaned. He looked out of the window, the dottle in his pipe sending up another rapidly whirling cloud of mingled smoke and sparks. "There are the horses, of course," he resumed, in a hopeful tone, answering his own question. "Girls like horses, don't they? We had to get rid of the dogs, after one of them was shot for worrying sheep on a local farm. I believe also there's a cat about the place — it's kept in the kitchen, for the mice. Might be feral, though, for all I know. Oh dear."

Strafford had a suspicion that, like him, Celia Nashe found something irresistibly comical in the old man's jeremiads; at least, she seemed to be having difficulty in keeping a straight face. He looked away from her and sat without moving and stared resolutely at the table top, afraid they would both burst into laughter if their eyes met.

Oddly, this non-exchange he felt to be the first instance of genuine communication he and the young woman had shared so far. Could it be that Miss Nashe had a sense of humour, after all? That she even derived a secret amusement, as he did, from the essential absurdity of the world at large? After a moment's reflection he came reluctantly to the conclusion that on balance this was unlikely to be the case. Miss Nashe was patently a Home Counties girl, in spirit if not by birth — from her accent she could have been born anywhere south of the Wash — and as such he rather doubted she would find life and its occasions much of a laughing matter.

"I don't imagine they see much excitement when they're at home," he ventured at last, keeping his eyes fixed on the table and rolling a crumb of bread back and forth under a fingertip. "I've always felt a little sorry for the royals, forever trying not to yawn in the midst of all that pomp and circumstance."

The duke glanced at him quickly, recognising sarcasm, even a hint of mockery, not only of the Royal Family but also, obliquely, of himself and his kind. Who was this fellow that he should feel thus free to comment on his betters?

Strafford: he turned over the name in his mind. Farming stock, most likely, come down in the world. The Fitzherberts of Clonmillis Hall were themselves hardly top-drawer. True, they had been, once — oh, from the highest of drawers! — but not any more.

Celia Nashe, meanwhile, had indeed brought out a packet of cigarettes — Senior Service of course — and was lighting up, without even a by-your-leave, so the duke had a glare for her, too. Clonmillis Hall might be neutral territory, like the rest of this exasperating country — his country, and yet not — but it had been invaded, nevertheless. For how long, he wondered gloomily, would the occupation last?

CHAPTER
TEN

Leisurely explorations of the Hall became from early on the chief of Mary's pastimes. She would wander about for hours in contented solitude, often talking to herself in a squeaky, singsong little voice that amused her, when she noticed it — for the most part she just prattled away unawares. She favoured especially the upper floors of the house, where the rooms were neglected and mouldy, and the air smelt, for some reason, of rotted apples; it was a smell, melancholy and evocative, that she liked, though she could not have said why.

One day, on one of these solitary ventures about the house, she stopped in a draughty corridor and lingered by a high window overlooking the stable yard. The panes of glass were cracked, and greyed over with dust. She leaned her forehead against the window frame. Mummy and Daddy had telephoned the previous evening, though as usual it was her sister they spent most of the time talking to. After the call she had cried herself to sleep, and if her sister heard her she made no comment.

There at the window, she was hoping to catch a glimpse of Billy Denton.

Billy was the young man with the shotgun she had seen walking down the drive that first day, and whose image had lodged firmly in her mind. He worked at the Hall in various capacities, one of his main tasks being the maintenance of the horses. Since that first sighting on the drive she had caught further glimpses of him on a number of occasions. He was, as she had noted straight off, very good-looking, though he always had a sulky expression. He had hazel eyes, and his curly black hair gleamed like wet coal. She had tried repeatedly to get him to talk to her, but he had brushed past her as if she weren't there.

It would be different, she was sure, if he knew who she really was, and often she felt like telling him, just to see the look on his face.

This morning she saw down in the yard not Billy but what she thought must be a tramp, though how a tramp would have got in there she couldn't think. It had rained in the night, but it was fine again now, and the cobbles shone in the damp, hazy light. The man, whom she first saw from behind, was squatting down on one knee, tying a length of rough yellow twine around one of the legs of his trousers at the level of the ankle.

He was short and squat, and wore a patched tweed jacket and a battered old grey felt hat and hobnailed boots. Even though his back was turned she knew that he was old. She was about to move on when suddenly he turned his head, or swivelled it, more like, as if it were mounted on a pivot, and glared straight up at her. It was uncanny — how had he known she was above him there, looking down on him? He had a broad face with crooked-looking features, and there was something peculiar about his eyes, which seemed not to match.

She stepped back quickly from the window, alarmed by the wild, fixed way in which he stared at her.

Maybe he was one of the people Miss Nashe and the detective were supposed to be on the watch for. If so, they weren't doing a very good job. The tramp, or whatever he was, could easily get into the house from the yard, for the doors were never locked, except at night, and often not even then. If he did break in, would Miss Nashe have to shoot him with that snubby, gleaming little gun of hers? This was a thrilling possibility. If it should happen, she hoped she would be there to see it. She had once seen a horse shot — it was at a point-to-point and the animal had fallen at a jump and broken a leg — but never a person.

She wondered if Miss Nashe had ever killed anyone. She didn't look as if she had but, then, how would a person look who had done a killing? Soldiers shot and blew each other up all the time, and they didn't seem any different from anyone else, except the ones who were shell-shocked, like old Jeavons, the gamekeeper's assistant at Windsor, who had been in the previous war and had the jitters and talked to himself under his breath without cease.

Goodness, she thought, do I sound like Jeavons when I talk to myself? She didn't know whether to laugh or be alarmed at the notion.

It turned out after all, and somewhat to her disappointment, that the old man in the yard wasn't a tramp, or an intruder come to kill her and her sister.

His name was Pike, and he was a general labourer in the employ of the duke.

She encountered him in person on the afternoon of the same day that she had spotted him from the window when he turned and looked up at her with that fearsome, cockeyed glare. This time she was sitting on the stump of a fallen tree at the side of what was called the Lower Paddock, which was nothing but a circle of churned-up clay enclosed by a rickety pitch-pine fence, and situated in a hollow next to the wood and out of sight of the Hall.

Her sister was doing her dressage exercises on a horse the duke had lent her. Prince, as the beast was called — what a stupid name! — was being uncooperative, not having got used to an unfamiliar rider, or so Mary supposed: she didn't like horses and therefore didn't understand them, although her parents insisted that she ride. This one kept shying to the left and jerking his head up and down and pulling at the reins, causing her sister almost to lose her seat.

The detective-she-wasn't-supposed-to-know-was-a-detective was at the far side of the paddock, wearing a gabardine coat and a pair of borrowed gumboots that were too big for him. He had taken up his place outside the fence, on which he had set his elbows, and was reading a book. She could see from the droopy way he was leaning there that he was bored — Mary knew all about boredom. He was so thin, she thought he must have TB. She wasn't absolutely sure what TB was or what the letters stood for — it was something to do with the tubes inside one's chest — but it was a disease that people discussed all the time, in hushed tones, or used to, until the German bombers came and gave them something more immediate to be afraid of and to chatter about endlessly.

All at once Prince stopped dead in his tracks, so that her sister very nearly came a cropper, and lifted his head and champed down hard on the bit and gave a frightened whinny, the whites of his eyes flashing.

Something had startled him.

Then Pike appeared, pushing a wheelbarrow, the single wheel of which gave out a small, anguished squeak once in each turn. Honestly, she thought, horses were such foolish animals — anything could set them off: a rabbit jumping out of a ditch or a tractor backfiring a mile away. Even a scrap of paper picked up by the wind could have them rearing and pawing at the air in terror.

Prince now was backing off sideways from Pike and the noisy wheelbarrow, throwing up his front hoofs and whinnying even more loudly than before, and her sister really had a hard time of it not to fall off.

The detective looked up from his book, frowning, just as the horse, having pushed open the gate with his rump and reversed all the way out of the paddock, turned about and galloped off swiftly by the side of the wood, his rider helpless in the saddle, and was soon out of sight.

Mary watched the detective with keen interest. What would he do? He jerked his head to right and left, a little as the horse had done — who was he looking for that he thought would help him? — then stuffed the book into the pocket of his coat and set off at a run after her sister and her bolting mount.

Pike, who had stopped near where Mary was sitting and set down his barrow, straightened up with a hand pressed to the small of his back, grinning as he watched the detective dashing along the slope of the meadow, his arms swinging and his knees going like pistons and his coat-tails flying.

"Begod, but that lad can run!" He laughed wheezily. "A champion sprinter!"

Up close, Pike was fascinatingly ugly. He looked exactly like a toad, with that wide flat mouth and the fleshy lips, the moist lower one of which hung slackly loose. His tobacco-brown teeth were gapped and broken. He was dirty, too, with little black specks, which made her think, disgustingly, of caviar, embedded in the pores of his cheeks and potatoey nose. It was his eyes that drew her immediate attention. They were each of a different colour, the right one grey and the left one an unreal sort of glossy bright blue. The blue one didn't move at all, only stared straight ahead as if it were fixed on some frightful prospect it alone could see.

"That young one has a grand seat on a horse," he said.

"Her name is Ellen," Mary sniggered; it gave her a funny little thrill, probably because it was a lie. But she had been told to tell it and therefore, supposedly, it wasn't wrong. "She's my sister."

"And what's your name?"

"My name?" She gave another small laugh. "Mary."

"Mary. Aye." He gazed at her vacantly for some seconds, moving his lower jaw in a circular motion, as if he were chewing slowly on something soft and sticky. Then he left his barrow and came and sat down beside her on the fallen tree trunk, grunting in discomfort and again pressing a hand to his back. He smelt of hay and soil and tobacco smoke, and something else she couldn't identify, which she supposed was just his old-man smell.

"I see you're looking at my eye," he said.

"Is it glass?"

"It is."

"Does it come out?"

"It does." He chuckled. "Will I tell you how I lost the real one?"

"Yes, please."

She wriggled inside her clothes in eager anticipation; she loved to hear accounts of gruesome mishaps.

"It was a great big old scald-crow that done it," Pike said, leaning forward with his hands on his knees and gazing before himself thoughtfully out of his one remaining eye. "I was over there in the Long Meadow, snagging turnips, and didn't he swoop down on me, thinking maybe I was an old ram that was after falling over and breaking a leg, and snap!" He clicked a finger and thumb in the air in front of the girl's nose. "Like that, he had the eye out of my head."

She turned to him with a look of deep scepticism. "Is it true?"

"Oh, true as God, miss," Pike assured her. "Sure, why would I lie to you?"

98

Just then a new voice broke in. "Don't believe a word of it."

Billy Denton had come up behind them unheard. He was wearing a shabby old jacket with a half-belt at the back, trousers that were shiny at the knees, and a peaked cap. He carried his shotgun in the crook of his right arm. He was looking away, in the direction of the trees. The girl saw straight off that he was one of those shy people who try to cover up their shyness by making themselves seem to be thinking all the time about something that was very serious and made them angry.

"He lost that eye," he said now, "when he fell into the ditch one night, coming back plastered from the pub."

This was the first time Mary had heard Billy Denton speak — he had a deep, plump voice, as if he were holding a peach stone or something carefully in his mouth — and she decided straight away that she had fallen in love with him. She stood up from the log so that he would be forced to look at her, but he gave her only the briefest glance, still solemnly frowning.

At that moment her sister reappeared, with the horse under control. She walked him across the paddock. The creature looked as if he wasn't in the least ashamed of himself and his obstreperous behaviour. He really was like something prehistoric, with that miniature flat face and huge, glossy black eyes.

"It's time to change for dinner, Mary."

"No, it's not!" the little girl cried indignantly. She had noticed how her sister avoided looking at Denton. Probably she was in love with him too; it would be just like her, fastening on to things that other people wanted, and not caring how they felt when she took them away for herself.

Prince's shiny coat was steaming after the gallop, and he was still worrying at the bit and making gagging noises. How could people who claimed to be fond of horses make them go about with a metal bar jammed between their teeth for hours on end?

"I was just remarking to the little one here, miss," Pike said, squinting up at Ellen where she sat astride the animal, "what a grand fine horsewoman you are."

"Thank you," Ellen said shortly, and dismounted and extended a hand impatiently to her sister. "Come along, or dinner will be held up, and Mrs O'Hanlon will be cross."

Mary scowled — one of her sister's ways of annoying her was to pretend to be convinced she was afraid of the housekeeper — but she allowed herself to be led away, Prince walking behind them with his head lowered, as if he were scanning the ground for something lost.

"Aren't they a grand pair of lassies, now?" Pike said to Denton, looking after the girls as they departed. "Only the older one is a bit stuck-up, by the look of her." He rose stiffly to his feet, sucking in air through his teeth as he did so. "Ah, the back is killing me today!" he exclaimed. "Have you a fag, at all?"

Denton brought out a packet of Player's and gave one to the old man, and struck a match and held it out to him, shielding the flame in the cup of his fist. "You'd better not let His Nibs hear you telling them those old stories of yours," he said.

"What stories?" Pike enquired innocently, drawing hard at the cigarette to get it going. The smoke brought on a bout of coughing that made him double over, with a fist pressed to his breastbone, his froggy face reddening and a tear springing up in his one functioning eye. Denton watched him dispassionately, and shifted the shotgun from his right arm to his left.

Strafford, knees and elbows still churning, came pounding up the meadow and into the paddock.

"Did you see the girl?" he demanded, panting, and pushing back the lock of hair that had flopped down over his forehead.

"We did indeed," Pike said, getting his own breath back after coughing so hard. "The two of them are gone off for their dinner."

"Christ," Strafford said, between clenched teeth. He turned to Denton. "We haven't met," he snapped. "I'm Strafford — with an r."

The two young men shook hands, Strafford making sure to smile — not good to alienate the locals — and Denton frowning and looking off to the side.

Pike's breathing had settled down sufficiently for him to risk another puff. He held the butt of the cigarette daintily between a thumb and middle finger. This boyo down from Dublin hadn't bothered introducing himself to him, he had noticed. "You needn't be worrying about that girl," he said. "It's a brave horse that would dare to land her in the muck."

Strafford was scuffing at the clay with the toe of a gumboot; the boots borrowed from the duke were three sizes too big for him, and the backs of his heels were already chafed and sore. He was angry with himself, and with the girl for losing control of the horse; he was angry, too, with these yokels standing before him, the older one of whom was making no attempt to curb his amusement at all that had happened, while the younger one glared at nothing as if he found everything offensive. It seemed to Strafford that the very day itself was mocking him. Silently he cursed Inspector Hackett for lumbering him with this absurd and futile posting; at this moment, as far as he was concerned, the wild men were welcome to break in and kidnap the pair of royal brats, if they cared to, and hold them to ransom for whatever sum they took it into their heads to demand.

He turned away. It was rare indeed for him to lose his temper like this. He must control himself. It was a time, if ever there was one, to keep a cool head. All the same, he stamped off, his hands clasped white-knuckled behind his back.

Pike regarded Denton with amusement. "Queer times, eh?" he said.

But Denton gave no reply, and he, too, departed, in the opposite direction from the detective. With a sardonic smirk the old man watched him go, then spat, and bent with a grunt and grasped the handles of the wheelbarrow and trundled it away.

CHAPTER
ELEVEN

It didn't seem a real scream, and for the first half-second of waking she thought she had dreamed it. But it hadn't been inside her head. It had come from somewhere close by in the house, cutting through the darkness, like the sound of a sheet of wrapping paper being ripped down the middle. A child's scream.

She registered dimly that she was already out of bed, having sprung up by instinct a split second before she was fully awake. She shrugged herself into her dressing-gown and fumbled to tie the belt of it as she ran to the door — she had brought slippers, too, but couldn't remember where she had put them when she was unpacking — and hurried barefoot along the corridor to the girls' room.

The curtains were open — hadn't she closed them? — and on a small table beneath the window stood a night-light with a low-wattage bulb that cast a faint, yellowish glow over the room. Mary was sitting up in bed, in the last stages of sobbing, wiping at her eyes with both her hands. Celia sat down on the side of the bed and took her in her arms. "Hush now, hush, it's all right," she said. "Did you have a bad dream?"

The child resisted her embrace; she was stiff with fright, but also trembling with resentment at being grabbed like this by a person she hardly knew, who was soppy like all adults, and smelt musty, the way all adults did, especially at night.

"I'm all right," she said, upset and cross at the same time. Her hair was all in a knot. She had been too hot under the heavy blankets but now she was getting chilled. She was annoyed at herself for screaming like that. She felt a fool.

"What frightened you?" Celia asked.

"There was someone in the wood, and the sky was on fire."

"It was just a dream, dear, just a dream. And it's gone now."

"It was not a dream!" the girl cried indignantly, and pulled herself free of Celia's encircling arms. "And he's still there."

"Who is?"

"I told you — in the wood! A man with a bird's face."

"A bird's face? What sort of bird?"

"How should I know?" Honestly, what a stupid question! "Just a bird, with a beak and glittering eyes."

Ellen, in the other bed, was lying on her side with her cheek resting on her joined hands. In the glow of the lamp her skin was shiny and sallow; she looked like an outsized doll. "She hates it here," she said quietly. "So do I. It's a horrid place."

"It won't be for long," Celia said. "Just until the bombing stops."

104

"It won't stop," Mary said matter-of-factly, and wiped her nose on the sleeve of her pyjamas. "The aeroplanes will keep coming until everything is blown up. Then they'll come over here and do the same."

"Oh, be quiet," Ellen said, putting on her weary-sounding, grown-up voice. "You're such a baby." With a violent movement she heaved herself on to her other side, so that she was facing the wall, and drew the bedclothes over her head.

Celia put out a hand to Mary but the child drew back, glaring at her narrowly, her eyes reflecting a tiny gleam from the light bulb.

"Go back to sleep, dear," the young woman murmured, striving to sound calm and comforting but not really succeeding — she was not the calmest herself. "It will be morning soon, and everything will look different in daylight."

The child lay down again, and she, too, turned her back, and would say no more.

Celia pressed her hands down heavily on her knees and drew herself wearily to her feet. They were right, the girls: this was an awful place. She wished Richard Lascelles hadn't left so soon. Him she trusted, though she was sure she shouldn't, at least not in certain areas: from the look in those hard, smiling eyes of his, it was plain he fancied himself a lady-killer.

She tiptoed away from the beds. As she was passing by the window she looked out into the darkness, and stopped. Had she glimpsed, beyond the dim reflection of the bulb on the pane, something moving down on the lawn? She put her forehead close to the glass, blocking off the light of the lamp with her hands, and peered out more searchingly into the night.

Below, the grass was grey in the moonlight.

Was the child right? Had there really been someone, or something, out there, or had they both been imagining things?

Perhaps it had been an animal, but she didn't think so. Yet what person would be walking around in the garden at this hour of the night? A soldier, maybe, come in to make a closer tour of inspection? But Lascelles had assured her that the patrols would stay well away from the house, and that she wouldn't even see them, unless she went out on to the road to look for them.

She glanced back at the girls, two motionless recumbent forms. She felt she should stay close, in case the little one's nightmare started up again.

The corridor was dark. She slipped along it, making not a sound, and went into her own room and closed the door. Her bare feet were cold. The window here looked down on the same patch of lawn that was to be seen below the girls' room. She stood a moment, sheltering behind the curtain, and peeped out through the glass. There was definitely nothing down there now, only the glimmer of moonlight on the lawn, and the dark wood beyond and, in the distance, the vague outline of a humpbacked hill.

No, there had been no one; her imagination had played a trick on her; it was the kind of thing that happened, at night, in a strange house.

But all the same —

She stepped into an old pair of corduroy slacks and drew on heavy socks and her lace-up walking boots, and put on a pullover and an alpaca jacket and a woollen cap that came down over her ears — when she had still entertained hopes that it was Scotland she was to be sent to she had kitted herself out for long, happy hikes through rugged but welcoming landscapes, with trout streams chuckling over the stones and the heather glowing in the autumn sunlight. Fat chance.

She took the Browning from the drawer and eased it out of its holster, the leather of which was still unhandily stiff, and put the weapon into her pocket, surprised again at how much it weighed, for its size.

Crossing once more to the window, she cupped her hands around her face and took another look out into the night.

Just the silver-grey moon-dust on the grass, the dark wood, and that far hill.

Was she being ridiculous? These were special circumstances, but that was no excuse for giving in to fancies. Yet she shouldn't take a chance: she had to be sure.

She went to the door and eased it open and stepped into the corridor, then stopped and stood quietly for a moment, listening. From the girls' room she heard the sound of one of them snoring — Mary, most likely. She hoped Ellen, too, had gone soundly back to sleep. She must do everything in her power to keep them from being frightened; frightened children, she knew very well, would be difficult to manage, and with these two, managing was about the best she could hope to do.

A man with a bird's head: she had to confess, the image it provoked in her had shaken her a little. How difficult it was to keep control of one's imaginings, especially in the middle of the night. Poor Mary, poor little thing — even if she gave all the signs of being a thoroughgoing minx in the making.

It was strange, Celia reflected, how quickly she had come to think of the girls by their new names, how quickly she had got used to it. Already, for her, the pair had ceased to be princesses; it was like the end of a fairy tale, when the witch's spell has been lifted and the changelings turn back into ordinary human children. They were just young girls, upset at being separated from their parents, and prey to bad dreams. She recalled her first days, and nights, at boarding school. She had begged to be taken home, back to the things she knew. But her pleas had not been listened to.

The staircase was unlighted, which reminded her that she had brought an electric torch with her. She returned to her room and found it in a hidden compartment in the side of her suitcase — why she had thought to hide it she couldn't remember. Her personal documents were there too, her identity papers and her ration card, and a passport the Service had issued to her but which she hadn't had the opportunity to use yet; she wondered if she would live through this war and see the pages of it stamped at this or that foreign port some day. For her, as for everyone else too, she supposed, the future had come to seem a strictly finite concept. She recalled the glow of the bombed naval yards at Pembroke that she had seen from the boat on the way over here.

What was it Mary had said? The sky was on fire.

She put the torch in her pocket, on the other side from the one the pistol was in, and crept downstairs.

It was never easy to find one's way about in unfamiliar surroundings, but in a house the size of Clonmillis Hall it was next to impossible. She tried to remember the route by which Mrs O'Hanlon had led them to this wing, when she first showed them their rooms. All she could recall was that they had gone up two flights of stairs; in her memory the rest was a jumble of endless passageways and blank walls and white doors.

On first arriving, she and the others had been taken into the morning room, and later there had been lunch in the dining room, both of which were on the ground floor, but with quite a distance between them. And where was the front door? Not that there was much point in her going out by that way, even if McLaverty had managed to set the door securely on its new hinges, for the strip of lawn overlooked by the girls' bedroom and her own, where she thought she had caught a glimpse of someone moving, was around at the side of the house.

All before her was dark, with not a chink of guiding light on show anywhere. She didn't want to use her torch, since the prowler, if there was one, would surely see the beam of it.

109

She moved from the foot of the staircase along what could only be a hallway. A draught from somewhere brushed her face with silky fingers. There was the tarry reek of a turf fire that had gone out hours ago; she seemed to catch a lingering whiff, too, of the duke's pipe tobacco.

Smells were what struck you first and most forcefully in new surroundings. She never noticed smells in her flat, except when she had been away for a long time, which she rarely was, and certainly had not been in the past year since the start of the war. She remembered the shock she had got when she came home for the first time from boarding school — she was eleven — and the pong, at once piercingly sad and shamefully embarrassing, hit her smack in the face the moment she stepped across the threshold and dumped her bag on the mat. She had been mortified to think that this smell was the first thing that met her friends when she brought them to the house!

She blundered about for some time, extending a hand in front of herself and knocking into various items of furniture. She barked her shin against a low table with a marble top, which she didn't see since the marble was black. She swore under her breath, and was glad of the thick corduroy of the trousers she had on.

Sniffing again for guiding smells, she ventured past a baize-covered door and along a narrow corridor, following the odour of cooked food and domestic gas, and found herself, sure enough, in the kitchen. She saw dimly that it was a large, square room with a low ceiling and, standing in the middle of the floor, a big pine table, across the top of which the moon in the window was casting a delicate quadrilateral of grainy light.

Odd, she thought, how full of menace the most homely things could seem in the dark of night — the black range, which looked to be a couple of yards wide, had the aspect of some large animal, a bull, say, or even a rhinoceros, crouched with its head lowered and about to make a charge at her.

The window with its many tiny panes looked out into a walled yard.

She stood motionless beside the table. Still there was not a sound to be heard from anywhere. She was aware of her own heartbeat.

The back door was bolted, though the key hadn't been turned in the lock. She withdrew the bolt, slowly and carefully, for fear it would squeak, and stepped out into the night, taking the big iron key with her and turning back to lock the door with it.

CHAPTER
TWELVE

It was unexpectedly mild out there, for the season and the hour. The sky was clear, a vast velvet dome strewn with more stars than she had ever seen before. There was moonlight, although she couldn't locate the moon itself — which must be low down, close to the horizon, or maybe somewhere above the wood yet hidden from her by the high tops of the trees. When she was little she hadn't realised that the moon rose and set; she had vaguely imagined that it was always in the sky, in a fixed position though seen from different angles, there even in daytime, when it was outshone and made invisible by the sun, and even that wasn't always the case, for sometimes a kind of transparent ghost of it gleamed up there in the bright blue sky, on certain autumn mornings and winter afternoons.

The yard was paved with cobbles, flat round ones set into the ground sideways, placed close together and at a slant and one overlapping another, like the scales of a fish, which made them difficult to walk on because of their sharp edges. She assumed they were arranged that way to keep the farm animals from straying into the yard.

112

How on earth could people bear to live in the countryside?

She felt her way along by the wall, skirting a gnarled and almost leafless wisteria with a trunk as thick as a man's thigh, and came to a narrow arched gateway. She expected the metal gate to be locked, but it wasn't; she would have to look into the question of locks and suchlike. Evidently Richard Lascelles hadn't reconnoitred the place with sufficient thoroughness. Maybe security wasn't part of his brief, but was left instead to whoever was in charge of the army patrols. She told herself she must find out who that was and speak to him as a matter of urgency. In the event, as it turned out, she never did.

She drew back the bolt of the gate — this one did make a protesting screech, but not a loud one — and stepped out under the arch and on to the lawn. The moonlight before her was a kind of dully shining, cobweb-like stuff covering everything; it was brighter here, brighter, surely, than it would be in the city; she supposed it was always like that, away from the metropolis, the light lighter and the dark darker.

The moon was somewhere behind her now, so that the wall at her back threw a sharp wedge of darkness on to the lawn where she was standing. She couldn't actually see the lawn, so inky-black was the shadow lying athwart it, and only knew it by the springiness of the turf underfoot.

She stood motionless, peering this way and that. The wood, off to her right, made a dense black mass, a seemingly impenetrable fastness, and she thought again of fairy tales, of the wicked witch and the apple, of Sleeping Beauty immured in her castle deep within a forest of thorns.

With both hands she hoisted up her corduroy slacks at the waist, for she was in danger of tripping over the hems — the trousers were dragged down on one side by the weight of the gun in her pocket, on the other by the torch and the big key from the back door — and again moved along beside the wall, the outside of it this time, thankful for its protective shadow.

In the wood a night-bird cried out piercingly, giving her a start. What was it? An owl? Truly, she had never cared for nature, or even thought about it much, and now the notion of there being wild creatures all round her, in trees, in the undergrowth, in burrows in the ground, gave her the shivers. She had grown up in Wimbledon, and was educated at Roedean School, from where on Sunday afternoons she and other girls of her year would take a strictly supervised and gratingly tedious walk on the Sussex Downs. On one such outing a seagull had done its business on the crown of her school hat. Her form mistress had not been amused, and had been quite sharp with her, which to Celia seemed thoroughly unfair.

No, you could keep nature, as far as she was concerned. Give her the busy thoroughfares of Piccadilly or Knightsbridge any day — or even Wimbledon High Street, come to that.

It began to occur to her that she had been foolish to set out in the dark on this wild-goose chase, on no good grounds other than a probably imagined glimpse out of the corner of her eye of a moving shadow in the depths of night. Didn't those ever-present wild things prowl about after nightfall, hunting and scavenging, and suchlike? Surely it was one of those that she had seen on the lawn, if she had seen anything. A deer, probably, or even a domestic animal — hadn't the duke said there was a house cat? — or some beast that had escaped from a barn. What a fool she would feel if she were to find herself, at the end of all this, with the muzzle of the Browning trained on a cow.

Was she losing her nerve, or if not her nerve then her judgement, that she should have been brought out here by the hint of a shadow? She reminded herself, once more, that she was a professional, and that the point of being a professional was that she should be prepared for and capable of seeing any assignment through to its end. But the last thing she had expected was that in the midst of a world war, when civilisation itself was under threat, she would be sent to this of all places to look after a couple of children. True, they weren't just any couple of children, but they were children, all the same.

"Don't forget to let me know when you've bagged your first Kraut," Corporal Lucas had said to her cheerfully in farewell.

Corporal Lucas was the young man at the shooting range who had taught her how to use the Browning: the right way to stand when she was holding it, and how to point it, and what to do with the trigger — "Don't pull it, love, stroke it," he had said, with a suggestive wink that she had chosen to ignore.

But neither of them had thought he was joking when he spoke to her of killing Germans, even though as he said it he had smiled at her, in the cheekily lopsided way he probably imagined no girl could resist.

Shooting people wasn't exactly the first thing she had had in mind when she decided to apply for a post in the Security Service, but she had joined up — or, rather, had been allowed in, with less than good grace — before there was a war, and now that the enemy was in clear sight she was perfectly prepared to use a gun on him, indeed on multiples of him, should the occasion call for it.

She might have looked like a prettier version of Vera Lynn — more than one young man had professed to spot a resemblance, except that Celia didn't have the Forces' Sweetheart's mouthful of tombstone teeth, thank goodness — though there was a side to her that was not only unafraid of the prospect of violence but secretly looked forward to it. Her father was right: she was tough, and she was eager for that toughness to be tested.

Given all this, it was as well she had not heard her boss, Leslie Manling, say of her, over lunch with a trio of his cronies at the Travellers Club, that whereas she thought of herself as a cross between Joan of Arc and the Amazon Queen, she was more like Miss Muffet, the poor thing. "Yes, and sitting on that pretty tuffet of hers," one of the others said, and they had all chuckled throatily.

All the same, she had a clear and concentrated awareness that everything she held dear was under the

116

gravest threat. She had grown up in an English garden, but the garden was a jungle now where the law, as in every jungle, was to kill or be killed.

Look where she had ended up, though! The Maginot Line was a long way from Tipperary.

This was not her first stint of babysitting, which was what these assignments were known as, in the Service — aptly, in this case. A year or so previously, just after the start of the war, the first secretary at the British embassy in Cairo, a person by the name of Watson-Wade, whose job naturally entailed a bit of spying on the side, had been caught passing information to his German counterpart. There was no ideological motive involved: the fellow had done what he had done purely for money — he had an expensive wife. London had recalled him for what he was told would be a routine debriefing, but the moment he stepped on to British soil he had been seized and bundled away to some secret and well-guarded hellhole in the isolation of deepest Cornwall, there to be put through the wringer by the boys from Internal Security.

Before leaving Cairo, Watson-Wade had asked if he could bring his wife home with him, and it had been judged advisable to allow him to do so, as he would surely have become suspicious otherwise and might even have made a bolt for it. The wife's name was Siri, and she was a Coptic Christian. Celia, to her secret embarrassment, had never heard of the Copts, and hadn't even known that a Christian sect existed in Egypt.

117

The woman was handsome, Celia conceded, though in what she considered to be a leathery, Levantine way, with smooth, dark-brown skin that had a hint of black intermingled with the brown — similar to Richard Lascelles's sun- and wind-burned complexion, in fact. She had high cheekbones, big inky eyes, as shiny as pools of water in an oasis, sinewy hands and long, tapering fingers adorned with heavy gold rings set with precious stones.

It was plain to see, from all that opulence, why poor Watson-Wade had been driven to selling secrets for cash.

Celia, being the only female available, had been assigned to look after Mrs Doubleyou-Doubleyou, as everyone called her — sometimes she was referred to like that even in official dispatches — who, as might have been expected, was of a highly strung, not to say hysterical, nature.

The two were put up together in Bayswater, in a depressingly cramped modern flat with plastic curtains that had to be kept drawn by day as well as night, for fear of inquisitive passers-by. They ate tinned food and drank endless cups of tea — Mrs Doubleyou-Doubleyou took hers black as tar — and, through the hours of the blackout, slept as best they could on camp beds, the ill-assembled frames of which cried out as if in pain at every slightest movement their occupants made. Mrs Doubleyou-Doubleyou did little other than pace the floor all day long, fingering what Celia took to be some sort of prayer beads and smoking foul-smelling Egyptian cigarettes — she had brought two dozen packets of them with her in her suitcase — and railing at the British authorities who had snatched her husband from her and taken him to God knew where to do to him God knew what. She had not been told what the charges were against him, but of course she had guessed — in fact, Celia suspected she knew very well what he had been up to.

On the evening of the third day of their sequestration, a couple of heavies in belted mackintoshes arrived, to Celia's relief, and took the dratted woman away, still complaining shrilly, in a car, the side and back windows of which were blacked out. Later Celia heard on the internal grapevine that Watson-Wade had been tried in camera, found guilty of treasonous activities and dispatched to Pentonville Prison, while his wife had been put on an RAF transport plane at Brize Norton, having been gagged beforehand to quell her cries of protest, and flown back to Cairo.

During those three long days they endured together, the woman had either ignored Celia entirely, or would stop in her pacing to hiss at her what were unmistakably curses, either in Egyptian or Coptic — if the Copts even had a language of their own — putting her face close up to Celia's with her lips peeled back from her teeth and spraying her with spittle.

There had been one passage of calm, however, when, exhausted and tear-stained — the kohl on her lower eyelids running down her cheeks in long black spikes — the frantic woman had thrown herself down in one of the two chintz-covered armchairs, in what was fancifully called the living room, and sat hunched there

119

for a long time, staring starkly before her with both fists pressed against her mouth.

"You know," she had said at last, in a voice cracked and hoarse after a day of almost ceaseless ranting, "you English think you are the rightful owners of the world, as if you, and not the Jews, were the Chosen People."

Celia, exhausted, too, from the unending tension and being incessantly shouted at, had flopped down opposite her in the matching chair beside the gas fire and, hardly having known what words would come out, heard herself say: "But we didn't mean it, you see. Somebody once remarked, Lord Curzon or someone like that, that Britain had accumulated her empire by accident."

At this Mrs Doubleyou-Doubleyou had snorted in rich contempt. "Ha! This is how you deceive yourselves, and smooth your conscience, if you have such a thing. But you are mad animals, like the rest of us, running at the world and tearing off bleeding pieces of it with your teeth and claws. Jackals, that's what you are" — and here she had again done that contemptuous inside-out thing with her lips — "jolly jingo jackals!"

Celia had been fascinated and appalled. The woman's voice had sounded suddenly as old as the country she came from, the voice of a sibyl, or a sphinx, implacable and terrifying, speaking out of the desert's parched, sun-blinded wastes. What was shocking was not what she had said, but the tone in which she had said it. Until that moment it had not occurred to Celia that England, her England, a place of rolling downs and country cottages, of Big Ben and the Pearly Kings and

120

Queens, of Yorkshire pudding and seaside ices, could be the object of such violent hatred and contempt.

Watson-Wade had died in Pentonville, not far into his sentence. He was found hanging by a length of torn-off, knotted sheet from the bars of the window in his cell one cold December evening; suicide, supposedly, but at the headquarters of the Service — at the time based temporarily, and ironically, in another prison, Wormwood Scrubs, which had been cleared out for the purpose — the whisper went from desk to desk that two men, in mackintoshes, had visited him earlier that day, and no one had seen them leaving, not by the front gate, anyway. It was only a few weeks into the war and, like last time, everyone was saying it would be over by Christmas; everyone, that was, except those who had been in it last time.

Could the war be lost? Celia asked herself. Could her country be overrun, her people beaten to their knees and enslaved? The possibility had not for a moment occurred to her, until she heard of Watson-Wade's death.

She didn't know why his dying, whether by his own hand or the hands of others, should be to her a cause of stark foreboding, but it was; and the thing had not faded, however far she pushed it to the back of her consciousness. It was always there, the thought of the poor man, traitor though he was, dangling by the neck in his cell, and his wife, now his widow, in a squalid Cairo room above a souk, wailing her grief to an open window where a moon the shape of a scimitar hung crookedly in a pale night sky filled with indifferent stars, while far off to the north, vast squadrons of men and machines advanced relentlessly westwards through the fields and towns and villages of a soon-to-be blood-soaked Europe.

If the Germans came, Celia knew, she and agents like her would be among the first to be shot.

Suddenly, in the darkness of the garden, she was jogged out of her bleak reveries. She shrank back into the black shadow of the wall, and gripped the pistol in her pocket, where it felt huge and unwieldy in her tiny, frail fist.

A figure stood, quite still, under a tree at the edge of the wood. She didn't know how she was able to make him out, since he, like her, was clothed in shadow, but make him out she did.

He was wearing what looked to her very much like a mackintosh.

CHAPTER
THIRTEEN

She was not afraid, not exactly. Every sense was alert. Her heartbeat, which she would have expected to speed up, had on the contrary slowed to a steady, almost a solemn, pace; it felt like the distant thudding of a funeral drum. She worried she might wet herself, not from fright but from the pressure of the adrenalin pumping through her veins.

She took the Browning out of her pocket and eased off the safety catch.

Now what? It all seemed unreal, like something in a Hollywood B-picture: a garden at dead of night, a mysterious figure skulking in the shadows, and a blonde girl with a gun in her hand. All that was missing was the wail of a police siren in the distance.

It would have been funny, except that it was not.

This wasn't the pictures: this was really happening. It could end up with someone dead out here, and she might be that someone, even though she was armed and on the alert. Yes, it was real, but somehow — well, somehow ridiculous, too.

When she first spotted him, she thought that the man under the tree must be a trespasser, but not necessarily a threat to her royal charges. At best he might be a poacher, but at worst — well, she wasn't sure what the worst would be.

Or maybe he wasn't an intruder at all. Maybe he was one of the household staff. For all she knew, there might be a time-honoured tradition by which some poor clod was deputed to stand on sentry duty out here all night, even in peacetime, even when there were no precious guests staying at the Hall in need of protecting. He might have a title — His Grace's Nightwatch, or something equally antiquated and absurd. She almost laughed; the tension was making her giddy.

Her wrist had begun to ache from the weight of the pistol — why did it have to be so heavy? — and she was increasingly anxious, dithering there and unable to think what exactly she should do. Somehow it seemed to her that the most punctilious behaviour was required at this moment, though why, she couldn't think.

"You!" she called out, her voice sounding oddly flat under the immensity of the night. "You there, by the tree — step forward!" The man in the overcoat gave a start, and turned his head quickly from side to side, evidently surprised, and clearly unable to tell exactly where the challenge had come from. "Step out." Celia called again, "step out from the shadows. Stand on the grass, where I can see you. I warn you, I'm armed."

Now that she had seized the initiative the situation seemed even more melodramatically unreal than it had up to now. It even crossed her mind that the whole thing might be a prank, got up to give her a fright and prove her to be the ninny she had earlier denied she was, and that in the morning she would find herself a laughing-stock before the entire household, upstairs and down. She had heard that the Irish had a passion for playing tricks on strangers and making them look foolish — wasn't there something called an "Irish bull"? — which was supposed to be part of their charm.

At last the fellow stirred himself out of his startled trance and took two steps forward into the faint quicksilver glow of moonlight, and stopped. He wore a hat, and his right hand was in the pocket of his coat. What if he, too, had a gun? He wouldn't even have to whip it out of his pocket: he could just shoot straight through the cloth.

But he wouldn't know where to aim, since he wouldn't be able to see her, crouching in the ink-black shelter of the wall — or would he?

"Put up your hands!"

She had never expected to hear such a thing actually spoken, in real life, and certainly not by herself.

"Miss Nashe?" the man on the lawn asked hesitantly. He sounded as if he might be about to laugh.

It was Stafford, or Strafford, or whatever his name was — the peculiar Irishman who didn't sound Irish. Damn it! She felt a thorough fool — good thing it was night-time or he would see her blushing for shame.

She straightened up, putting on the safety catch and easing the gun back into the pocket of her trousers. She walked clear of the protective shadow, out on to the lawn. She could see better, now that her eyes had become accustomed to the night. Everything was sharply defined by moonlight yet somehow the wrong way round, as if she were seeing the scene as in a photographic negative.

"What are you doing here?" she called, sounding more peevish than anything else.

"I might ask the same of you," Strafford said.

He seemed not at all put out, after his initial surprise at being challenged in this unexpected manner, in a garden, in the middle of the night. Indeed, she suspected he was smiling.

She stood peering at him, trying to identify the expression on his face.

The surge of adrenalin had subsided, and she was suddenly conscious of the rawness of the air.

"Why are you out here?" she asked again.

"I thought I heard something," he replied. "A cry of some kind."

It must have been Mary's scream he had heard. She was surprised — his quarters were at some distance from the Hall, all the way across the stable yard. He must have remarkably good hearing; she was impressed, too, by his alertness. If it had been she out there by the stables, and asleep, would she have caught even so piercing a scream from that far off?

He seemed to read her thoughts, for he added, "I was awake, reading. I'm a bit of an insomniac, I'm afraid."

She didn't believe this, thought it must be a white lie, told in case it might seem he was claiming to be always awake and vigilant while everyone else was asleep. Quite the gentleman, then. She wasn't accustomed to such tactfulness, in her line of work. It made her suspicious: was he making fun of her? She told herself not to be so defensive. It was a weakness of hers to worry that she was being ridiculed. She hoped it didn't indicate a deep-seated uncertainty — she would have to put up with a lot of male mockery, if she was to have any kind of career in the Service.

"You probably did hear something," she said. "It was a scream. The little one, Mary, had a nightmare. She dreamed there was a man in the woods, and that the sky was on fire."

"Ah, so that's why you're out here."

"There wasn't anyone about, was there? Other than us, I mean. Did you see anybody, any intruder?"

"Not a soul."

"She said the man had a bird's head."

"Well, I certainly didn't see anyone like that. Didn't see the sky on fire, either."

"I've told you," she said crisply, "it was a dream."

"Yes, of course," he answered, in a meeker tone.

And yet she could sense that he, too, felt himself at something of a disadvantage. It would be embarrassing to be surprised out here like this, lurking in the dark under the trees. Perhaps he had been doing a pee; in her experience of them, men had only to quit the confines of any four walls to feel an immediate urge to unbutton their flies and point themselves at the trunk of the nearest tree or on to any patch of greenery. Primitive creatures. Well, if he was feeling awkward, for whatever reason, she was glad. It evened the balance between them, which had dipped quite badly on her side yesterday morning when she had allowed herself to blurt out her doubts and uncertainties. She could make a new start with him now, on an equal footing: they had both made fools of themselves.

"Have you got a gun, really?" he asked.

He sounded both impressed and sceptical, and faintly amused, too.

"Have you?" she countered.

"No. That's to say, I have one, I mean I was issued with one, but I haven't got it with me. I was remiss in that, I suppose."

She found his diffidence irritating and yet oddly reassuring: yes, they were both at a disadvantage.

"It will be dawn soon," he said.

"Yes."

"Is she all right, the child?"

"Of course. I told you, she was just dreaming."

A quarter-moon had risen behind the wood and hung above the massed trees, looking as if it were reclining in an invisible hammock. Strafford cocked his head and considered it. "Would you have shot me?" he asked mildly.

"I hope I wouldn't have shot *you*, but someone else, yes. An intruder."

"Have you done it before? Shot someone, I mean."

It had struck her that she must be older than he was. By how much? she wondered. Three, four years? More, perhaps? It was a bit of a shock, to think of. Most of her friends were already married.

"It's getting cold," she said brusquely. "We should go in."

128

CHAPTER
FOURTEEN

She had been right in thinking she had caught him at a disadvantage, and right, too, in guessing that he had lied in saying he had been awake when he heard the scream. He did suffer from bouts of insomnia, some of them lasting for months, but he had been sound asleep when the child's cry roused him. It had been silly to pretend otherwise, and he wasn't sure why he had done it.

When the scream pierced the night he had started up from his narrow bed — its slack springs making a raucous jangling — and had not recognised his dim surroundings.

It was a scream he had heard, he was sure of it. A rabbit, maybe, pounced on by a fox? He had heard such sounds often when he was a boy, growing up at Roslea. They had never failed to freeze his blood, as he lay in bed watching the shadows of foliage moving on the wall and heard the night wind moaning under the eaves of the old house, and thought of the tiny creature dying bloodily in a muddy furrow in some far field.

But supposing what he had heard at Clonmillis was not the sound of an animal in its death throes but some human creature caught up in terror?

129

Shivering in the chill damp air — even this year's hot summer had left no warmth in the stones of these stable walls — he had dressed himself in a pullover, and a pair of trousers, which he drew on over his pyjamas, and put on his trench coat and belted it tightly, and took up his hat and, still half in a daze, made his way out into the night.

The air outdoors was soft and mild, almost balmy. The sky was clear and the moon hung low above the wood, looking like an eye glinting under its lid, following his movements with vindictive interest; he had always found the moon uncanny, a stealthy witness suspended up there, watching everything.

He walked across the cobbled yard to the house. All the windows were unlit, and the back door was locked. He stood listening, but heard not a sound.

Maybe he had imagined the scream, after all, or dreamed it.

He went around by the side of the house, making his way with ease in the moonlight, and stepped on to the lawn, walking across to the edge of the wood before turning back towards the jutting West Wing. No lights in any window there, either. He could not place where the girls' room was situated. Maybe he was at the wrong side of the house altogether.

Something flew past, above his head but quite low, making a heavy, hushing sound in the darkness. An owl, he guessed, on the hunt.

He moved back, into the shadow of the trees.

It was a long time since he had been out like that, in a country garden, in the depths of night. He could see a surprisingly long way, across fields and meadows. A long trail of white mist lay in a hollow beneath a far hill, motionless, as if the land had expelled one extended last sigh before falling into sleep. He smelt the rich brown fragrance of loam and fallen leaves. The moon glinted through the foliage above him. Something seemed ready to be expressed, some large, intimate truth, and Strafford's mind reeled in a kind of muted ecstasy, awaiting the secret that was surely about to be revealed.

Then the woman's voice had called out a challenge, and he had started in fright and sudden self-awareness, the back of his neck gone hot and the tips of his fingers tingling.

He recognised Celia's voice. He was impressed by her coolness. She was a singular presence, standing there before him all webbed over greyly by the moonlight, at once substantial — that bulky jacket, those concertinaed trousers — and not quite real, like one of Shakespeare's woodland sprites stepping briefly into the limelight for the space of a scene. Her hat, with the ear-flaps lifted at either side, gave her something of the look of an out-sized furry toy animal.

Who was she, really, Celia Nashe? What was she? Did they really have young women like her, so clean of limb and earnest of character, in the undercover services? He had thought it would be all blue-jawed ex-colonials, the Lascelles type, or trigger-happy half-mad veterans of the veld and Flanders Fields.

When she had remarked on the cold and suggested they go inside he had agreed, even though he didn't find it cold at all and his trench coat wasn't half as thick as hers. He wondered if he might be succumbing to a touch of fever.

"I could do with a cup of tea," Celia added, turning back towards the house and the gate into the walled kitchen yard.

She led the way across the cobbles and they entered by the back door.

After the moonlit outside, the kitchen seemed plunged in impenetrable darkness. They felt along the walls for switches, but there was no electricity down here, below stairs. Strafford managed to locate an oil lamp and lit it, the bulbous glass shade springing into blossom, like the head of a giant gold tulip. Celia, in her turn, put a match to half a dozen candles in a holder on the table. Around them, shadows pranced on the walls.

The range had died down many hours ago; it was still too warm to touch, though not warm enough to heat a kettle. There was a gas stove, a spindly, blackened affair standing on four oddly dainty little wrought-iron feet. Strafford set one of the burners going and put on a kettle to boil, while Celia laid out mugs, spoons, a sugar bowl and a milk jug. The milk turned out to be sour, but it didn't matter: they would drink their tea black. Celia thought of poor Mrs Doubleyou-Doubleyou, and wondered where she might be at this moment. Perhaps she had put Britain and the British out of her mind; perhaps she had made herself forget her dead husband, and was married again — she hadn't seemed the kind of woman who would stay single for long.

132

Celia spooned tea into a china pot, and Strafford poured in water from the kettle.

They sat one at each side of a corner of the enormous pine table.

"It's like a midnight feast at school," Celia said, "only without the sausage rolls and the buns. Did you have them, midnight feasts, when you were a boy?"

"I went to a Quaker school," Strafford said. "We didn't go in much for jollifications of that nature."

"Oh dear. Sounds grim."

"Not really. Quite a decent place, all in all."

"You were lucky. My brothers both had a terrible time. Dotheboys Hall, and all that."

Here, Strafford thought, was an opportunity to learn something about her origins and her background in general. Yet he hesitated. Did he want to know her at any level other than the professional? He had no idea how long he would be required to spend at Clonmillis in her company — or in her vicinity, at least, since what would constitute company seemed really not on offer.

She had struck him, from the start, as not the kind of person he would find particularly interesting. Nice enough, and admirable — fanciable, even — but far, far from fascinating. She appeared to him to be of that perfectly pleasant, bland variety of well-bred young Englishwoman to be met occasionally on this side of the Irish Sea, usually at hunt balls during Dublin Horse Show week, when little bands of them came over from London, like lady explorers bent on seeing something of the lives and customs of the natives of a legendary, exotic isle, Hy-Brasil of the Unblest, as a friend of his, a recently graduated pathologist and a man of mordant humour, used to say.

It always surprised him to think that he had never been romantically involved with anyone, or not seriously so, at any rate. He had no girlfriend at present and no prospect of one either; even that word, "girlfriend", had an unlikely ring to it, for him, being vaguely suggestive, to his mind, not of passion and the toils of love, but rather of boarding-school girls, of noisy hockey games, of "crushes", and scented *billets-doux*, and little boxes tied up with pink ribbon. Strange.

It wasn't that he was not interested in women, quite the contrary. It was only that courtship and all it entailed seemed to him an excessively complicated and encumbering business. That, too, was strange, he supposed, but then, most of the time he felt a stranger to himself.

There was an actress he had been introduced to recently, by his friend the pathologist as it happened, but after a first edgy date — afternoon tea at the Shelbourne, a susurrus of reedy voices in the high-ceilinged lounge and rain on the trees across the road in St Stephen's Green — she would hang up when she heard his voice on the phone; later he was told she had taken up with someone else, some Englishman, apparently. He had not been much put out: he would have been lost in her rackety world of first-night parties, mid-morning hangovers, and endless theatrical gossip.

At least, that was what he told himself.

134

Isabel Galloway, the young person in question — or out of the question, rather, as he wryly reminded himself — was theatrically brittle and bright, but she had a brain, and was nobody's fool. Should he have persisted with her? The mere thought of all that effort provoked in him a weary sigh, which in turn made him annoyed with himself. His father often joked, in his sly but not unfond fashion, that of the two of them, father and son, the son often seemed the older.

"I take it you didn't choose this posting, any more than I did?" Celia Nashe asked now.

Through the window Strafford saw a faint, soiled glow above the woods. An October dawn. "We don't get to choose, in my line of work," he said.

"Nor in mine," Celia swiftly responded, as if to scotch any notion that in her "line of work" she had any easier time of it than he did in his.

She searched the pockets of her woollen jacket and brought out a packet of Senior Service, and lit one. When she made a tight little circle of her mouth and angled it upwards to blow a stream of smoke in the direction of the ceiling, she had for a moment the look of an East End urchin whistling "Colonel Bogey". Strafford smiled to himself. Now she took off her hat and her jacket. In general she had a boyish look, slim-hipped and long-legged, that he hadn't registered before now. Yes, she was attractive, in many ways, he had to admit. Ah, well.

But what would happen if he were to fall for her? He didn't for a moment imagine he would, but all the same, what if he did? She would break his heart, there

135

was no doubt of that. She was just the kind of girl to do it, decisive and brisk, a person in no doubt of the significance of her role in the scheme of things, and not at all prepared to tolerate a drag on her prospects, such as a spurned and woebegone admirer trotting at her heels. He couldn't see himself even as her friend, much less her lover, but were he to fall, and were she to catch him, if only for a brief interval, to amuse herself, he could all too clearly imagine her leaving him — *Oh, pull yourself together, for goodness' sake, it's not the end of the world, you'll meet someone else.* Yes, he could picture that moment, all right.

Celia, who had set an elbow on the table and propped her chin on her hand, said, "I wonder why it is the Irish hate us so."

"Us?" he asked, in some surprise.

She looked at him. "The British, I mean."

"Ah."

He had thought she must be referring to something else: secret agents, for instance, or guardians of law and order in general. He had an early-morning feeling of light-headedness, and there was a faint burning sensation just under the skin, as if his flesh were inflamed. His eyes stung, too.

"Have you heard of the Desmond Rebellions, here in Ireland?" he asked, his gaze directed towards the window, and tapping a soft little rapid tattoo on the table with the fingers of his left hand — it was an old habit.

"No," Celia said, in a less than eager tone that he seemed not to notice. "When was that?"

136

"There were two rebellions, in fact," he said, warming to the topic; he had always been keen on history, in school and then at university. "In Munster, in the south-west of the country, in the 1570s and again in the following decade. The Earl of Desmond was the head of the FitzGerald clan, rather confusingly. The Geraldines, as they were called, even more confusingly, had come over with the Normans in the twelfth century, and in time became, as the saying went, more Irish than the Irish themselves. They were still feudal lords, and wanted their independence from the Crown. Also they didn't care at all for the Reformation, which was no reform as far as they were concerned, so the thing was partly a religious war, the first such in Ireland, but by no means the last."

He made that little tattoo again on the table.

"They were defeated first time round, in the 1570s," he went on, "but survived to rise again. Twice was too much for the English. Troops were sent down from Dublin and proceeded methodically, and with great cruelty, to slaughter every man, woman and child they could find. They killed their animals, and laid waste the land — for years afterwards there was famine throughout Munster, the people dying by the tens of thousands. The Earl of Desmond was hunted down, and butchered. His head was sent to Queen Elizabeth in a sack, according to the custom of those days, and the rest of him was put on show on the walls of Cork City." He paused, and gently smiled. "The Irish have long memories."

Celia studied the burning tip of her cigarette, frowning. "Yes, I'm well aware that terrible things were done —" she began.

"And there was Cromwell, later on," Strafford said animatedly, or with what in him passed for animation. "Let's not forget Cromwell, your chief of men, but our devil incarnate."

The young woman sighed. It was not that she didn't care about Ireland and all the wrongs her countrymen had done to it, but these horrors had taken place so long ago. What about the equally horrible things that were happening now, across the Irish Sea, where every night hundreds of those same fellow-countrymen — men, women and children — were being slaughtered by German bombs?

Strafford sighed too, but he was smiling, in the faintly melancholy way that he did. He was aware of the collar of his pyjamas peeping out above the sweater he had put on. "I'm sorry," he said. "I shouldn't have gone into all that, about the rebellions, and Cromwell and so on, but you did ask why the Irish hate so fiercely, some of them."

"'Them'?"

He smiled. "Us."

Celia's frown had by now made two parallel vertical wrinkles above the bridge of her nose. "Do *you* hate us?" she asked. "You're more like us than you're like them, as far as I can see."

"Ah, but you don't know me, really," Strafford was amused.

138

"That's true," she said. "In fact — I've just realised — I don't even know your first name," He told her. "Oh," she murmured.

"Yes, that's how most people react."

"It's just that I've never known a St John, before."

"Neither have I. It's spelled as two words, by the way, 'Saint' and 'John'."

She was certain he was making fun of her. But this time she didn't mind.

He really did look impossibly young, much too young, surely, to be a detective. He reminded her a little of the first boy she had gone out with, when she was seventeen: his hair used to flop over his forehead in the way that Strafford's did. Freddie was the boy's name, Freddie Dixon; she found it strange to be thinking of him now, here, in this kitchen in a house at the edge of the wood in a wholly foreign country that yet was just a little way across the water from her homeland. Life is odd, she mused, very odd.

There was a scrabbling off in a corner, and a cat appeared, a large white one with pink-rimmed eyes, which looked at them coldly before stalking away into the shadows.

Dawn was strengthening, making the candlelight turn pale. Something they hadn't realised was open had closed between them, and they were both aware of it shutting. It was something like a window, a thing that had been a space of possibility for a moment and now was a barrier, transparent but impenetrable.

A mid-autumn night's dream, Strafford thought, with a strange quick stab of sadness.

He rose from the table and carried his mug to the sink and rinsed it under the tap and set it upside down on the worn oak draining-board.

"I don't see how it could be possible to hate an entire people," he said. "Certain individuals, yes, even lots of them, but collectively, no. All the same I understand, in my bones, the bitterness there is in this country against what you call 'us' — I mean the British." Now he turned his back to the sink, and there was something strained in his look. "I don't know what they were thinking of, your people in London, to send those two girls here. Of all the places —" He broke off, lifting a hand and dropping it again in a gesture of futility. "Anyway," he went on, "they're here now, and it's up to us to keep them safe."

CHAPTER
FIFTEEN

A long week passed, and another began, and the mild autumn weather persisted, with mists at morning, and smoky afternoons, and the night skies crowded with stars and traversed by a slowly burgeoning moon, a tarnished silver arc with patches of faintest gold. Strafford was mildly startled when he looked at the calendar and realised how much time had gone by since he had first arrived at Clonmillis. What had he done with those days? He could hardly recall. When he looked back it was like peering into a fog, with people and objects hazily visible only to a certain depth, and all beyond that lost in an ice-white blur.

He had filled much of the time engaged in reading, his favourite pastime. He had taken the bus to Clonmillis, which turned out to be an anonymous market town much like any other, and gone in search of the Carnegie lending library that Celia Nashe had spoken of. It was housed in the upper reaches of the County Hall, a vast mock-Gothic nineteenth-century Ruritanian castle, with turrets and arrow-slits and even a fake drawbridge over a grass-grown moat that had never known water except for repeated falls of midlands rain. He entered upon a hallowed silence and signed up for a temporary borrower's card.

The librarian, a Miss Broaders, dowdy, harassed-seeming, with something of the nun about her, regarded him, the stranger, with a gleam of interest, but made no attempt to find out who he might be or how and why he came to be in these parts. Later he was to discover that she was a widow; all librarians were labelled "Miss", he supposed. When he was filling in the form for the card, he considered giving a false address, but instead simply wrote down "Clonmillis Hall", at which Miss Broaders arched an eyebrow, but still made no enquiry.

In time she was to prove more accommodating, indeed more kindly, than the undemonstrativeness of her manner would have led him to expect. When he asked for Lawrence's *Women in Love* she informed him, with a flicker of angry amusement — her anger, as he understood, was directed not at him but at the censorship laws of the country — that the book was banned in Ireland. Then she turned to the sub-librarian, a timid-seeming girl with a tendency to blush, and asked her to look after the desk for a few minutes, and led Strafford down to the car park, and to her car, a Morris Eight with a bad dent in the front bumper. There she rummaged among a jumble of books on the back seat and came up with a copy of the novel he had asked for. "Don't say you got it from me," she murmured, and Strafford fancied he detected, not a wink, exactly, but a faint flutter of her left eyelid, accompanied by another brief, amused grimace at the grubby act of complicity they had been obliged to engage in.

He accompanied Miss Broaders back to the library — they went up, as they had come down, by a clattering metal fire escape, which somehow added to the clandestine nature of the transaction that had just taken place — and there he collected a further armful of books. He was supposed to take out a maximum of three volumes, but an exception could be made, Miss Broaders said, since he was staying outside the town; this arrant flouting of the rules caused the sub-librarian to glance sideways at her superior in surprise and shock.

On the way back to Clonmillis Hall, Strafford sat at the back of the bus, grinning like a schoolboy, with his trove of books lined up beside him on the seat. Life's littlest treats were disproportionately cheering, he always found.

At the Hall he laid claim, silently but firmly, to the library. The big square room was musty and the air felt damp, and he persuaded Mrs O'Hanlon to direct Maggie the maid to light a fire for him in the chest-high, red-marble fireplace. When lunch was out of the way — mealtimes did not become any less oppressive with the passing of the days — he would retire there, and spend the afternoon happily leafing through the stack of books Miss Broaders had magnanimously permitted him to borrow.

He hadn't exercised much discrimination in his choices. There was the Lawrence, which was a disappointment, and something slim and thrillingly sordid by Simenon; volume one of Schiller's history of the Thirty Years' War; *The Swiss Family Robinson*, a favourite from childhood; and some others. Over the coming week he would read them all with equal appreciation and, at times, equal inattention, as he let his thoughts wander from the lines of cursive print and drift off in any direction they fancied. The doings of the cheery Switzer castaways — could Robinson really be a Swiss name? — hardly called for sustained concentration, and due to his slipshod reading habits he came away from Schiller's volume knowing as little about the religious conflicts of the seventeenth century as he had before, though he was interested to note that the book had been translated by a Captain Blaquiere of the Royal Irish Artillery, and that the edition he had borrowed had been published by one N. Kelly in Dublin in 1800. These marks of propinquitous antiquity warmed his essentially old-fashioned heart.

He wondered what Inspector Hackett would say if he could see him lounging there by the fireside with his nose in a book. Inspector Hackett, he suspected, was not much given to literature.

These self-indulgent afternoons reminded him of a time in his boyhood when he had been kept home from school for an entire winter term, suffering from — what was it? Rheumatic fever? Diphtheria? Mumps? Whatever the malady, the chief symptom of it was a chronic and not entirely unpleasant enervation, which made him feel as if he were stretched out and suspended in the warm, sweaty depths of a sort of celestial goose-down mattress. Now, in his armchair in

144

the library of Clonmillis Hall, beside the crackling fire, he allowed himself to sink into the same state of cocooned, feathery and only slightly guilty contentment.

In those days of bibliophilic bliss he saw little of the girls, or of Celia Nashe. The duke would come and talk to him now and then, insinuating himself into the room on the pretext of looking for this or that volume, which both of them knew he had no intention of opening, much less reading.

What did they talk about, in the course of those visitations? Strafford could never quite remember what the topic had been, once the duke had departed in his carpet slippers and his bright-red scarf — this last he wore every day, from morn till night, complaining that the autumn made his wounded knee ache, besides being a perilous time for his lungs, still suffering the effects of the gas attack he had been caught in during what he invariably referred to as the "first show", as though the Great War had been, for him, a long-running and extremely loud music-hall performance.

Sometimes Strafford would look up to the mullioned window opposite the fireplace and catch a glimpse of the Princess Elizabeth — he knew he should be training himself to think of her exclusively as "Ellen", but often he forgot — cantering past outside on the horse the duke had allowed her to select from his stable of half a dozen mounts. Of course she had picked the finest of the bunch, a beautifully proportioned animal named, by what seemed to Strafford a happy chance, Prince. The magnificent creature was greyish-brown in colour, with a pure Arab head and a coat that rippled like a field of barley played over by a warm summer wind.

At fourteen the girl was already, as even Strafford could see, a fine horsewoman; it was a peculiar kind of pleasure, of aesthetic transport, almost, to watch the two of them, the rider and the ridden, moving over the lawn in perfect physical accord, the animal seeming to touch the merest tips of his hoofs to the turf, and the girl standing up a little in the saddle and canted forward at a perfectly maintained tilt, transformed into a being made not of mere flesh and bone but of some far more insubstantial materials, supple and fluid as the misted air itself through which the pair fleeted like phantoms.

It was plain the girl loved the horse, possessively, passionately, with all the force of her secretly ardent young soul. He was her indulgence, her joyful release from the strictures of being who and what she was. Years later, when she was grown-up and had assumed the crown, she would recall the delightful, beautifully formed animal with a pricking of tears of regret and remembered happiness. He was her friend, her guide, her saviour; he was what had made bearable her time at Clonmillis Hall; he was, in short — she would laugh at herself shamefacedly to think it — her prince.

She knew very well that her sister saw, with her usual beadiness, the instant bond that she and the animal had forged between them. Mary — the Princess Elizabeth, like Strafford but more diligently than he, strove to remember to think of herself and Margaret always under their assumed or, rather, their imposed names —

had a passable seat on a horse, but that was as far as it went.

Mary knew this, too, and didn't care. For her, a horse had no personality, was just a big, blundering brute, a force in the world more physically powerful than she was and yet a thing hardly worth a moment of her consideration. It wasn't animals that interested her, but people, though the ones who interested her most were the strange ones, the ones who were nearest to being animals themselves. That was why she liked it when the family was at Balmoral, where the staff, the ground staff especially, who were all Scots, spoke as if they were fighting with each other all the time, and half the time were. It excited her when people were in contention; nothing was more dispiriting to her than peace and tranquillity and, especially, accord.

But, oh, she did miss her parents. One night when she could not sleep she had gone to Miss Nashe's room and crept into the shelter of her bed and snuggled herself against the young woman's warm, silk-clad back. She knew she should be furious with herself for being so weak, but the dark had seemed particularly dark that night, and the shadows around her more frighteningly lifelike, and the bombs nearer, and the sky on fire just beyond the horizon. Miss Nashe had woken up but had said nothing, only made herself into an accommodating S-shape, and presently, together, they had fallen asleep. In the morning there was no mention of what had occurred in the night, as Mary had feared there would be; and she was grateful, and tried to forget the unkind nickname she had thought up for her discreet nocturnal comforter.

CHAPTER
SIXTEEN

Another night, and again Strafford was woken in the early hours, not by a scream this time but by the urgent dinning of a telephone from the next room.

He lay for some moments staring into the darkness, his heart hammering. He thought of his mother. She was still in her forties when illness had struck. It was summer. The doctors gave her six months to live and, sure enough, by Christmas she knew, as she said herself, that her time had come. She moved downstairs to a bed old Kate the maid, the last remaining servant — the estate had been going steadily downhill for decades — had fixed up for her on a big floppy sofa in one of the back rooms looking out on to the lawn.

There the dying woman had passed her final weeks, the windows sealed against the winter's cold and a fire of beech logs blazing day and night in the blue-tiled fireplace. She kept a hand bell on the floor beside her, a large, handsome instrument, brass, with a wooden handle polished from long use, like the one the prefects in Strafford's school would ring, with malicious vigour, to mark the end of breaks and the resumption of classes. His mother used it to signal for her "medicine", as she called the tots of brandy she took at frequent intervals throughout the day and late into the night, to assuage the pain of her already decaying body.

It was a convention that the brandy bottle not be kept in the room with her but, each time she rang for it, must be carried from the sideboard in the dining room, disguised, supposedly, in a hot-water-bottle cover. Strafford was home from school for the Christmas holidays, and he was most often the one who answered the summons, since his father had descended into a disabling state of premature mourning, and often Kate did not hear the bell. He saw again now the dying woman's lips trembling on the rim of the glass, and the stray drops of brandy fallen on to the front of her nightdress.

They had never got on, he and his mother, he wasn't sure why; somehow he had been a disappointment to her, in ways it seemed she could no more identify than could he. He experienced a flush of guilt now, remembering how impatient he had been with her for taking so long to die.

He dragged himself from the low metal bed, taking up a blanket and draping it over his shoulders, and went into the other room — it couldn't really be called a living room, if only for the fact that he did so little living in it — in his stockinged feet, swearing under his breath.

A field telephone had been set up to keep him in touch with the platoon of soldiers guarding the perimeters of what was known as the Home Farm. He was the military's point of liaison with the house. A much more sophisticated machine had been installed in

Celia Nashe's room, linking her directly to the embassy in Dublin, and onwards from there to MI5's London headquarters at the Scrubs.

The contraption Strafford had been issued consisted of a substantial square oak box with a telephone receiver on a cradle attached to the front, and a metal crank-handle at the side that powered the batteries; a fine black rubber cable leading from it had been fed through the window and played out all the way across the lawn and through the wood to a hide camouflaged among trees close by a sentry box, also under camouflage, on the Clonmillis road. It was a clumsy arrangement, but apparently it worked since the thing was ringing. It squatted on the table, shrilling insistently; Strafford was reminded of an infuriated baby screaming for its bottle. He snatched up the receiver.

"Yes, yes, what is it?"

The voice that spoke to him was difficult to make out behind the static. It seemed to be coming from the other side of the globe, as though it had traversed mountains, plains and valleys and snaked along the ocean's deep floor to emerge at last, a sort of faint, elven piping, from the Bakelite seashell pressed to his ear.

"Major de Valera here," it said.

Strafford thought either he had misheard, or it was a joke. "This is Strafford. Who's that again?"

"De Valera — Major Vivion de Valera."

"I see. Any relation?"

"What?"

"Doesn't matter."

Éamon de Valera was the taoiseach, the head of the country's government, a famous and controversial figure, and no friend of the British — some months before he had turned down an offer of Irish unity, from Churchill himself, in return for Ireland joining the war and opening its ports to the Royal Navy.

After a break in the connection, the voice on the phone came squawking out again more strident than before.

"What's that?" Strafford said.

"We've apprehended an intruder!"

"Ah. Right. You apprehended him, did you?"

"What?"

"Nothing, nothing. Who is he?"

"Won't give his name."

"Can't you beat it out of him?"

"Pardon? What's that you said?"

Strafford sighed. Drollery was not called for here. "I'll come and have a look at him. Where are you?"

"We'll bring him along to the front gate."

It had been agreed that members of the military guard were not to venture within the boundary of the Home Farm. This was part of the elaborate charade meant to shield the princesses from the fact that they were under watch round the clock. Strafford thought it a ridiculous rule, but it would be futile to protest. "All right," he said irritably, "I'll meet you there. Give me time to get down the drive. It's a bloody long way."

He hung up the receiver and pushed the box back against the wall, not without effort for it was a heavy piece of gadgetry. He consulted his watch: five thirty. He dressed, and put on his overcoat and his hat and wound a woollen scarf round his neck and stepped out into the dark.

The sky was overcast and there was no moon, and he had to use an electric pocket torch to light his way. Earlier in the night it had rained hard, and as he set off down the drive he smelt the sodden fields on either side of him, and felt the rinsed air cool against his face.

An armoured car was parked crookedly outside the gate, its blunt back end jutting into the road. Four or five soldiers stood beside it in a huddle, one of them holding a storm lantern that threw an unearthly glow upwards and turned their faces into Halloween masks with jutting jaws and empty eye-sockets. Two of the men were armed with carbines that, to Strafford's eye, looked worryingly antiquated.

Strafford identified Major de Valera — he still couldn't take the name seriously — by his cap with its shiny peak and some sort of pips on the shoulders of his uniform. He must be Dev's son, all right, for he had the look of the Chief, a younger, less severe version of him. He wore horn-rimmed spectacles, his eyes were watery and red-rimmed, and his nose was long and curiously fat at the tip. An outsized, awkward-looking holster was attached to his Sam Browne belt. He seemed not much of a soldier — in fact, he looked exactly what it was plain to see he was, a civilian in an army uniform. Why on earth had they chosen him, of all people, to guard the King of England's daughters? Not that the major had been informed of the identity of

153

the two girls — whoever was in charge of the operation had shown that much good sense. Why it had been considered all right to let the duke's housekeeper in on the secret, while it was kept from the officer in command of the guard duty, was a mystery to Strafford — another among the many mysteries of this harebrained operation.

"You're Stafford, are you?" the major said shortly. He sounded ill-tempered and on edge. Probably he had been on duty since nightfall, struggling to stay awake and not let the men realise how sleepy he was.

"That's right — Detective Garda Strafford. Where's this fellow you nabbed?"

They had put their captive to sit in the armoured car and shut the door on him, presumably to prevent him from running away. He was in his late twenties, thin and rat-faced, with a nose as long as the major's but tapered at the tip, and with a deep dent below the bridge where at some time in the past he must have been struck quite hard with a sharp-edged implement.

Strafford opened the door and put his foot on the running board. "Your name?"

"Who wants to know?"

After a pause, Strafford said softly, "I do."

The man looked him in the eye, and swallowed; Strafford, for all his disaffection, could do a nice line in menace, when menace was called for.

"Harte," the captive said. "Joseph Harte." He smelt strongly of drink.

"And what are you doing out at this hour of the morning, Mr Harte?"

The fellow, getting his nerve back, snickered. "Taking the air," he said, and ran a forefinger rapidly back and forth under his pinched nostrils. He was clutching a small sack in his lap, and suddenly inside it something squirmed convulsively.

"What's that?" Strafford asked. "What's in it?"

"Nothing."

"Give it here," Major de Valera said.

Harte was unwilling to part with the sack, but at a signal from the major, one of the soldiers stepped forward, shifting his grip on his rifle, and grabbed it from him.

"Mind out," Harte said, with a sly grin. "You'll get bit."

The soldier looked uncertainly to the major.

"What is it?" de Valera, in his high-pitched voice, asked of Harte. "A ferret?"

Strafford was watching the sack, inside which the animal was wriggling violently. How had the major and his men failed to notice before now that their captive was in possession of a bag with a ferret in it?

"I suggest you take him to the guards in Clonmillis," Strafford said. "See if they're interested in bringing a charge against him."

He had been instructed to keep clear of the local constabulary. The superintendent in Clonmillis was a notorious drinker, hence not to be trusted; the story that had been spun to him was that there had been rumours the local IRA was planning to attack the Hall and burn it, hence the armed patrols around the place.

155

"A charge? What sort of a charge?" Harte demanded indignantly.

"Quiet!" the major snapped. He turned to one of the soldiers. "Sergeant, take this man into Clonmillis and deliver him to the Garda barracks. Say we caught him poaching."

"Yes, sir," the sergeant responded.

The sergeant was a large, moon-faced, jolly-looking fellow with a tin helmet set crookedly on an outsized head the shape of a medium-sized cabbage, and it was apparent he was finding it difficult not to laugh: no doubt he had the measure of Major de Valera. He and one of the soldiers went round to the other side of the car and climbed in. The soldier started up the engine — it made a noise like the honking of a jennet, then backfired — and steered the machine on to the road and off it went, sputtering exhaust smoke into the air behind it.

Strafford bade farewell to the major, who snapped back his shoulders and delivered him a whiplash salute. One of the remaining soldiers put up a hand to follow his example, and in doing so managed to lose hold of his rifle. It fell on to the tarmac with a tremendous clatter. Strafford was surprised it didn't go off — that would have been a perfect end, he thought, to this dreamlike nocturnal adventure.

He went back up the rained-on drive, a ten minutes' slog over slippery gravel and tussocks of sodden grass. In his bedroom he pulled off the wellington boots and lay down on the narrow bed, still in his raincoat, sweater and trousers. In an hour Maggie the maid

156

would come with a kettle of hot water — or lukewarm, rather — for his morning shave. Then he would cross the yard, his cheeks chapped and stinging from the razor, the duke's horses eyeing him sceptically from the stable doorways, and enter the house by the back way and sit down to breakfast.

Later, at mid-morning, Celia Nashe and the two girls went for a walk in Clonmillis Wood. The wood was long and only a couple of hundred yards wide, running past the house and down the flank of a gentle slope, with cow-scattered meadows on the house side and skirted by the Clonmillis road on the other. Having struck off crosswise, they had got halfway through when the deciduous trees gave way to ranked stands of evergreens, and the ground became an even layer of pine needles that felt like rush matting underfoot. They followed a barely discernible track that wound its way steadily along the side of the low hill.

Here, in the depths of the wood, there was a deep quiet, with no sound of bird or breeze, and the air under the trees was a dense blue-green haze. The girls walked ahead, the younger one close on the heels of the elder, with Celia a dozen paces behind.

Celia often wondered what it was the sisters talked about when there was no one nearby to overhear them. They seemed to get on best together when there were just the two of them; the presence of other people provoked them into squabbles. It surprised her, the violence and cruelty of some of the things they said to each other. She had no sisters herself.

These musings were occupying her mind to the exclusion of her surroundings when suddenly, close behind her, at her very shoulder, so it seemed, there was a tremendous crash of sound that plunged her into a helpless panic, her heart racing and her knees atremble. In the first moment she couldn't imagine what had caused it, but instinctively, and before turning to look, she had flipped back her coat and reached for the Browning in its holster at her left armpit.

She heard the soft step of someone emerging from the pines, and now she did turn, still not knowing what to expect. The girls had stopped too, and were looking back to see what had happened. Celia's hand, clutching the butt of the pistol, was hidden by the flap of her coat, but all the same she was sure Mary had caught a glimpse of the holster — that watchful little body missed nothing.

Billy Denton, stepping sideways from the trees on to the path, dipped the barrel of his shotgun so that it was pointing at the ground. Celia caught a lingering whiff of gunpowder. She gave a tight, brittle little laugh. "Ah, you startled me!" she exclaimed.

The young man wore a threadbare Norfolk jacket, a collarless and not very clean white shirt, brown cord trousers and stout leather lace-up boots.

"Sorry," he said, though he didn't sound it. "Thought there wasn't anyone out here."

"What are you doing?"

"Shooting rooks."

"Rooks?" They were a kind of crow, she thought. "Why?"

158

"They're a pest."

Celia frowned; she hadn't known that birds could be pests, at least not ordinary birds, like crows and rooks. She supposed it must be that they ate grain, or some such — or was it a countryman's joke at the expense of a city-dweller? There was certainly no trace of humour in the young man's look. He was handsome, in a sullen sort of way, with shiny black curls and milk-pale skin and a saddle of tea-coloured freckles over the bridge of his nose.

"My name is Nashe, by the way," she said. "Celia Nashe."

She held out her hand but he pretended not to notice it.

"Denton," he said.

She withdrew her hand. He regarded her with a blank expression, the shotgun resting easy on his forearm.

"And that's Mary," Celia said, "and her sister, Ellen. We're staying at the Hall."

"Aye, I know."

Still his stony expression did not soften. He seemed not so much hostile as determinedly indifferent.

Mary came running back to where they stood, while Ellen remained behind.

"How many did you shoot?" Mary asked breathlessly. She was looking up at him with a smile, hazy and excited, that was most unlike her, Celia thought.

Billy Denton frowned. "How many what?"

"Crows — isn't that what you were shooting?"

"Rooks," he corrected her. Celia seemed to detect a slight adjustment in his manner, a slight softening now. "Not many," he went on. "They're clever enough: they see the glint of the barrel as soon as you lift it, and then they're gone."

The girl had many more things she would have liked to say to him, but without another word he stepped back into the bluey shadow of the wood and, in a moment, was gone from sight. Mary turned to Celia Nashe with her eyes narrowed and her lips tightened to a thin line; it was clear she held Celia responsible for driving the young man away.

"You've gone white," she said accusingly.

Celia blinked. "What?"

"Haven't you ever heard a shotgun fired before?"

"Of course I have."

"I thought you knew all about guns."

"Oh, do be quiet," Ellen said, coming back along the path and taking her sister's hand. "Let's go."

She walked on, dragging Mary behind her. Mary looked over her shoulder at Celia with a thin malignant smile, as if to say, I'll pay you back, don't think I won't.

"Oh, God," Celia murmured to herself, and touched a hand briefly to her brow. Her ears were still ringing from the gun blast. In fact she hadn't heard a shotgun fired before. It made an astonishingly loud noise, and it was borne in on her that her nerves were in worse shape than she had thought.

Billy Denton turned off from the path and made his way between the tall, slender trunks of the trees. He felt

160

uneasy, he wasn't sure why. It was only a young woman and a couple of girls — why should it have upset him to chance on them in that way? It was like something out of one of those old pishogues that Pike was fond of telling, the woman a witch disguised as a maid, the two young ones her enchanted captives, and himself the innocent woodsman with his gun. Yes, that was how Pike would have told it.

It amused Pike to play the part of the wise old bird, full of rural lore and tales of "bygone times" — he was a walking *Ireland's Own*, and just as much of a fake as most of the things that were written about in that rag of a magazine. Behind the blarney and the blather, Pike was as sly and slippery as a rat in a gutter. Even the way he spoke — always generously sprinkling in "sure" and "bedad" and "amn't I?" — was put on. He talked the way Americans expected the Irish to talk.

Here was the limit of the evergreens — the duke had put in this plantation years ago, convinced it would make his fortune, and then had lost interest in it. Billy turned and walked along a firebreak separating the pines from the original native trees. He heard something move in the foliage ahead of him, and stopped and raised the shotgun shoulder-high and squinted along the barrels.

Then, slowly, he lowered it again.

Peering out from the green tangle in front of him was a pair of eyes set in a soot-daubed face topped by a helmet camouflaged with oak leaves; the tip of a rifle barrel was poking up through the brambles. He took a step back, and set the butt of his own gun on the ground. The soldier rose from where he had been lurking in the undergrowth and retreated slowly, still facing him, still at a crouch, until the trees swallowed him and he was no more to be seen.

Denton waited a moment, in case there were more soldiers. Then he laughed, shaking his head, and set off in the direction of the Clonmillis road.

This was not his first encounter with the military. He had spotted them three or four times in the past week, lying on the ground under cover with their rifles at the ready — for what? — or creeping through the trees and signalling to each other, waving each other on or back, and generally looking like a squad of actors in a war film. He couldn't take them seriously. If they weren't careful, someone was going to get shot.

CHAPTER
SEVENTEEN

Joey Harte often thought what a pity it was that people didn't wear cloaks any more, or not without the risk of being laughed at, anyway. He would wear one, if he could. Joey liked to think of himself as a man of mystery, a lone wolf on the prowl, a sort of secret agent. He maintained a self-consciously furtive air, keeping always to the inside of the pavement and slipping along silently in the shadows. In fact, Slipper was his nickname in the town.

He lived in a one-room whitewashed cottage — or grey-washed, as some local joker had once remarked, and everyone remembered it — on John's Street, wedged between a butcher's shop and a blacksmith's yard, which he rented from the butcher for a few shillings a month. His father was a drunkard who beat Joey's mother, until she ran away with a tinker, and from then on Joey got her share of the walloping as well as his own. Eventually he had to be removed from the family home, such as it was, for fear the father on one of his extra bad nights might do for him.

And so Joey had passed his teenage years in various foster homes and so-called industrial schools, and in every one of them he had been bullied, and interfered with by the priests and the Christian Brothers, and generally kicked around. He had never had a job, and lived on the dole, cadging drinks and smokes and doing a bit of poaching and the odd bit of thieving. The town tolerated him; he was one of its "characters".

He had got in early with the Lads, as they had come to be called — usually with a glance thrown up to the ceiling, a click of the tongue and a tight-lipped, indulgent smile — and in time became their unofficial courier. This involved not much more than running to the bookie's on Saturday mornings, and ferrying bottles of porter to thirsty throats — they did a lot of talking, did the Lads — in the upstairs back room over Redmond's pub, which was general headquarters, supposedly.

There the Lads met once a week, with the door locked, to discuss whatever there was to be discussed, such as what way they might go about procuring funds from America, how to get their hands on a few guns, or plans for another foray up to the Border to throw stones at the windows of customs posts on the far side. The Lads were "politicals", pledged to drive the British out of the North and reunite the country. They had never actually set foot in Northern Ireland, and would have been hard put to name the six counties that made up the province. Everyone thought they were a bit of a joke, except themselves.

The spell of fine weather had broken, and it had begun to rain again that afternoon when Joey dodged in at the side door of Redmond's, with his collar turned

164

up and his cap pulled low over his eyes, imagining himself every inch the cloaked conspirator.

The pub inside had a raw, tousled look to it, as it always did in the daytime, and smelt of stale beer and staler cigarette smoke. There were no customers in yet. Old Redmond himself was behind the bar, in shirtsleeves and braces, leaning on his elbows, picking his teeth with the split end of a match and reading a copy of last week's *Nationalist*. He was fat, with a puffy red face and a few remaining strands of sandy-grey hair plastered across a bald and pitted skull. He lifted his pink-rimmed, lashless eyes and gave Joey a blank stare.

Joey rubbed his hands together vigorously, as if he were cold; it was a thing he did, and it irritated anyone who had to be around him for more than five minutes. "Is the man himself above?" he asked, jerking his head in the direction of the stairs at the back.

"He is."

"On his own?"

But Redmond had returned to his newspaper. Joey went out of the bar and climbed the back stairs.

A scorch-marked pale-green paraffin stove stood in a corner of the upstairs room. The window was fastened and the curtains were pulled shut to keep out the afternoon light, and the air was foetid.

Tom Clancy, known to all as the Boss Clancy, sat at a table in front of the empty fireplace. A weak, unshaded bulb burned above the table, which as usual was covered with sheaves of documents, on which Clancy as usual was pretending to be hard at work. No one knew what the important affairs were that he was supposed to be engaged in, that required the processing of so much paperwork, but whenever anyone came into the room, there he would be, hunched over the stacked pages, with a pencil in his hand, frowning and moving his lips as he read, his tobacco pipe sitting in the tin ashtray in front of him.

"Joey, *a chara*," he said, without warmth and without looking up. "Are we winning?"

Clancy was the self-appointed leader of the Lads. He was a thick-set, bullish man of forty or so — old enough to know better than to be playing at toy soldiers, as people said, behind his back — with a head the shape and size of a shoebox set atop a neck that was as wide as his forehead, and oiled black hair combed back so fiercely it seemed to pull his eyebrows upwards, giving him a look of permanent, ill-tempered startlement. He wore a white shirt and a red tie, and a light-brown tweed jacket, all three buttons of which he kept fastened most of the time. He had a pasty look to him, with skin the colour of a blanched vegetable. He seemed to be bulging out of himself, and was constantly in a sweat. Mrs Redmond, the publican's wife, a taciturn woman of dour aspect who nevertheless came out with occasional nuggets of sarcastic wit, swore that if you looked close enough you could see the perspiration oozing out of the lace-holes of his size-eleven shoes.

Joey had been drinking the night before, and consequently had a raging thirst today, but judged it unwise even to hint at the possibility of a restorative pint. Clancy was in one of his puritanical phases, and lately had been trying to get the Squad to take the pledge — Clancy always spoke of his little band of volunteers as "the Squad", and flew into a rage if he heard them referred to as "the Lads", a term he considered disparaging: his men were no "lads". He was a man to be reckoned with in Clonmillis, for as well as being a secret insurrectionist — though it was a secret known to pretty well everyone — he ran the town's biggest hardware store and was a member of the County Council.

He put down his pencil and looked at Joey where he hovered just inside the door.

"If you're coming in, come in, for God's sake!" he said sourly.

Joey advanced to the table, removing his cap and holding it before him with both hands. The fumes from the stove had already deposited an oily smear on his lips, which he tried to wipe away with the side of a forefinger, but couldn't; he hated the stink of paraffin, and didn't know how the Boss could bear to sit there breathing it in for hours every Saturday afternoon and most weekday evenings, working at his papers and smoking that pipe of his, which smelt even worse than the stove.

"How are you doing, Boss?" he ventured.

"I'm grand," Clancy responded brusquely. "What have you to tell me?"

"They're still out there, the blonde one and the two youngsters. The English fellow in the fancy car didn't come back."

"But the Free Staters are still guarding the place?"

The "Free State" was how the rebels contemptuously referred to de Valera's Irish Republic.

Joey glanced aside uneasily. "So I hear," he muttered.

He had no intention of telling the Boss about his run-in with the soldiers in the armoured car on the road behind the Hall in the middle of the night. He would probably get to hear of it anyway — two of the Lads were civic guards, and supplied regular reports to the Boss on what the Free Staters were up to. Joey had been brought by the soldiers to the Garda barracks on Hill Street, but as soon as the arrest party were gone the desk sergeant had let him go, with a warning to stay off the Duke of Edenmore's lands or next time he'd find himself facing a charge of loitering with intent, if not something more serious. The sack with the ferret in it was ignored.

Clancy's pipe had gone out, and he took it up and lit a match and applied it to the ashy dottle in the bottom of the bowl. "So, if the Englishman is gone and Dev's so-called army is still on duty," he said, "then it wasn't him they were guarding." He puffed out tobacco smoke. "Maybe it's the blonde one, then, the wife."

"And the two youngsters."

"No, no." Clancy shook his head. "A whole bloody platoon to look out for the family of some fellow that works at the embassy? The Brits are not that considerate of their lackeys, or even their lackeys' womenfolk. What about the other fellow from Dublin, the detective?"

"Strafford is his name."

"Stafford?"

168

"No, it's Strafford, with an r. So he said."

Clancy looked at him with narrowed eyes. "How do you know what he said?" Joey's forehead went red, and he was relieved when the Boss went on, "I suppose your sweetheart was able to tell you his name, and all about him and his doings."

"That's right, that's right, yes," Joey said eagerly, with a nervous laugh.

Clancy regarded him for some moments, chewing the stem of his pipe. Something wasn't right, here: Joey was keeping something from him. But, then, the Slipper was a dedicated liar, the kind who lied even when it wasn't called for, just to keep in practice.

"When did you see her last, your lovey-dovey?" Clancy asked, deliberately casual.

"The other night," Joey answered.

"What other night?" Clancy was smiling — at least, the expression on his face was what, with him, stood in for a smile.

"Wednesday. No, Thursday."

"I see," Clancy said.

He might as well let it go. Sooner or later Joey would blurt out whatever it was he was keeping silent about — he had no backbone, just like his wastrel of a father. When the time came for shooting, the Joeys would be the ones to send in first, if for nothing else than to use up some of the enemy's ammunition. That's what volunteers were for, as he had remarked to Sean MacBride — he had only once met the great man, when he was still the IRA chief of staff, but it remained the single most memorable encounter of his life, and he

169

never failed to find a pretext for mentioning it at the weekly strategy meeting with the Squad.

"What about our fellow out there on the estate?" he asked now. "Is he keeping an eye on things?"

Joey snickered. "Oh, he is."

Clancy, whose sudden rages were notorious, took the pipe from his mouth and picked up his pencil and bit on the end of it, as a substitute for grinding his teeth.

"Jesus Christ," he snarled, "we have him and your young one, the two of them, on the bloody premises, and still we don't know what's going on."

"I've a date with Maggie this evening."

"Have you, now," Clancy said, opening his eyes wide in the pretence of being impressed. "A date, no less, and you only after seeing her the other night. She can't get enough of you, seemingly."

"She lets me in by the back door."

At this, Clancy turned his smile into a leer. "Oh, I'm sure she does that, all right," he said.

Joey looked down, his brow going red again. Whatever Clancy thought of him, there was no cause for sneering at the girl he was sweet on, or dirtying her name with suggestive remarks. He thought of saying something, of making some protest, but he hadn't the nerve.

"Anyway," Clancy said, with harsh finality, "see what she has to say about the situation out there, and let me know."

He had caught the momentary flash of resentment in Joey's downcast look. Joey was full of surprises, today. A minute ago he was blushing at the mere mention of

170

his sweetheart, and now he was in the sulks because of a bit of a joke at her expense. Wasn't she only a skivvy at the Big House? The Boss couldn't understand what it was about fellows and their girls. But, then, he didn't have much truck with women himself.

He turned back to the table, and his papers. He had been sending regular dispatches to the people in Belfast — Head Office, as he would say, with a wink — keeping them informed of developments at Clonmillis Hall since the arrival of the mysterious party of five in the maroon-coloured car, and the deployment of a military patrol to keep guard on the place. They were saying in the town that Dev's own son, Major Vivion, was commander-in-chief out there. That little snippet would have made the top brass in Belfast prick up their ears, if he had chosen to tell them, which he hadn't; it was always well to keep a little something back. He had been trying for he couldn't remember how long to get the Belfast boys to acknowledge the readiness of him and his men to engage in subversive action, but they had paid him no heed — not until now.

Joey hadn't moved.

Clancy looked at him. "Was there something else, Slipper?"

"No, Boss."

"Tell Redmond I said to give you a pint, and put it on the slate."

"Ah, thanks, Boss," Joey said, breaking out in a smile. "I've a thirst on me that would —"

"Right, right — off you go."

Clancy addressed his paperwork again, smoothing a hand over his hair. Jesus, think of the calibre of the men of 1916, scholars and poets every one of them, while all he had to aid him in the Cause was the likes of Joey Harte.

CHAPTER
EIGHTEEN

Strafford was sunk happily in his armchair in the library, his long legs stretched out before him and his toes toasting in front of the fire, when he heard faint strains of music coming from somewhere on the upper floors. He had been reading *Eustacia Goes to the Chalet School*, the one of his choices that had made Miss Broaders raise an eyebrow on his latest visit to the Carnegie library. Now he closed the book, keeping a finger between the pages to mark his place.

The music was a waltz, he recognised it, though he couldn't remember the title; something by one of the all too many Strausses, no doubt. Grown curious, he laid the book face down on the floor beside the log basket. The fire was low, and he stirred the fading embers with the poker and piled on a handful of kindling and a couple of logs; in a minute or two it would be going nicely again.

He stretched, and yawned. There was, he recalled, a word for doing that: pandiculation. How in God's name did he know that? His mind retained all sorts of odds and ends; he feared it was another sign of his essential unseriousness.

173

He heard voices from the adjoining room. Celia Nashe was in there with Mary, testing her knowledge of French verbs; the unrelieved tedium was driving them all to extremes.

Outside, it was raining.

The ballroom was on the first floor, and ran from the front of the house all the way to the back. Strafford stopped before the open doorway, just short of the threshold, careful not to make a sound. Suddenly the name of the tune came back to him: it was not from the quill of any of the Strausses, but was by Franz Lehar — "The Merry Widow Waltz". It had been one of his mother's favourites; that was how he knew it, for he was not at all musical himself. She used to hum along to it, and for a moment now he could almost hear her again: *Daah da-da dah, daah da-da dah, dah — dah — dah*.

The room he could see through the doorway was vast, and was made to seem all the more so by being almost entirely unfurnished. There were not even curtains on the three arched, oddly ecclesiastical-looking windows. The vast expanse of wooden floor looked as if it had not been polished in half a century, and was striated all over with fine grey loops and lines, like the surface of the ice in an ice rink. The fireplace, of green Connemara marble, was tall enough for a man to stand up in, and the ceiling, too, was high, and decorated with elegant plaster moulding that was badly in need of cleaning.

The gramophone, an old-fashioned wind-up model with a florid brass horn, had been placed on the floor underneath one of the windows. The red-labelled record spinning on its turntable was the only thing moving in the room — that, and the girl dancing.

It was Ellen. She was wearing a blue dress with a pleated bodice, white ankle socks and black patent leather pumps with a strap that buttoned over the instep. Her hair was done in her usual tiara style, and a tortoiseshell slide was fixed in it at one side. She was waltzing fluidly in time to the music, her eyes closed. In her arms, in place of a partner, she was carrying a Victorian ball-gown of diaphanous white lace slightly yellowed with age, the collar pressed to her throat with one hand, while with the other she held, extended far out to the left, its empty limp right sleeve. The rain-light from the window formed a luminous mist around her, and the hissing of the gramophone needle in the groove reminded Strafford of the sound of a far-off sea running over pebbles at the shoreline.

He had begun to retreat backwards on tiptoe from the doorway when the music came abruptly to a close, and the girl halted in the dance and her eyelids clicked open, and the pair found themselves staring straight into each other's eyes, both of them equally startled, in their different ways.

"Oh, I'm sorry," Strafford said hastily, "I didn't see you there."

This was such an obvious falsehood that he had to shut tight his own eyes for a second, wincing in embarrassment. The girl immediately rolled the white

175

dress into a ball and, holding it pressed to her midriff, crossed quickly to the gramophone and knelt on one knee and lifted the needle clear of the record and drew the heavy playing-arm aside and clipped it on to its metal support.

Strafford, still teetering awkwardly in the doorway, had no alternative but to come forward into the room. The girl straightened up from the gramophone and turned to face him, pale and rueful and a little cross. Somehow she had made the ball-gown disappear — she must have cast it aside somewhere. She brushed her hands down the front of her skirt to rid it of non-existent creases.

This young person, Strafford told himself, in the manner of one pinching himself awake, was a princess of the blood, the first in line to the throne of England and future sovereign of the British Empire, and yet at the same time she was just a girl, caught out in a private fantasy, an adolescent dream of sophistication and romance.

"I'm sorry," he said again. "I didn't mean to —"

He wasn't sure what it was he hadn't meant to do. They stood facing each other in vague desperation, the tall, lean young man and the even younger girl, in her ankle socks and neat, shiny shoes. He had thought she would hurry away, once she had got rid of the lace gown — what had she done with it? — but she seemed as helpless as he was to break the spell that was holding them together here in this painfully awkward situation.

The three tall, rained-on windows afforded an undulant view over the tops of trees to the mysterious

176

far hill that seemed to be visible from whatever part of the house one was in.

"It's cold," Strafford said, giving an exaggerated shiver to illustrate the point. "I don't know how people manage to live in houses like this."

"Yes," the girl said, and after a pause added, "My people have been living in houses like this for as long as any of us can remember." Again she paused. "Where did you grow up?"

"Well, also in a house somewhat like this one, actually, only smaller, of course. A place called Roslea. Not very far from here, but in another county."

"Ah," She nodded. "But you are Irish, yes?"

How grave her manner was, he thought, for one so young.

"Yes, yes, indeed," he said. "Or Anglo-Irish, anyway. That's what the Irish call us." He smiled. "The British, of course, don't quite know what we are."

"It's all very complicated, isn't it?"

They both looked aside at the same instant. Strafford felt acutely the discomfiture of the situation, from which neither of them seemed to know how to escape. Of course, he could just murmur some polite word and turn and leave. And yet he lingered. It was as if an invisible circle had been inscribed around them on the ballroom floor, from which they would not be allowed to escape until one or the other hit upon the magic formula.

"What's that smell?" Strafford said. "It's like —" He couldn't think what it was, yet he knew it well.

"Mothballs, I imagine," Ellen said. "I've got the smell of them on my hands, from that frock."

"Of course. Very" — he searched for the word — "very evocative."

"Yes."

Some day, years from now, he thought, I'll catch a whiff of camphor and on the spot relive this moment.

Rain whispered against the windowpanes. The shiny wet tops of the trees outside were grey-green, gold, russet, blood-red.

"Are you all right?" he heard himself ask.

She appeared to be not at all surprised by the question. She gave it a moment or two of solemn consideration. "Yes, I think so," she said. "Why?"

"I just wondered. I thought you might be missing — well, lots of things."

"Yes. But we're trained not to."

"Not to what?"

"Miss things."

He smiled again, putting his head to one side. "Trained?" he said.

"Bred, then. But it's the same thing, really, isn't it?" The girl was silent for a moment, frowning, as a teacher would frown when she is about to formulate a proposition she knows will be beyond the comprehension of all but one or two of the brighter pupils in the class. "It's part of our job, you see."

"Part of —?"

"Yes. Part of it is not to give in to weakness, not to want things, or feel sorry for oneself."

Strafford couldn't think what to say to that.

The girl's look brightened. "I should imagine it's teatime," she said. "Shall we go down?"

They went out together, and descended the staircase, side by side. There was still the faint odour of mothballs.

After his first few days at the Hall Strafford had quietly given up the taking of afternoon tea. It was this one in particular among the numerous observances by which the day at Clonmillis Hall was portioned out that he found the most tedious. After his encounter with Ellen, therefore, instead of repairing to the first-floor drawing room, where the tea ceremony was celebrated, he instead returned to the library.

The fire he had relit had caught, and the logs were blazing away in their self-absorbed, arabesque fashion. He took up his book and dipped again into the story of vengeful Eustacia, who was preparing her plan to wreak havoc on the School at the Chalet. After a quarter of an hour in the armchair, lulled by the warmth of the fire and the placid cadences of Miss Brent-Dyer's prose, he grew heavy-lidded, and presently fell into a half-sleep.

He had not been dozing for long when he was woken by the sound of a throat being noisily and pointedly cleared.

The duke was standing over him with a reprehending scowl. Oh, Lord, Strafford thought, asleep on guard duty!

"Sorry to disturb you," the duke said, with ponderous irony. "Wanted to have a word."

"Yes, of course," Strafford said, putting his book away hastily and pulling himself more or less upright in the chair. "Won't you sit down?"

"Prefer to stand."

Strafford by now, despite his forebodings, was agog to know what the matter could be. Had he violated one of the unwritten protocols of the house? Was it his disdaining of the tea ceremony that had piqued the old boy? No: something more serious.

"Thing is," the duke said, shifting his glare to the fire in the grate, "the girls have been complaining — well, the older one has, on behalf of both of them."

It was time for Strafford to stand up. He had the advantage of being almost a head taller than the duke. "Complaining about what?" he asked, in the mildest of mild tones.

"Perhaps 'complaining' is too strong a word."

The old man fished his pipe out of his pocket, along with an old leather tobacco pouch, and a small steel implement bristling with prongs and blades and scrapers, and commenced the pipe-man's ritual of reaming, tapping, filling, tamping, lighting. Life, Strafford reflected, is essentially a succession of small and for the most part unacknowledged diversionary tactics.

"What they say, what *she* says" — the pipe emitted a billow of transparent, light-blue smoke, and a horrible gurgling sound, like a death-rattle, came out of the bowl — "is that they are subjected to altogether too much supervision."

Strafford had been hoping for something much more exciting. "Supervision?" he said.

"Yes. You and Miss Nashe, she says, are forever fussing over them, and watching, and listening, and so on."

"I see." Strafford felt as if he were being tickled, and had a strong urge to laugh, which he knew he must resist at all costs. "But, then, of course, it is our job," he said, "to watch, and listen, and generally — well, generally keep an eye on things."

"I understand that," the duke said, making an impatient slicing gesture with the side of a hand. "Of course I understand. But dammit, man, they're children, they need a bit of freedom, to play and — and — and be themselves, and so on."

The duke was not intrinsically funny, yet he never failed to provoke in Strafford this giddy urge to break down in merriment.

And whence came the old boy's sudden access of concern for the girls' well-being?

"As a matter of fact, sir, I wanted to have a word with you myself on the very same topic."

"Eh?" The old man stared, one eyebrow lowered and the other hoisted high, which gave him the look of an infuriated cyclops. There was a spill of tobacco ash on the front of his tweed waistcoat. "What do you mean?"

"Well, I feel — and I suspect Miss Nashe would agree with me — that there's rather too much coming and going here at the Hall, and about the grounds especially."

"Coming and going?" The cyclops eye glittered.

"Yes. There's that young chap — what's his name, Denton? He seems to have free run of the place."

The duke, his nostrils flaring now, gave himself an indignant shake, wriggling his shoulders and flapping his lower lip. "Of course he has free run of the place! He's practically my steward."

"Wasn't his mother shot by the Black and Tans?"

At this the duke reared himself backwards from the waist and stared up at the young man, his brow turning a shade darker. "How do you know that?" he demanded, in a menacing growl.

"Well, we were given some degree of briefing, you know, Miss Nashe and I — separately, of course — before being deployed here."

The duke broke off his stare and walked in a tight little circle with his hands clasped behind him, shaking his head and making a low humming sound, as if a wasp were trapped in his throat.

"For God's sake," he said, "that was all a long time ago and, besides, the military denied it was they who shot her." He ceased to pace and glared into the bowl of his pipe and jabbed at it with one of the blades of his smoker's companion.

"All the same, you take my point, sir," Strafford mildly said.

"I do, and I think it absurd. Do you really imagine Billy Denton could be a — what would you call it? — a security risk? And my housekeeper, Mrs O'Hanlon? Do you think she carries messages to the IRA hidden in her bloomers? And me, what about me? What's to prevent me telling all and sundry that the two children staying here are in reality —" He stopped and set himself in front of Strafford again. "My dear fellow, really. This

182

isn't the East End of London — this is the Irish midlands."

His pipe was going strongly, and now he walked in another tight circle, more slowly this time, trailing shunts of smoke behind him, like a railway engine.

"It's not so long since they were burning down houses just like this one," Strafford said, hardening his voice; he was suddenly tired of being lectured to. "They haven't all gone away, you know, the gunmen."

"But the people, man! They haven't got the people with them, not any more. The fight has gone out of the Irish — poverty saw to that, poverty and the priests, along with the realisation of what it takes to run a country when you no longer have someone else to blame when things get sticky. And remember what Napoleon said: march without the people and you march into night."

Strafford said nothing to that, only raised his eyebrows and puffed out his cheeks in a small show of surrender. The duke seemed an unlikely proponent of democracy but, after all, he probably knew the country far better than Strafford himself did.

That evening, before the house sat down to dinner, Strafford approached Celia Nashe and told her of the afternoon's exchange with the old man. To his surprise, she sided with the duke.

"I had been thinking of saying something to you myself," she said, with a sort of bright steeliness.

They were in the upstairs drawing room, standing by a window that looked out, not on rolling greensward, as

183

such a window might be expected to do, but down into the back garden of the Hall and across to the stable yard. Dusk was closing in, the rain had stopped, and a mist was settling on that ever-present distant hill — Strafford wondered if it even had a name — making it seem as flat and insubstantial against the sky as if it were painted on a stage backdrop in a wash of lavender-blue.

Celia was smoking, darting at the cigarette and not so much taking puffs as giving it quick little pecks, like a blackbird at feed.

"I had the impression we were not to let them out of our sight," Strafford protested weakly.

"Oh, I think they could be allowed at least a little leeway, don't you, and given a bit of time to themselves? It must be so oppressive, knowing one is being watched at all hours of the day and night. Besides, we're completely surrounded by a platoon of armed soldiers, aren't we?"

Strafford said nothing, but his look was dubious. Evidently she had more confidence in Major de Valera and his men than he was able to muster, as well as imagining them to be more numerous than they were. But she was the senior figure here, he reminded himself, and let the subject drop.

All the same, as they descended the staircase together, they were aware of an uncomfortable silence between them; it was almost as if they had been engaged in an outright squabble. He supposed she was more conscious than he was of how in this operation the usual order of things was reversed, first of all by her being a woman, and second, by her being older than he was. He might have been her younger brother, whom she had been obliged to allow to accompany her on an adult undertaking. He found the notion absurd and unsettling, in equal measure, and yet there it was, a thing they had to bear between them.

They came to the door of the dining room. There were sounds from within of chairs being drawn forward, of cutlery being taken in hand, of crystal goblets clinking. Dinner had begun.

"Deep breath, eh?" he said lightly.

But Celia was not to be drawn so easily into collusion with him, and pretended not to have heard, and, anyway, she was already going ahead of him into the room.

CHAPTER
NINETEEN

The new relaxed security regime, which the girls had demanded, which the duke had backed and which Celia Nashe had sanctioned, was put in place next morning, and within an hour a small disaster had occurred.

It was early, and Billy Denton had been out replacing a fence that ran along by the edge of the plantation, walking with a roll of barbed wire from post to post and stopping at each one to fix the new wire to the wood with a couple of U-shaped metal cleats. The morning was misty and mild under a low sky as white as pipe clay. He had got as far as the edge of the Long Meadow when he heard an unexpected sound. Someone nearby was sobbing. He set down the roll of wire and the hammer and the tin of nails and made his way into the wood.

He found her in a clearing in the pines, sitting on a low hillock and clutching her left leg at the ankle with both hands. It was the older one, Ellen. The horse, Prince, stood at a few yards' distance, unconcernedly grazing on a patch of sweet grass flourishing in a little oasis amid the covering of pine needles.

When she heard his step Ellen looked up quickly, her eyes widening in alarm. "Oh, it's you," she said, relieved.

He stopped in front of her. "What happened?"

She brushed the tears hurriedly from her cheeks. "Prince bolted again. He must have thought he had seen something in the grass, a snake or something."

"No snakes here," Denton said curtly. He had leaned over and was peering at her ankle, trying to decide how serious the injury might be. "Can you put your weight on it?"

"I don't know, I haven't tried. I was feeling dazed, after the fall. I'm all right now."

"Let's have a look," He knelt before her and took her foot in his hands and rotated it first to the left and then to the right. Ellen gasped, and bit her lip. "Is it that sore?" She nodded, frowning in the effort of holding back another effusion of tears. "We'll have to get that boot off. Come on."

He lifted her up, with one arm under her shoulders and the other under her knees. She was forced to put one of her own arms around his neck. She had left her riding hat and her crop on the ground. He would get them for her later, he said. He smelt of creosote.

"What about Prince?" the girl asked.

"He'll be all right here for a while."

They set off through the trees.

Ellen was mortified, to be carried along like this, helplessly, like a survivor being rescued from a burning house, or something equally undignified. Strangely, though, it was also the first time since she had come to Clonmillis that she felt entirely safe.

It looked like a cottage in a fairy tale, tiny, one-storeyed, with a picturesque plume of smoke coming out of a crooked chimney. It stood in a glade in the older part of the wood, hidden from view a little way back from the main road. There were clumps of moss on the roof, and rosebushes under the windowsills; the limbs of an ancient, gnarled wisteria were twined around the frame of the front door, like thick, clutching fingers.

Billy managed to get the door open even with the girl in his arms. He carried her to the sofa and laid her down on it. She wriggled herself into a sitting position, and held herself as straight as she could; she was who she was, after all. Billy Denton looked down at her, frowning, his head to one side; he might have been figuring out how to fix a machine that had broken down, she thought. The thought was comforting: she liked to be treated impersonally, as if she were — well, as if she were, on occasion, just like everybody else.

He knelt on one knee and lifted her leg with a hand under her calf, and with his other hand grasped the heel of her boot and gave it an experimental tug. She drew in her breath again with a hissing sound, and again bit her lip. He sat back for a second, then leaned down and, without warning, gave the boot a quick, deft tug, and drew it free. Ellen released a little squeal of pain — she couldn't help it.

188

"Sorry," Billy Denton said gruffly. "Only way to do it. That, or cut off the boot." He peered closely at the swollen ankle, catching the warmish, woolly odour of the girl's sweat-damp sock. "Well, it's not broken, anyhow," he said.

He set her foot on the floor and rose and went to the sink, telling her to take off the sock. She did as she was told, while he ran water from the tap into a white enamel basin. She watched him covertly. He had removed his raggedy Norfolk jacket and put it to hang on the back of a chair and rolled up his shirtsleeves. His sleeveless Fair Isle pullover had moth holes in the back of it. The linoleum floor was littered with chevrons of dried mud that had fallen out of the ridges in the soles of his boots.

Everything here was so simple and homely, and for a second she saw how rigid were the rules by which she was required to live and felt a stab of resentment.

Billy Denton brought the basin and set it down in front of her. "You soak that ankle for a few minutes, while I go back and get the horse."

"Will you remember my hat, too, and my riding crop?"

He put on his jacket again and went out. There seemed to be a limit to his available responses so that he was compelled to dole them out judiciously.

A low, narrow bed stood in one corner, covered with a red blanket, well tucked in round the edges. There was a wooden work bench with a vice mounted on it, and on the wall behind it tools hung from nails, ranked according to type and size. There was a smell of lubricating oil. A brace of pheasants were strung up by their feet from a beam in the ceiling. An iron stove was lit, the flames a dull red flicker behind the sooty glass panel in the door.

Her ankle throbbed, and the icy water was making her toes ache. All the same, she felt like Snow White, though blessedly without the Seven Dwarfs. She laid her head against the back of the sofa and closed her eyes. Everything was topsy-turvy, her world turned upside down, yet still there was that feeling of being in a place of safety.

Perhaps, after all, her parents had done the right thing in sending her here.

She had fallen into a doze by the time Billy Denton returned. The sound of his step in the doorway woke her, and once more she drew herself upright hastily. Billy knelt on one knee again and examined her ankle. The water in the basin was no longer cold, and the skin of her toes had gone all white and crinkled, like, she thought with amusement, the top of a steamed suet pudding. She could hear Prince grazing outside, tearing up clumps of grass, his tack tinkling.

"We'd better take you back," Billy Denton said. "They'll be wondering where you are, or if you got lost altogether."

He picked her up, quickly but not roughly, and bore her in his arms again, all the way to the Hall. Her hat and crop rested on her lap, she carried her boot with the sock stuffed into it in one hand, and in the other she held on to Prince's bridle. The horse clopped along

190

behind them, snorting now and then. He was bored, she thought. Horses found everything a bore, except eating and galloping and, of course, the other thing they liked to do when they were put to stud.

What would have happened if Billy Denton hadn't come along and heard her crying? She might have been on her own in the wood for ages, until nightfall, even; she might not have been found for days. But, no, they would have sent out a search party for her. All the same, she rather liked the idea of being abandoned and alone, among the trees, as the shadows of evening gathered round her. It would have been a test of her courage, of her strength of character. She thought it right that she should be subjected to repeated testing: she needed to be hardened for the duties that lay ahead of her.

She was a very serious girl; being serious was another part of her job.

All the same, later on, when she was at the house again and lying on a sofa with a blanket over her and people fussing all round her, she could still feel, in the backs of her knees, the warmth and pressure of Billy Denton's left arm.

It was Strafford who spotted them first, or heard them, rather, the two of them and the horse, as they came into the stable yard. He had allowed himself the luxury of a late shave, and was standing at the sink in the lean-to bathroom at the back of his quarters. At the sound of the horse's hoofs on the cobbles he tilted the shaving mirror at an angle — a crack ran athwart the glass so that his face seemed cut in two by a deep, silvery, bloodless gash — and saw reflected in it the young man with the girl draped over his arms, and Prince clopping along in their wake. He went out into the yard, unwinding the towel he had slung round his neck and wiping his face with it. His shirt was collarless — the metal collar stud glinted in the morning light — and his braces hung down in two deep loops beside his thighs.

"Hello," he said, speaking to the girl. "Take a fall, did you? Nothing broken, I hope."

"It's just a sprain," Billy Denton muttered, seeming to resent Strafford's having popped up suddenly like this. "The horse took a fright and threw her."

Strafford nodded. Celia Nashe would be beside herself — so much for her policy of relaxed vigilance, he thought with satisfaction — but for his part he had no intention of making a great thing of it.

He was wondering why Denton should seem permanently aggrieved, with that scowl, and the sullen, evasive look he wore. Was it his mother's violent death, even though it had happened when he was an infant, that had left him so embittered?

What if, Strafford asked himself, his own mother had been murdered by a gang of drunken soldiers on a rampage? Would he have forgiven the class of people whom the soldiers had supposedly been sent over here to protect? He recalled himself telling Celia Nashe of the Desmond Rebellions and their ruthless and bloody aftermath. What had got into him? He felt the cruelty of those antique struggles and the monstrous warlords who had put them down, but he could not find it in himself to hate the nation or the people those warlords had come from.

Yet as a descendant of the land-grabbers who had flooded over from England three centuries before, was he not himself suspended between two worlds, two sets of sensibilities, two impossible choices? Poor Ireland, poor divided little country, gnawing away at immemorial grievances, like a fox caught in a snare trying to bite off its trapped leg.

For all Denton's dourness of manner, Strafford felt instinctively that he could be trusted. He was a decent enough fellow, surely, behind the rancorous exterior.

"I'm perfectly all right, really," the girl said.

Strafford noted with amusement the haughty tone in which she spoke these words, so at odds was it with the fact of her being slung between the arms of a young man who clearly wanted nothing more than to put her down somewhere; nor did a dangling, bare and swollen pink foot do anything to bolster her aspirations to imperium.

She was borne into the kitchen and put to sit in Mrs O'Hanlon's wicker armchair beside the range, with her injured leg elevated before her on a three-legged stool and resting on a soft cushion. This, did she but know it, was a marked honour, for no one in living memory, other than its rightful occupant, had been allowed to sit in the housekeeper's special chair.

Mrs O'Hanlon herself put a saucepan of milk on the range to heat, so that the young miss might have a drink to warm her, and went so far as to bring out a biscuit tin in which she kept the remaining half of a homemade plum cake her married sister had presented her with on a recent visit.

Meanwhile Maggie filled another basin of cold water for the girl to give her swollen ankle another soaking. Florence the parlourmaid came to have a look at her, but held back in the shadows, her long pale hands entwined at her waist and her big eyes wide and glowing with a tragic light — Florence was known to have romantic tendencies, and regarded even the smallest accident in the household as a portent of an imminent and general disaster. With that stricken stare, the long neck and those pale hands, she reminded Strafford of a Pre-Raphaelite figure, a Guinevere or a Mary Magdalene. Even Poor-Elsie found an excuse to emerge from her lair in the scullery and take a peep at the fallen horsewoman. It was clear that everyone below stairs secretly welcomed this brief disruption of the unvarying pattern of the house's day.

Ellen herself, despite her pretence of displeasure at being the centre of so much attention, could not but find the whole thing faintly enjoyable. It was, after all, a form of misrule, a state of things from which so far she had for the most part been strictly protected.

Billy Denton, the hero of the hour, had slipped away without anyone noticing.

At last Celia Nashe appeared. "Oh, heavens, child," she wailed, "what happened to you?"

Mrs O'Hanlon, nostrils distended, gave her a histrionically accusing stare — where had she been, the cold-eyed autocrat, when her charge was alone and injured in the woods? And wasn't her show of dismay just a touch overdone?

Strafford agreed. Guilty conscience, he said to himself, and tried not to smile.

It seemed to him the best course was to follow Billy Denton's example and quietly withdraw. He had finished with Eustacia and her misadventures at the Chalet School, and was about to plunge into a biography of the Emperor Nero; bound to be some spice there.

He hoped Maggie had lit the fire in the library.

Mary was with Pike down at the pigsties when Billy Denton passed by on his way back to his cottage and told her, in little more than a dozen words, of the mishap that had befallen the rider in the wood. She was not surprised that the beast had thrown her sister: although she was no expert, she had had only to take one look at Prince to know he was a bolter. She was annoyed not to have been there to witness the upset.

She was lounging in a wheelbarrow on a bed of straw with her legs dangling over the end, between the handles. Pike's smelly old coat was folded behind her back for a cushion, and she was smoking one of his Wild Woodbine cigarettes. He had charged her a whole penny for it, the old crook — she knew for a fact you could get a packet of five for tuppence.

This was the third cigarette she had smoked since she had been at Clonmillis Hall. Already she was getting the hang of it, though the first draw or two after lighting up still made her cough every time. When Billy

Denton had appeared she had dropped the cigarette into the straw, and nearly set fire to herself, but after he had gone she had retrieved it, and was lying back now and puffing away happily at the last half of it, thinking how much she must look like Marlene Dietrich, who was her favourite film star of the moment.

"Will they have to shoot him, do you think?" she mused aloud, watching the shivery blue line of cigarette smoke flowing straight up through the morning's motionless air. She was wearing a wool coat with a fur collar, fur-lined bootees, and a silk headscarf she had borrowed from a drawer in Miss Nashe's room, without Miss Nashe's permission.

Pike, with a pitchfork, was heaving straw over the low stone wall of the pigsties. Inside the pen, the pigs were making wonderfully disgusting noises. She liked the smell of pigs: it reminded her of Balmoral — of all the castles her family lived in, Balmoral was her favourite. Her sister had told her it belonged to her parents, not to the Crown, which she was rather glad of; she had read up on the French Revolution, and knew what could happen to royals when the people got fed up with them. Scotland would be a good place to retreat to, should the necessity arise: the Scots were terrifically loyal, despite all the battles the English had beaten them in.

"Shoot who?" Pike asked, without pausing in his work.

"Prince, of course," Mary said. "The horse." She couldn't tell whether Pike was as stupid as he seemed, or if he was only pretending in order to be able to make fun of her and get away with it. She suspected that really he was a crafty old codger. "If she had died he would certainly be put down, wouldn't he?" she said.

The old man did suspend work now, and straightened up, squinting off with his one eye at the blue hill on the horizon.

Just before Billy Denton had come along Mary had asked Pike to show her how he took out his glass eye. When he did so she was pleasantly revolted — the eye itself seemed enormous, when he let it plop on to his palm and held it out for her to see, but what was truly squirm-makingly awful was the collapsed empty eye-socket, which looked exactly like the little puckered hole in the centre of a pig's bottom.

"Well, before they could shoot him," the old man said pensively, "there would have to be a trial."

"A trial?"

"Aye. Did you never hear tell of a horse being put on trial?"

"You're just teasing."

She had smoked the cigarette down to the last half-inch, and now she held it out for Pike to finish; she liked the way he screwed up his face and pressed the sodden butt expertly to his pursed lips to suck in the last few lungfuls of smoke.

"Oh, true as God!" he said, swivelling his eye sideways and giving her an arch look. "There was a stallion over at Tuckerstown one time that threw his master and broke his neck. Brought the beast into the courthouse, they did, before old Judge Gilhooley and a jury. Three days the hearing went on. It'd have gone hard for the stallion if a mare that was sweet on him hadn't come forward to testify on his behalf."

The girl cackled in derision. "You're such a liar!"

Pike shook his head sagaciously, wagging a finger. "It's not a word of a lie I'm telling you," he said. "Got him off, scot-free, she did, the same filly, and hasn't left his side to this day."

He took up the pitchfork and heaved another swatch of straw over the wall of the sty, to the approval of the snorting, snuffling animals on the other side.

"Do pigs really eat their young?" she asked.

"They do, the heartless brutes."

There was a pause. Mary swung her legs where they dangled out over the end of the wheelbarrow. Now it was her turn to gaze off thoughtfully in the direction of the dream-blue hill.

"It's a good thing she wasn't killed," she said, and carefully picked off a flake of tobacco that had got stuck to her lower lip.

"That's true," Pike said drily, and grunted as he bent and plunged the fork once more into the mound of lightly steaming straw. "The killing of her would have been a terrible thing."

"Because then she'd never be Queen."

Pike gave a wheezing laugh. "A queen! Is that what she's going to be? I declare to God!"

"Not a queen," Mary said scornfully, "*the* Queen. That's what she'll be when our father dies."

Pike had stopped in mid-heave, and now turned his eye on her once again, but more keenly this time.

"And who, may I ask, would your father be?"

She gave an exasperated sigh and threw a look skywards. "The King, of course! You really don't know much about anything, do you?"

She folded her arms across her chest and looked away in disdain; it was a thing her sister used to do, folding her arms and looking aside and clicking her tongue, before she became so selfconsciously hoity-toity and practically stopped doing anything except hold herself as straight as the statue they would put up to her after she was dead. But, then, Mary had to concede that, since her sister *was* going to be Queen one day, she if anyone had the right to be hoity-toity. It was annoying, but it was the case.

She asked Pike why he tied string around his trousers at the ankles.

Pike was only half listening. "It's not string," he said distractedly, "it's twine."

"Yes, but why do you do it?"

"To keep the rats from running up my legs and biting me on the arse."

CHAPTER
TWENTY

It was on that day, or rather the night of that day, that Joey Harte was shot. This was the event that dispelled the strange, dreamlike atmosphere that had held Clonmillis Hall in a kind of enthralment since the arrival there of the two princesses. No one in the house even heard the shot that killed poor Joey, but death sauntered in anyway, quietly, by the back door, as it were, and nothing was to be quite the same thereafter.

Up to that moment of sudden violence it had been a night much like any other. Since it was the weekend, the girls had been allowed to stay up a little later than usual, but by ten minutes to nine Celia Nashe was ushering them out of the dining room and upstairs to bed. As they were going out Florence, all in black as usual, with a scrap of lace at her throat, was wheeling in a serving trolley on which stood an enormous wireless set — the duke never missed the evening news on the BBC Home Service. Behind the maid came Mrs O'Hanlon, bearing a cut-glass decanter on a silver tray, which she placed on the table at his left-hand side.

The duke turned to Strafford. "You'll take a glass of port, I suppose?" he said, in a grudging tone. The duke still regarded Strafford as an only slightly elevated servant, and resented the fellow's assumption that he should be allowed to share in the nightly ritual of the wireless and the decanter.

"Oh, yes, thank you," Strafford said cheerfully, with a smile. He didn't much care for port — the combination of alcohol and what tasted like a child's sticky, sweet, slightly rancid drink struck him as perverse — but it afforded him a mild amusement to irritate the old boy who, he knew, would have much preferred him to withdraw at dinner's end along with the ladies.

Florence was down on all fours beside the sofa, plugging the wireless into the electric socket in the wall; why, Strafford wondered idly, did no one think to move the sofa a few inches to the side?

Mrs O'Hanlon poured the port, which was one of her little privileges. "Will there be anything else, Your Grace?" she enquired, as she did every night, and was ignored, as every night she was. She left the room.

The duke switched on the wireless and waited for the valves to heat up. "More reverses, I suppose," the old soldier muttered gloomily, taking a drink from his glass. "I sometimes wonder about the conduct of this war. Too much interference with the generals from the civilian side, I don't doubt. If they left the PM and the army to it, the thing would be over and done with in a month."

The wireless crackled into life.

"— is the BBC news, read by Alvar Lidell. German air raids on London and Coventry are continuing. In the capital, extensive damage has been reported in the East End and to the London docks. No casualty figures

201

have been released but it is feared that many people remain trapped under collapsed buildings. In a speech earlier this evening to the House of Commons, the prime minister spoke of the gravity of the situation facing the country, but said that —"

The duke reached out with an angry grunt and switched off the set. "The same every night," he muttered. He took another, longer, sip of his port. Then he held up the glass and gazed at it sadly. "Fonseca 'ninety-three," he murmured.

"It's very fine," Strafford said dutifully.

The duke nodded. "My father laid down a pipe of it for me when I was still a schoolboy. Only a few bottles left." He paused. "Everything running out." He turned to Strafford. "I don't envy you, your generation, I mean, or" — he glanced towards the doorway where the girls had gone out — "theirs. When the war is won, I wonder if there will be any empire left at all, for that child to reign over, when she grows up."

"Oh, something will survive, I imagine," Strafford said lightly. "The world always recovers, somehow."

"Does it, now?" the duke said, in a sort of snarl, and turned away from the young man with an expression of contempt, grinding his jaws. "Does it?"

He really was an extremely irascible old gentleman, Strafford reflected, and gingerly took another nip from his glass. Fonseca 1893, eh? No wonder it tasted musty. A sickly drink.

Upstairs, on the landing, Mary was leaning with her arms folded on the banister rail and her chin resting on

202

them. She had hung back to try to hear what was on the news, but only fragments came to her, though enough to let her know that London was being bombed again. She wondered if it would ever stop. Surely they would run out of bombs, sooner or later.

Miss Nashe came to fetch her then — "Don't dawdle, Mary" — and led her off to the other wing. Why she and her sister had to sleep so far away from everyone else she didn't know. It was as if they had a contagious disease.

Ellen was already in bed, sitting up and reading a book. She had a cushion under her leg to elevate her ankle. The sprain had turned out not to be serious at all, as Billy Denton had predicted, though for some days Ellen would continue to walk with a limp, which Mary was convinced she was putting on so that everyone would keep asking her how she was, leaning their heads to one side and doing that clown's sad smile with their eyebrows wrinkled and the corners of their mouths turned down, as people always did when they were pretending to be sympathetic to someone. The book Ellen was reading was *A Tale of Two Cities*. Oh, my, Mary said to herself, how very, very grown-up!

She undressed and put on her pyjamas, but was too restless to get into bed. She could hear Miss Nashe moving about in her room. She made a call at this time every night from the special telephone that had been installed by her bed. Who was it she spoke to? Probably that Mr Lascelles, at the embassy: she was keen on him, which had been quite plain the first day, before he left so rudely, not bothering to say goodbye to anyone.

There couldn't be much to report to him — nothing ever happened here.

Mary had picked up the phone receiver, one day when Miss Nashe was out, just to hear what kind of sound it would make. She got a shock when a bossy woman's voice came on, demanding a "colour code", whatever that might be. She had dropped the phone and fled.

She leaned her forehead against the cold window. How dark it was outside, and how the night seemed to gleam behind the glass.

Did Celia Nashe check her gun every night, to make sure it was in working order? Mary was extremely envious: imagine having a pistol in the same drawer as your knickers and your socks!

"I do wish you wouldn't fidget," Ellen said, in her dear-me-I'm-so-jaded voice, without looking up from her book.

Mary took no notice: she was picking congealed bits of grease from the side of an unlit candle in a candlestick on the window-sill. Why was a candlestick called a candlestick? It wasn't anything like a stick. On the other hand, what was it like?

"How long do you think we'll have to stay here?" she asked. Ellen gave no response. "Pike says they'll have to shoot your horse."

"What — Prince, you mean? Don't be ridiculous."

"Well, that's what he said."

"You shouldn't listen to that old man, to the nonsense he talks and his horrible stories."

Mary climbed into bed and lay on her back with her hands folded, gazing up into the thickly crowding shadows. "If a bomb falls on the Palace, will Mummy and Daddy be killed?"

Her sister heaved an exaggeratedly loud, irritated sigh, keeping her eyes determinedly on the page before her. "A bomb won't fall on the Palace," she said.

"How do you know?"

There was the faint sound of bedsprings from along the hallway, which meant Miss Nashe had settled down for the night. What sort of things, Mary wondered, did grown-ups dream about?

She closed her eyes.

"I hope they do shoot him," she said drowsily.

Ellen counted in silence, slowly, to a hundred, to allow her sister time to fall safely asleep. Then she closed her book and got up quietly and turned off the reading lamp and went to the window and lifted a flap of the curtains at one side. The moon was racing through clouds, turning them icy-white at their edges.

What if a bomb did fall on the Palace? She wished she could be there now, even if there was a raid going on. If her parents were to be killed, she would want to die with them. At least, she couldn't imagine wanting to go on living if they were dead. She shuddered. But they wouldn't die; they couldn't. And some day the war would be over.

She was about to return to bed when down at the side of the house a light blossomed. The kitchen door opened, and a figure appeared there. It was Maggie the maid. She was peering out into the darkness and, after a second or two, another person flitted across the yard and into the light — a man, it looked like — and together the two went inside and the door was shut and the night closed over again.

Ellen turned from the window when a small voice spoke out of the darkness. "Is he out there?"

"What?"

Her sister's eyes gleamed up at her. "The man with the bird's head."

"There's no man with a bird's head. That was in a dream you had."

"No, it wasn't," Mary said, with implacable certitude. "You'll see."

CHAPTER
TWENTY-ONE

Maggie had been making a loaf of soda bread when she heard Joey Harte's low whistle outside in the yard. She stopped kneading the ball of dough and glanced across at Poor-Elsie, who was leaning over the big chipped white sink in the corner doing the washing-up. As well as being soft in the head, Poor-Elsie was a bit hard of hearing, so it was a fair bet she hadn't heard the whistle.

"Are you nearly finished?" Maggie called across to her.

"No, I had my supper. I'm not hungry," Elsie replied placidly, without turning.

It took Maggie a second or two to figure that one out.

"Are *you* *finished*?" she yelled. "Not *famished*!"

She was amused and exasperated at the same time, as was most often the case in her dealings with Poor-Elsie. How was it deaf people always fixed on the unlikeliest version of something they had misheard? When had she ever been known to use the word "famished"?

"I'm nearly done. There's just these last few plates," the girl said, still looking down into the sink.

Sometimes it crossed Maggie's mind that maybe Elsie wasn't touched at all, or deaf, but was only putting it on to have a private laugh.

"Leave the plates on the board to drain and go on up."

"Can I?"

"It's what I said, isn't it?"

Elsie stuck out her lower lip. She wiped her forehead with the back of a hand. "I'm wall-falling, I'm that tired," she said.

"Go on, then, go to bed." Maggie had to make an effort not to let her impatience show. Poor-Elsie was a trial, but who would have the heart to be cruel to her? "I'll put them away for you when they're dry."

"You're awful good to me, Maggie," Elsie said.

"Ah, go on with you."

Maggie watched the girl straggle up the narrow back stairs that led through several flights from the kitchen all the way up to the servants' bedrooms under the eaves three floors above. Usually Elsie would find some excuse to dawdle until Maggie was ready for bed — she was frightened of the dark places where the staircase turned at the top of each flight. Tonight she seemed too tired to be afraid.

Maggie waited until she could no longer hear the heavy, dragging footsteps ascending, then went to the back door.

Joey Harte came in rubbing his hands in the annoying way that he did. Maggie had got used to it, and had given up nagging him about it. She took a last quick look across the dark yard — if anyone saw her

208

letting Joey in, it would be as much as her place at the Hall was worth — and shut the door and put the latch on it, and turned the key in the lock. She still had flour under her fingernails — old Hynes the butler always said that bread-making was the best way to clean your nails, his one and only joke — and there were dabs of white all over the front of her dark-blue apron.

Straight away Joey headed for the range to warm himself. He was always cold — because of the thin blood he had inherited from his mother, so he said. He did look chilled tonight, his face the colour of skimmed milk and the tip of his nose red and raw and chapped. He was a sorry specimen, Maggie reflected, but he was decent enough at heart, despite his wanton ways; besides, with her big bum and her flat feet she wasn't exactly a raving beauty herself.

Of course, Joey couldn't get across the room without knocking something over, for he was the clumsiest man Maggie had ever encountered. This time it was the legs of the three-legged stool he got his foot caught in, and the thing upended with a clatter on the tiles and went skittering away under the table.

"Ssh!" Maggie hissed at him. "The girl is only just gone up. She'll hear you, you big lummox."

He grinned at her over his shoulder, meanwhile offering his spread palms to the warmth of the range. "Have you anything for me?" he asked.

"What sort of anything?"

"I wouldn't say no to a ball of malt."

"I'll give you balls of malt!" Maggie snorted. She had formed the dough into a loaf and set it on a buttered tray to go into the oven, and now she moved across the room towards the range, carrying the tray. "There's tea made, if you want it."

"How old is it?" he asked suspiciously, lifting the lid of the big iron teapot and peering inside. "It smells stewed."

"Go thirsty, then," Maggie said, making a feint at him with the sharp edge of the tray.

He stood back and she bent to slip the tray into the oven. He laid a hand lightly on her backside — he liked a girl with a bit of flesh on her, but knew better than to take too large a liberty.

She had been going out with him, on a more or less steady basis, for nearly six months. Of course, no one upstairs knew he was her fella, and certainly not that he was in the habit of coming to the house to visit her of an evening. She had asked him more than once how he managed to get past the soldiers, but he only looked crafty and said that was for him to know and no one to find out.

She knew all about his thieving and poaching, but that was something she could cure him of. His drunkard of a father was living still, mouldering away in the County Home, and when he kicked the bucket, which he was bound to do any day now — his liver must have rotted away entirely — Joey would inherit the farm out at Cullabawn. It wasn't much of a place, consisting of a dozen or so scrubby acres and a run-down slate-roofed cottage, but it would do for a start for the two of them, when the time came.

210

They tended not to speak about the future. It was out of shyness, Maggie supposed, or maybe so as not to tempt the Fates. Anyway, she had made up her mind what the future was going to be, for Joey as well as herself, whether Joey knew it or not. She was determined to make him settle down and be a farmer; she had no doubt she could persuade him to it. He wasn't the worst, not by a long chalk; often he would say to her, fondly, that she had him wound around her little finger.

She passed him a mug from the sideboard and he poured the tea and sat down with it at the deal table. He added milk and sugar and took a cautious sip. As he did so he made a face, wrinkling that rat's tail of a nose of his, which made the deep dent in the bridge of it almost close up — the dent was the result of his da hitting him one time with the edge of the blade of a chisel.

"Tastes like ditch-water," he said.

He seemed distracted. Maggie watched him. She poured out tea for herself, into her own special cup — Royal Doulton, with flowers and birds painted on it — that the duke had given to her as a Christmas box one year. She sat down at the table and examined Joey closely. Yes, there was something on his mind, definitely; she could always tell.

She looked at the big white-faced clock on the wall above the range. This was Mrs O'Hanlon's whist drive night, but she would be back no later than eleven, and Joey would have to be gone by then. The old rip had it in for Maggie, after a run-in between the two of them years ago over a sum of money that had gone missing and that the housekeeper had insinuated Maggie had taken, even though it turned up later; it was only a few shillings, anyway.

Joey took another slurp of tea, however bad it tasted.

"All right," Maggie said, laying one hand flat before her on the table. "What's up?"

"What?"

There was a scar, a sort of nick, in the pale skin at the outer corner of his left eye, another gift from his sot of a father. It gave him a slightly cock-eyed look when he stared at you straight on. It was one of the things about him, of which there weren't many, that she found endearing.

"You're up to something," she said. "I know by the look of you."

He blushed, and lowered his eyes; that was another thing she liked, the way he would blush for the slightest reason. For a while he only fiddled with the handle of the tea mug.

"I was talking to the Boss," he said, in a mumble.

"Who — Clancy?" She glowered at him. "Haven't I told you to stay away from that fellow?"

This was a ritual denunciation, which he brushed aside as he always did.

"He was asking about" — he jerked his head in the direction of upstairs — "the crowd that's staying here."

"Oh, he was, was he?" Maggie had a pendulous, rounded chin and a tiny mouth, and when she clamped her lips shut, as she did now, grimly, it made her look as if she hadn't a tooth in her head. "And why would he be interested in what goes on here at the Hall?"

Joey traced with a thumbnail a wavering line in the grain of the table. "He's wondering why the army was sent down here from Dublin to guard them."

"And what business is that of Mr Tom Clancy, may I ask?"

"He's curious to know who they are, that's all, and what's so precious about them."

Maggie suppressed a smile of secret satisfaction. She had guessed who the visitors were and why they needed an army patrol to guard them. The day they arrived she had overheard the duke calling them "Their Royal Highnesses" and quickly correcting himself. Then, later on, when she had finished hanging out the laundry, she had listened at the open window of the morning room to the duke and the Englishman; it was only for a few seconds, but long enough to get the gist of what they were talking about. Of course she had no intention of telling Joey, since he would go running immediately and blab it to the Boss Clancy and his famous Lads. Those boyos were probably the very reason the soldiers were here patrolling the place.

"Is it the blonde-haired one?" Joey asked now, in a low voice, still not looking at her. "Is she someone important?"

Maggie was stony-faced, her chin jutting and her mouth shut so tightly it almost disappeared into her head. "How would I know?"

Joey gave her his most cajoling, crooked grin. "Ah, now, Maggie, there's not much goes on here that you don't know the ins and outs of."

"I know a lot of things, none of which I'm going to tell you or anyone else."

Joey took up his tea again. "It's gone cold," he said.

"Pity on you," Maggie answered tartly. She sat up straight and square as an Indian squaw, watching the white-faced fellow before her, who was trying hard to seem relaxed and unconcerned.

"The fellow that was here in the red car," he said, squinting off now towards a far corner of the ceiling, "is there any sign of him coming back?"

This time Maggie set both arms on the table in front of her and leaned forward slightly, grim-faced and tense, so much so that it seemed she might rear up and spring at him. He was a little afraid of her when she got into this mood, watching him out of eyes that had gone small and glittery.

He turned away from her fearsome stare and looked about the room somewhat wildly, drawing up his chin and waggling his neck, as if the collar of his shirt had suddenly become too tight. "Is there no drink at all in the place?" he demanded peevishly.

"You'll have to go in a minute. Mrs O'Hanlon will be back from her whist."

He tried his wheedling grin on her again, showing the black stump of a broken tooth. "What about a drop for the road?" He knew she had a half-bottle of Powers hidden behind the shelf where the meal bin stood. "To

214

keep out the cold of the dark night," he added, in a comically mournful voice.

Maggie sighed, and fetched a glass from the cupboard above the sink and took down the bottle and poured out a small measure of whiskey. "Drink that down and then hop it."

But he had a surprise for her, one that he had been holding back until he judged the moment just right. He was watching her with a crafty look, and now as she set the glass before him he whipped out a scrap of paper and slapped it down on the table beside the glass, like a card player producing a winning ace out of nowhere.

"What's this?" she asked, suddenly uncertain.

"Have a look."

She seated herself again and took up the tattered piece of paper. It was a reproduction of a photograph, torn from a page of the *Irish Independent*. It showed a group of people standing on a balcony, some of them in cocked hats with white plumes, and all of them waving to what must have been a big crowd below, looking up at them. Rings had been drawn with a pencil around two of the figures: two young girls, one taller than the other.

"You know who they are, don't you?" Joey said.

Maggie bit her lip. She was afraid she would do something to give herself away. Of course she recognised them — weren't they staying here in the house?

"I see who they are, so I know who they are," she said airily, though she had to clear her throat. "What about them?"

Her heart was pounding. She was angry, more than anything else, angry and disappointed. Her secret had been taken from her, or what at least she had thought was her secret. She had clasped the knowledge to her like a diamond ring she had found by chance and held on to, knowing she could never wear it in public but could keep it and give it to the daughter, or even the granddaughter, that she was certain she would have one day. And now here was Joey Harte, with no doubt the Boss Clancy behind him, as good as telling her that everyone knew she had the ring, and not only that but they all had one just like it themselves.

Holy God, she said to herself in horror, probably even Poor-Elsie the halfwit knew what was what.

"It's them two that are staying here, isn't that so?" Joey said.

"What two?"

"Don't play the dummy with me, Maggie Ryan."

She put on her stupidest expression, which she was good at, when she tried.

But he wasn't fooled: he knew he was right.

He had a thrilling sense of vindication. It hadn't occurred to the Boss Clancy who the girls might be, but Joey had guessed, all by himself, even though he had only once had a glimpse of the pair, when they were walking in the pine wood with the blonde-haired woman and he was dodging soldiers. He had been struck, too, by the smugly secret air Maggie had taken on since the strangers had come to stay. Now, judging by the fright in her look, which had replaced the smugness the instant her eye had fallen on the photograph, he saw that he had been right. Tomorrow he would go round to Redmond's and slap the photo down in front of the Boss, the way he had slapped it down on the table here a minute ago.

"I don't know what you're talking about, I'm sure," Maggie said.

She was truly furious; she wanted to hit him. He drank off the whiskey in one swallow and put down the glass with a bang and nodded for her to pour him another. Oh, the grin on him! Maggie thought bitterly. She refilled his glass, almost to the brim this time; she knew he had no head for spirits, and maybe he'd fall over his own feet on the dark road, the clumsy oaf, and give himself a good crack on the head, for he surely deserved it.

They heard, distantly, the sound of the front door opening and closing again. It was another of Mrs O'Hanlon's little privileges that she was allowed to enter the house by the front way, instead of coming in through the kitchen like the rest of the servants — not that she thought of herself as a servant, not a servant like the rest of them.

Joey took a draught of the whiskey. If he didn't stop doing that thing with his hands, Maggie thought, she really would give him a clout across the ear.

"There's Mrs O'Hanlon coming in," she said.

"I'm going, I'm going." Joey waved his hands in front of her face. "Don't start."

He tossed back the rest of the drink and put on the dirty old scarf he wore summer and winter, and knotted it tightly round his neck. But she wasn't ready to let him off yet.

"What's going on?" she said. "Tell me."

He took on a look of wounded innocence. "What do you mean, what's going on? There's nothing going on that I know of — except that by all accounts we're being paid a royal visit, though we're not supposed to know it."

He gave her an archly knowing look, then started towards the back door. Maggie jumped up from the table. "Joey Harte, you come back here!"

He had drawn the bolt on the door, and paused now with his hand on the key. "A minute ago you were telling me to hop it," he said, "and now you're telling me not to go."

Oh, he was enjoying himself, all right.

She crossed the floor quickly and planted herself in front of him and grasped him by the lapels of his coat. The crown of her head barely came up to the level of his chin, but all the same when he looked down at her she caught a flicker of nervousness in his eyes, too. She knew she frightened him, a little — as far as he was concerned, there was no telling what she might do. He wouldn't put it past her to snatch up the rolling pin and come after him with it.

But then her anger with him suddenly drained away. That look in his eye wasn't just fear of her. He was all brave talk here in the kitchen, with a feed of whiskey in him, though it would be different when he had to face the Boss Clancy. It was one thing for her to be worried,

218

but if he was worried too, they could both be in trouble.

When she spoke, her voice was low and steady, the words evenly spaced and precise, like a succession of little bright nails each one of which she drove home with a single neat tap.

"You tell the Boss Clancy and that gang of bowsies he's supposed to be the leader of to stay away from this house and from the people in it."

They stood there in the doorway, squared up to each other, the little plump maid with her fearsome but all the same uncertain glare, and in front of her the anxiously smiling skinny creature she couldn't believe she intended to marry. Then Joey laughed and gave a sort of cowboy whoop and snaked one of his long, bony arms around her non-existent waist and pulled her against him and kissed her, or tried to, since she turned her face aside at the last moment and his lips landed on her ear instead of her mouth.

"By God, Maggie Ryan," he said, "but you're a fine armful of a girl!"

And then he was gone. She stood a moment, with the door open, facing into the clammy dampness of the night, and a shiver passed along her spine. She had let drop the precious diamond ring, and how was she to find it again, in all this darkness?

CHAPTER
TWENTY-TWO

It was the telephone in the house that rang this time, bringing dire news. One of Major de Valera's men had tried to get through to Strafford's quarters, but Strafford was still at the Hall. Dinner had finished some time before and he had retired to the library, intending to drink a cup of tea and read a book beside the fire for an hour or two before taking himself off to his unloving quarters in the stable yard.

The jangling of the phone made the house itself seem to draw back in startlement and fright. Who could be calling at this hour? Strafford assumed it must be for the duke, and went back to his library book — *The Waning of the Middle Ages*: not exactly bedtime reading, but he had been meaning for some time to have a look at it. The ringing of the telephone made a nice coincidence with Huizinga's lyrical opening passage on the bells of northern Europe pealing the hours. Then there was a tap at the door and Hynes came shuffling in, his shock of wild white hair wilder than ever.

"Excuse me, sir," he said, his voice as always a thin creak, like the sound of a rusted gate being pushed to and fro by a wintry wind, "there's a person on the telephone for you."

Strafford stared at him in surprise, and experienced at once a shimmer of foreboding. He closed the book slowly and put it aside.

"Who is it?" he said.

"A man, sir."

"What sort of a man?"

"An army man, I'd say."

"Is it de Valera?"

Hynes peered at him out of watery blue eyes, obviously suspecting a joke.

"Oh, no, sir, it's not Mr de Valera," he said, in some puzzlement. "I doubt he'd be telephoning the Hall, here, this late at night, or" — he paused, and the corners of his mouth twitched in the ghost of a grin — "any other time of day or night, for that matter. Mr de Valera would not have much time, I'd say, for His Grace, and the rest of us here at the Hall." Again he stopped, seeming suddenly to have forgotten the reason for his being in the library. Then his brow cleared. "No, this is a military person, as I say. A Sergeant Brody, I think he said. Or Brady —" His voice trailed off.

Strafford walked behind the old man out to the hall. The phone was an old-fashioned upright affair. He picked it up, and applied the little cold cup of the receiver to his ear.

Sergeant Brody, or Brady, could hardly contain his excitement. It took Strafford a good half-minute to understand that there had been a shooting. He imagined at first that an accident must have occurred

221

— he recalled the soldier dropping his rifle on the road that other night — and for some reason got it into his head that the victim was Major de Valera himself.

"No, no," the sergeant babbled, "not the major — it's the same fellow we caught the last time, the fellow that was out after rabbits."

"Ah. I see." He remembered him clearly: tall, thin, shifty-eyed, a sharp nose with a dent in it, kept rubbing his hands, and had a ferret in a sack. "What's his name, again?"

"Harte, sir. Joseph Harte."

"Is he dead?"

"He wasn't when I came away — it was at the edge of the woods he was brought down — but I have to say he didn't look too hot. Got it in the throat. You'd better hurry, sir. I'll come and meet you at the gate, like the last time."

Oh, God, Strafford thought miserably, all that rigmarole again! And this time, as seemed likely, with the addition of a corpse.

Should he inform the duke of what had happened? Probably he should, but he couldn't face it. Anyway, the old boy had surely toddled off to bed by now — it was close on midnight.

His coat and hat were in the hall. Hynes held the coat while he fitted his arms into the sleeves. He chose a pair of gumboots from the selection under the hat stand and pulled them on with some difficulty; whereas the last ones had been too big, these were too small.

It was only then that he thought of Celia Nashe — certainly he should let her know what was going on.

Yes, he certainly should. But he didn't, and the not doing of it afforded him a tiny vindictive and shamefaced satisfaction.

He opened the front door and stepped out into the darkness.

The weather was mild still, though the air was thick with autumnal vapours. There were the usual smells of clay and wet weeds and already rotting leaves. No wind, and not a sound to be heard save for the rubbery squelch of his boots in the gravel.

The armoured car was waiting for him at the gate, as promised. Sergeant Brody — not Brady, it turned out — was the big, round-headed fellow he remembered from the last time, a countryman, slow-moving, soft-voiced. He was standing beside the car having a smoke, and now he threw the butt of his cigarette hastily into the ditch and sketched a fat man's sloppy salute. The excitement he had displayed on the phone had evaporated by now, and he seemed to be in control of himself.

"Bad business, sir," he said.

"What happened?"

"He was challenged twice, and refused to identify himself — he was charging all over the place in the pitch-dark. Then he tried to leg it, and one of our lads lost the run of himself and fired off a round. It was meant to go over his head and make him stop, but instead it caught him in the side of the throat. It must have severed an artery or something."

"Lot of blood?"

"Lot of blood, sir."

"But you tell me he's not dead?"

"He will be by now, I'd say. It wasn't the kind of wound you'd recover from."

"I see."

They climbed into the armoured car. Strafford had never seen a man shot. He was interested to know how he would feel when he came to view the body. Didn't someone always vomit at the sight of a blood-soaked corpse? He didn't think he would be sick, but he couldn't be sure. One knows so little about oneself, at the visceral level, he reflected.

At any rate he hoped he wouldn't make a fool of himself. Had Major de Valera seen a man die by violence before? Certainly his father had: de Valera senior had been one of the leaders of the 1916 Rising. The British would have shot him, had he not been an American citizen. It was rumoured he had suffered a complete, if temporary, nervous collapse when he and his men were under siege in Boland's flour mills. But, however badly he had been affected, it hadn't prevented him from going on to wage a particularly brutal civil war half a dozen years later.

A fox appeared on the road ahead, and turned tail and ran away full tilt in the twin beams of the headlights, keeping to a straight line for some way before veering off into the ditch.

They drew up at the camouflaged sentry box by the side of the road. Sergeant Brody led the way into the wood. There was no path. "Mind where you step," the sergeant said. "It's boggy in places, and there's rabbit holes."

224

They could see the glow of a storm lantern among the trees a short distance ahead of them. There was the sound of hushed voices, too.

Was Major de Valera's fleshy pale face a marked shade paler tonight? He turned to Strafford crossly, with an accusing edge of brusqueness in his tone. "Ah, you got here."

"We couldn't have made it any faster," Strafford replied, in his diffident fashion.

"I thought you'd better see the fellow's remains before we proceed with anything else," the major snapped. "You're the policeman, after all." He made it sound like something for which Strafford should be prepared to apologise.

Joey Harte lay on his front in a humped position, both his arms trapped under him and his face half buried in sodden leaf-mould. Strafford immediately thought of a photograph he had seen once of a lava-encrusted corpse that had been excavated from the ruins of Pompeii.

He didn't feel in the least like being sick, although he was aware of a curious buzzing sensation in his head, which he didn't think had anything to do with the effect of looking at the dead man.

Three soldiers with rifles stood huddled in a knot in the lamplight. A fourth held himself apart in the shadows, nervously smoking a cigarette; he had taken off his helmet. His weapon was nowhere to be seen.

"Are you the one who fired the shot?" Strafford asked him.

225

Major de Valera twitched as if from an electric shock, and gave a barking cough.

"I don't want you questioning my men," he said, his voice pitched so high he seemed almost to shriek. "I only brought you here out of courtesy. This is a military matter. The man was challenged and wouldn't stop."

"Was he running away?"

"As I said, he was challenged and refused to halt. He was fired on. He was hit."

"How long did he live for?"

"Some minutes only."

"He said nothing, I suppose?"

The major gave a low snort of what in other circumstances might have passed for laughter. "Hardly. Look at the wound."

Strafford hunkered down beside the corpse. He had remembered to bring his torch, and now he clicked it on and trained the beam at the upper parts of what was left of Joey Harte. The head was turned partly to the left, and one startled eye seemed to be staring up into the emptiness of the night sky. A scarf knotted about his neck was soaked with blood that in the lamplight was not red but a shiny shade of purplish-black.

Gingerly, with an index finger, Strafford drew back the edge of the scarf where it was most thickly soaked. There was a jagged hole in the left side of the throat; it looked uncannily like an open, rounded mouth — like, in fact, the mouth of a particularly vociferous yodeller, Strafford thought. In his short time on the Garda Force, he had learned that the last thing a tragedy looks is tragic. "This must be the exit wound, yes?"

226

"Of course it is," Major de Valera snapped. "The bullet entered from the right."

"He must have been looking back over his shoulder?"

There was an awkward pause. Strafford supposed no soldier would care for it to be known that he had shot a man from the back — or was that another myth got up by writers of war books?

"He should have halted, when he was called on to do so," the major said. "The command was clear and unmistakable — I heard it issued."

Strafford tried to gauge the mood of the men standing before him in a half-circle. It seemed mainly one of sullen resentment, tinged with embarrassment and, on the major's part, a definite note of defiance. It came to Strafford that he was not wanted there; his presence was only making a bad situation worse. It was as if they had been engaged, the little group of men, in some private rite, calling for darkness, lamplight and a wooded clearing, and he had stumbled upon them by unhappy accident.

None of them, including the major, seemed to know what to do next.

An ambulance should be called, Strafford supposed, although he had never understood why a service designed to tend the living should be squandered on the removal of the dead. The back of the armoured car would do as well, if they had something to wrap the body in to keep it from bleeding on the metal floor. But, then, the vehicle was designed for the battlefield. Why be concerned about blood on it?

"Shouldn't we get on to the guards in Clonmillis?" said Major de Valera, who seemed to be waxing more and more annoyed. "They'll be the ones to deal with this, given that it's a civilian who has died."

It had ceased to be a military matter, then. It occurred to Strafford that the major had decided to palm off a tricky situation on some authority other than himself, so that he could get back to the serious business of playing at soldiers.

"I think I had better call Dublin," Strafford said. He rose to his feet, experiencing a brief stab of pain in each of his stiffened knees. His head was still buzzing; all in all, he was feeling markedly peculiar.

What sort of pain would this poor Harte fellow have suffered? Strafford was always sceptical when he heard it said of this or that dead person that he had died instantly. How could anyone know? The instant of death might be an eternity of agony and anguish for the one who was doing the dying.

He made up his mind. "Leave one of your men to watch over the corpse," he said to the major, "while the sergeant here takes me back to the Hall. Better not to have the local force involved." Hadn't someone said the superintendent in Clonmillis was a drunkard? "I'll telephone to my superior in Dublin and have him send some people down."

The major only sniffed, which Strafford decided to take as a token of sulky acquiescence.

Strafford moved towards the armoured car, followed by Sergeant Brody. They climbed in. After a mile or two the sergeant said again: "A bad business."

228

"Very bad indeed."

Another mile went by.

"It won't go down well in the town."

"No," Strafford said. "It won't." Nor would it go down well with Inspector Hackett, he assured himself.

It was all very worrying and uncertain, yet he felt curiously detached from the entire affair. The scene in the wood — the men gathered under a dome of lamplight, the hunched figure on the ground, the killer off by himself, worrying at a cigarette, and all about the tall black sentinel trees — had recalled to his mind a painting he had seen somewhere. What was the subject? A pause in some nocturnal battle? The execution of Maximilian I? Something like that. Night, vague faceless figures, an act of violence.

He knew very well there would be all sorts of awkwardness to be dealt with in the morning, but he could not work up the interest to think about any of that just at the moment. He wished the buzzing sensation in his head would stop.

"There was a smell of drink off him," Sergeant Brody said.

"Do you think he was drunk?"

"I wouldn't say so, sir, no. But he had taken drink, that's for sure."

"Is there a pub round about here?"

"The nearest one is Gaffney's, eight or nine miles along the road ahead of us, close to the town."

Strafford nodded, to himself more than to the sergeant.

"So you think he'd been at the house, I mean at Clonmillis Hall, and that was where he got the drink and where he was coming from?" Sergeant Brody shrugged, keeping his eyes on the road and the leaping headlight beams; it wasn't his task to speculate. "Any sign of the ferret?" Strafford asked. In other circumstances he would have laughed at the absurdity of the thing; indeed, he very nearly laughed now.

"I didn't see it."

"So he wasn't out for a night's poaching." Again the sergeant was silent. Strafford tried again. "Do you know if he had associates in the town — hotheads, troublemakers?"

"Couldn't say, sir. We don't have much contact with the town." The gateway of Clonmillis Hall came in sight. "Will I drive you up to the house, sir?"

"No, better not, but thanks all the same. The headlights would wake everybody up. By the way" — the question hadn't occurred to him before — "where's your billet? I mean where are you stationed?"

Sergeant Brody eased the vehicle on to the half-circle of gravel in front of the gate and stopped. The machine stood juddering and wheezing, like an old horse at the end of a hard race. The two men were enveloped in a miasma of diesel fumes, warm and cloying.

"There's a barracks on the other side of that hill, an old British Army place," the sergeant said. "That's where we are."

"What's it like?"

"Damp."

"Ah."

230

Thus the conversation, such as it was, trickled to an end. Strafford sat immobile for some moments, then stirred himself. "Thanks for the lift, Sergeant."

He opened the door and stepped down on to the gravel. The positive balminess of the moist night air surprised him anew. Would this unnatural season never end? He found himself longing for winter. He was about to push the door to behind himself when Sergeant Brody leaned across the seat and spoke to him. "Watch out for yourself, sir, if you don't mind me saying it. There'll be ructions over this. It's not every day the army shoots a man." Brody paused, seemingly struck by the incongruity of what he had said. "Not in peacetime, anyway," he added.

"You're right, no doubt," Strafford said. "Not these days, anyway, in neutral Ireland."

"Goodnight, sir."

Strafford banged the door shut and turned and set off up the driveway.

Oh, yes, there would be ructions; ructions galore.

CHAPTER
TWENTY-THREE

He skirted the house and let himself into his quarters at the corner of the stable yard. The air was chillier here indoors than out. By now he was feeling very odd indeed. His head was still filled with the whirring sensation — it was like the faint buzzing of a faulty electric light bulb — and he felt dizzy, and his limbs were so unwieldy they might have belonged to someone else. He undressed clumsily, fumbling with buttons, struggled into his pyjamas and crawled into bed.

He would have a little rest, just a little rest. Then he would go across to the house and telephone Headquarters in Dublin. And he would tell Celia Nashe what had happened: it was very important that she should be told. Yes, he would do that, he would tell Miss Nashe, and then he would get on the phone to Dublin. Resolving to do these things, he fell into a leaden sleep.

In the middle of the night he woke in terror when a half-heavy four-footed something landed silently on his chest. He scrabbled for the switch of the bedside lamp and sat up, blinking, to see the white kitchen cat wading away from him over the bedclothes, its tail stiffly lifted. It was a battle-scarred creature, Pangur by name. It had a split ear and, as he noticed now, one of its eyes was blinded and white as polished marble. It often came to visit him, especially since he had begun to smuggle out scraps from the dinner table to feed to it. He didn't much care for cats, but this one was of a misanthropic aspect that he approved of — cats should never try to be nice. In the near total darkness it padded on soundless paws, pale and glimmering, like the ghost of itself.

He lay down again, with a sort of gasping sigh. His forehead was burning. He couldn't think what was the matter with him. He had a vague, oppressive sense of having left important things undone.

Later on he heard faintly, or thought he heard, the sound of a car approaching up the drive, coming around the side of the house, but sank back at once into the yielding, comatose dark.

Then, after another interval of hot-limbed stupor, he was wakened again, this time by a knock at the door. He thought at first he had been subject to one of those abrupt, peremptory alerts the panicky mind sometimes issues, like a gunshot in the dark, when it takes fright at the sleeping body's deathlike stillness.

But, no, it had been a knock, all right: there was someone out there, banging insistently on the door.

He struggled up, his brain in a fog, and pulled on his trench coat — why hadn't he thought to pack a dressing-gown before he came down here? — and padded across the stone-cold tiles.

It was Hynes the butler, all in a flap, his rheumy eyes alight with excitement. He had dressed hastily, and the celluloid collar of his shirt stuck up at one side, like the Mad Hatter's, was it? He spoke in a gabble, and for the first few moments Strafford couldn't make out what he was saying, but at last understood that he was summoned to the house, and must come immediately.

He looked past the old man's shoulder and saw behind the nameless distant hill a faint penumbral glow: dawn was applying its makeup and getting ready to go on.

"Yes, all right," he said to the old man wearily. "Tell them I'll be there in a minute."

As he was getting dressed it came to him what he had forgotten to do, before collapsing into bed and falling asleep. He had been supposed to telephone headquarters in Dublin and summon assistance, as he had told Major de Valera he would do. Which meant Joey Harte's corpse was still lying out there under guard in the wood, and had been there all night. He peered at himself blearily in the cracked shaving mirror: he looked like someone else, a dishevelled and bewildered stranger who had woken up in wholly unfamiliar surroundings.

He entered the house by the back door. Maggie, already dressed but still sleepy-eyed, was in the kitchen, on her knees in front of the range with kindling and a box of matches and a bucketful of anthracite. She looked over her shoulder at him in surprise — why was he about so early? — and a shadow of fright fell across her features. He paused briefly and stared at the coal in the bucket, at the evil glitter of it. Then he went straight through to the hall and the telephone. Despite his muddle-headedness he knew that before he did anything else he must ring Dublin.

It was some time before the operator in Clonmillis came on the line; from the furry sound of her voice he knew he had got her out of bed. He had to wait again for the Dublin exchange to respond. The desk sergeant at Pearse Street sounded sleepy too, and at first could not take in what Strafford was telling him. Killings occurred even yet, not often but they did occur, in the stubbornly lingering struggle between the IRA and the forces of the state, but the violent death of a civilian was still a rare thing in neutral Ireland.

"Are you telling me to call Inspector Hackett at home, at this hour?" the desk man asked; he sounded thoroughly frightened at the prospect of such a daring undertaking.

"Yes. Tell him we need people down here," Strafford replied, and hung up.

There was the sound of voices from the first-floor drawing room. As Strafford went up the stairs he seemed less in control of his legs than ever.

Despite the fog swirling in his head he had the sure knowledge of being seriously in trouble, which created a peculiar feeling, at once oppressive and inconsequential. It was as if he had just come out of the examination hall and realised there had been a compulsory question on the paper he had left glaringly unanswered. Why, *why* hadn't he made that call to Headquarters last night, before letting himself blunder into that fever-sleep?

Richard Lascelles, impressively attired in pinstripes, bow tie and handmade brogues, stood by the fireplace in the drawing room, with one hand in his trousers pocket, smoking a cigarette. The gold watch chain looped across the front of his waistcoat had, to Strafford's eye, an unnaturally sharp and somehow insidious gleam. Everything was too sharply lit, the watch chain, the anthracite down in the kitchen, the brass base of an electric lamp on a table here by the window. He put a hand to his forehead and felt himself waver for a moment, like a reed bending before a breeze.

Celia Nashe was there, too. She had the slightly disordered look of a person who had been made to scramble out of her bed and get dressed in a hurry. When Strafford came in they had both turned their heads and looked at him, Lascelles with a brittle smile and Celia plainly furious.

"For God's sake, where have you been?" she demanded.

"I was in the hall, making a phone call," Strafford replied.

It was the only thing he could think of to say, though from the look the young woman gave him, her lips white and her eyes ablaze, he realised how insolently disingenuous his words must have sounded, but perhaps he had meant to insult her. He felt so odd, he couldn't be sure of anything.

"Why didn't you tell me a man had been shot?" she demanded.

This time he could think of no response, insolent or otherwise. He turned to Lascelles, who heard his unasked question and said: "Your Major de Valera let us know — he sent a dispatch rider to the embassy. I came down at once."

"I see," Strafford said. He was not quite sure that he did.

But it must have been Lascelles's car he had heard on the drive in the night.

"It's a damned disgrace," the duke said. Strafford hadn't noticed him until he spoke. He was seated in a strange sort of simian crouch in the depths of a chintz-covered armchair, wearing a dressing-gown and carpet slippers; he looked for some reason as if he had shrunk two or three sizes overnight. He, too, like Celia Nashe, was plainly in a fury; it wasn't immediately clear what exactly it was he considered to be a disgrace, but Strafford felt certain it wasn't the death of Joey Harte.

"There's an ambulance on the way," Strafford said, to no one in particular. "And some Forensics people. I was on the phone just now, to Dublin."

"A bit late in the day, I should have thought," Lascelles remarked drily, and tipped the ash from his cigarette on to the tiles in front of the fireplace. He turned to Celia Nashe, evidently taking up the thread of what he had been saying before Strafford's entrance. "We don't think it's a question of violence, necessarily, of attempted assassination or the like. Piecing together what crumbs of intelligence we've managed to gather — and, my God, but it's hard to find a fact in this blessed country — it seems more likely some kind of kidnap attempt is being planned."

"What, here?" the duke almost yelled, in a tone of outrage.

Lascelles ignored him, and so did Celia Nashe. The latter said: "Do we know who would be behind it?"

"Well, the IRA, or whatever it is they call themselves nowadays. There's a fellow in the town, name of Clancy, who seems to be in charge of the local lot. They're pretty harmless, or have been up to now. The worry is that Clancy may call in reinforcements."

"Reinforcements?" Strafford asked, his own voice adding another level of vibration to the buzzing in his head.

"Yes, reinforcements," Lascelles answered, examining the tip of his cigarette. "From Belfast, most likely. Belfast is where the serious people are."

Strafford nodded. The pulsing in his temples was getting worse. He supposed he must have flu. How absurd to be ill like this at such a time! "Was Joseph Harte involved?" he asked.

Lascelles slowly turned on him a look of lazy disdain. "Possibly," he said. "Though the fellow seems to have been mostly a layabout. Can't see he would have been much of a threat to anyone."

"It's possible he was here, at the house, last night," Strafford said. He told of Sergeant Brody's having smelt drink on the dying man's breath.

"He would hardly have needed to be here for that," Lascelles said. "It's not exactly difficult to find a drink in Ireland, even in the middle of the night."

Strafford turned away from him, and spoke to the duke. "I don't suppose anyone spotted him?"

The duke gave him a glare. "Don't you think I would have said so before now, if anybody had?"

"One of the servants might have let him in."

"Well, it would hardly have been anyone else! You don't imagine we're in the habit of inviting the likes of Joseph Harte into the drawing room for a glass of sherry and a chat of an evening?"

Celia Nashe had gone very pale, and her eyes glittered with a nervous light. "What kind of kidnap attempt might they be planning?" she asked.

Lascelles considered. "We don't know," he said. "That's the trouble. But let's say the girls might be seized and whisked away from here altogether, over to the west coast, perhaps, where there could be a submarine waiting for them at some quiet fishing harbour. Next thing we know Their Royal Highnesses are being paraded on the balcony of the Reich Chancellery, with a beaming Uncle Adolf patting them on the head."

He stopped. All that could be heard was the faint hissing of the clods of damp turf smouldering in the fireplace.

"For goodness' sake, man," the duke said at last, "it's just too far-fetched."

"Do you think so?" Lascelles asked, as if he actually expected a reply. "You've got to understand, sir, this is how the German mind works. Too much exposure to the operas of Richard Wagner, I say. They believe in the power of drama, of the spectacle. Bombing Coventry is

239

one thing, but capturing a couple of royal princesses, now that, *that*, they'd say, would surely deal the killer blow to the morale of a nation already under devastating nightly attack. Reeling under the shock, all spirit gone, poor old Blighty would be ripe for invasion. Then it's storm troopers in the Strand and panzers in Pall Mall."

He seemed positively to be enjoying himself, as he laid out this frightening scenario in his clubman's exaggeratedly plummy tones.

"But what would be in it for the Irish?" the duke demanded. His cheeks had turned an apoplectic shade of mottled crimson.

"The firing squad for de Valera and his government, first of all, I should say," Lascelles replied.

"You think the Germans would cross the Irish Sea, if the mainland fell?"

"The Wehrmacht doesn't pay much heed to the notion of neutrality. Fine deep ports here, many of them in the west, facing the Atlantic. As for your Irish Republican Army, I hear they quite approve of Hitler — my enemy's enemy, and all that. No doubt they'd expect to be put in charge, when Jerry got here, in recognition of their kidnapping coup if nothing else, and probably they would be. They'd make a fine puppet government."

"It sounds like a fantasy out of a novel," Celia Nashe said faintly, aghast in wonderment.

"Yes, doesn't it?" Lascelles calmly agreed. "But the most fantastic things do come about in wartime. Look at Dunkirk."

240

A silence opened like a hole in the air, into which three of the people in the room starkly stared, while the fourth, Lascelles, with seeming unconcern, tossed the butt of his cigarette into the fire.

"What is to be done?" Strafford asked. "Get the girls back to London right away?"

"Oh, no," Lascelles said, with his lazy smile. "No, I think not. On balance, they're safer here. It's very bad in London now, and going to get worse, according to those in the know. No, let's — what is it they say here? — let's let the hare sit, for now."

Celia Nashe was lighting a cigarette. Strafford noticed again the slight tremor in her hand, which made the match-flame shimmer. Despite the tension of the moment, he felt more remote than ever from his surroundings. It was hardly surprising, after all, that he should be not himself: he had been summoned out of bed in the middle of the night and led out to survey, in a dark wood, by the light of a storm-lantern, the body of a man shot fatally through the throat. That would be enough to make the soundest constitution falter, surely.

A rippling shiver ran down his back under the suddenly scratchy stuff of his shirt.

Lascelles turned to him. "I spoke to your minister, by the way."

Strafford greeted this news with a dull stare. "Dan Hegarty?" He was surprised, though he supposed he shouldn't be.

"Yes, Hegarty," Lascelles responded, selecting another cigarette from a slim silver case, "the chap you and I had lunch with in the Kildare Street Club. I must say, he wasn't best pleased to hear what I had to tell him, after his wife or whoever had managed to wake him up. He didn't sound entirely sober. I also had a call from an Inspector Somebody" — he was looking at Strafford — "your boss, I think?"

"Yes. Inspector Hackett."

"That's it. The minister had called him after speaking to me. It's been quite the busy night" — he paused for a second, showing his large square teeth in a chill smile — "for some of us, at any rate."

Strafford absorbed the barb. Long ago, in his earliest schooldays, he had taught himself to maintain a front of uncomprehending blankness in the face of sarcasm and worse.

"I left instructions just now for him to be called at home," he said.

"No need. He has come down himself — I expect he's out there, by now."

"Hackett?" Strafford exclaimed. "Ah. I had better go and report to him."

Lascelles had lit his cigarette, and now directed a cone of smoke towards the ceiling. "I'll run you out," he said. "You can show me the way."

The duke made to rise from his chair. "I should come too."

"No, no," Lascelles said smoothly, with another mask-like smile, "no need for that. You stay here, too, Miss Nashe."

Celia nodded distractedly into the fireplace. She had thrown her unsmoked cigarette into the turf and was making a nervous kneading motion with her hands.

"The girls will be getting up soon," she said. When she looked up, for some reason it was Strafford she addressed. "I'm not going to tell them," she said. "About the shooting, I mean."

The duke snorted. "Doesn't matter whether you do or not," he said, with a sardonic twist of the mouth. "They'll hear it from the servants soon enough."

A shaft of pale damp sunlight struck through the window and made a trembling puddle of brightness on the hearth. Lascelles headed towards the door, touching Strafford briefly on the elbow as he passed him by. "Inspector Hackett will be getting restive," he said.

CHAPTER
TWENTY-FOUR

In the Bentley Strafford, who had an uncommonly acute sense of smell, caught a faint after-trace of perfume. Lascelles must have been on a date last night. Or maybe there was a wife, a Mrs Lascelles, though that seemed unlikely, somehow.

"Good God, man," Lascelles said, laughing, as the big car rumbled down the drive, "what were you up to that you didn't alert the ice maiden, or anyone else for that matter, as to what was afoot?"

"I was called out by a sergeant from the guard detail," Strafford said. On the windscreen, a weak wash of early-morning sunlight palely glistened. His fevered blood simmered, racing along his veins. "I had a look at the body, and then came back."

Lascelles laughed again. "Yes, but didn't it occur to you to call someone straight away, me, or your inspector, or whoever, to say someone had been bloody well shot?"

Strafford did not reply. It puzzled him that Major de Valera had not contacted him on the field telephone when the hours went past and no one had come to deal with the body of Joey Harte. But then, as Lascelles had just pointed out, he himself had also failed to make a vital phone call. This was embarrassing, though already his blushes were cooling. It would be futile, he thought, to make excuses for his behaviour or offer extenuations: he had blundered, and would be called to account for it in one way or another — Inspector Hackett was an easygoing fellow, but there must be a limit even to his forbearance.

For all that, Strafford was no more than mildly curious as to what form of reprimand might await him. He was not one to dwell for long on his failures, or feel the weight of them particularly. His general disregard for the formalities and demands of police procedure, which somehow never quite amounted to insubordination, was a puzzle to his superiors, who consequently avoided dealing with him altogether, so that for the most part he was left to his own devices. Inspector Hackett couldn't understand him at all, but didn't seem to care. Strafford had potential, Hackett would say, to anyone who questioned the young man's fitness for the job; he had a future ahead of him, there could be no doubt of that.

Strafford himself was not so sure.

The Bentley turned out at the gate and slid smoothly along the narrow road, making a silken sound. There was a skim of last night's dew on the tarmac.

"I thought you might have been busy putting Miss Nashe in the picture," Lascelles said. He shook his head in rueful wonderment. "Instead of which you hadn't even let her know what had happened," He paused, and then resumed: "Are you two at loggerheads, or what? Has there been a division in the ranks?" He glanced sideways at Strafford with a smirk. "Have you tried your hand there yet, by the way? She's a toothsome piece, and quite the goer, I should say, once one had got past the chilly exterior. Plenty to take hold of, too, in the top and tail department."

Strafford shifted uneasily in his seat. He was embarrassed, not so much by Lascelles as for him. He did not care for this kind of mildly indecent talk, not out of prudishness, or delicacy of spirit, but because it seemed to introduce between him and the Englishman a humid, spurious form of intimacy.

"I'm afraid Miss Nashe doesn't hold me in particularly high regard," he said, in a voice deliberately cool. "I think she finds me more a hindrance than a help."

"Well, you certainly didn't cover yourself in glory last night," Lascelles said cheerfully. "I imagine you're in for a right old talking-to from your boss — stripping of your colours and the like."

"I imagine so, yes."

It wasn't something he wished to think about, at the moment. In fact, he hadn't the strength for thinking of anything much, since all of his energies were required for the ordinarily simple task of keeping his burning eyelids open. He craved sleep, as a thirsty man craves water; in fact, he craved water, too.

On a straight stretch of the road Lascelles opened up the throttle and the car seemed to draw into itself for an instant, like a runner tucking in his elbows, then bounded forward into a tunnel of trees and sped along

246

under a high, arched canopy of gold and crimson foliage.

Day was slowly strengthening.

They coasted around a dipping curve and came in sight of the armoured car parked at a tilt by the side of the road. There was also a squad car, with a Garda driver at the wheel, his shiny-peaked helmet pushed to the back of his head, and a square, blunt-nosed Garda ambulance with mesh-reinforced glass in the back windows, which in the force was never known as anything other than the "meat wagon".

Lascelles pulled up behind the van and he and Strafford got out. At the sight of Detective Strafford the driver in the Garda car sat hastily upright and straightened his cap. Lascelles was wearing his double-breasted overcoat and, like Strafford, a pair of borrowed wellingtons. They could hear low voices from within the wood. Lascelles looked about with a morose expression. "Christ," he muttered, "the messes I find myself caught up in — and I'm supposed to be a bloody diplomat!"

He had mentioned to Strafford the Paris posting that he had been in line for and would probably have had but for the outbreak of war. Yes, Strafford reflected, in the matter of style, elegance and *douceur de la vie*, Clonmillis was about as far from the Champs-Élysées as an ambitious diplomatist could get.

They stepped across a leaf-clogged ditch and went forward cautiously under the trees. Lascelles took the lead, and more than once a bent-back twig he let go of lashed Strafford stingingly across the cheek. This was where Strafford had walked last night, in darkness; already the passage of feet had laid down the beginnings of a rough track.

He saw ahead a group of figures standing together under the trees, and recognised Inspector Hackett's soft black hat and permanently sloped shoulders. The other two were Major de Valera and Sergeant Brody. By daylight the major's face had a raw look; his eyes behind the heavy, horn-rimmed spectacles seemed more watery than they had in the dark, and the fat tip of his nose was shinily red and sore-looking.

At the sound of footsteps Inspector Hackett turned and gave Strafford a sour glance; he was out of patience not only with the detective, it seemed, but with everything his eye fell on. He was a young-old man, hardly into his thirties but already of an ashen, exhausted aspect.

"So, you decided to grace us with your presence at last," he said, with syrupy sarcasm.

Strafford thought it superfluous to reply, and therefore said nothing.

For his part, Lascelles stepped forward and put out a hand to Hackett and introduced himself. Hackett nodded; Strafford could see he was unimpressed by the embassy man.

A sheet of canvas, grey and creased from the night's dew, had been spread over Joey Harte's corpse, covering it completely save for one elbow, which stuck out at an unnatural angle; Strafford thought again of Pompeian mummies.

"You had come across him already, before last night?" Hackett said, nodding towards the humped form on the ground.

"Yes," Strafford said, and glanced towards the major. "He was out poaching. Major de Valera and his men caught him at it."

Hackett sucked in his lower lip. He didn't seem particularly interested in Joey Harte's misdemeanours. Under an unbuttoned heavy black overcoat he wore a blue suit that had seen better days, a greasy blue tie and a fawn pullover that someone must have knitted for him. Strafford glimpsed also a shoulder holster, from which jutted the nicked and polished butt of what he judged to be a snub-nosed Smith & Wesson .38. He had never known Hackett to appear on duty armed before.

"We didn't 'catch him at it'," Major de Valera insisted heavily.

"He was spotted prowling about in the wood and one of my lads called on him to halt."

"And did he?"

"Of course."

Hackett nodded grimly. "Pity he didn't do the same last night."

From the major's pop-eyed stare, Strafford could see he was preparing to take offence, but then seemed to decide it would be better if he didn't.

The men from Forensics had been and gone.

"They were their usual enlightening selves," Hackett said. "They were able to tell us the poor fellow is dead, otherwise we'd never have known."

249

Lascelles leaned down and lifted a corner of the canvas to reveal the side of Joey Harte's face and the gaping wound in his throat. Strafford caught a glimpse of the dead man's staring eye, greyly filmed over by now.

"He's from the town, yes?" Lascelles said. "What was the name again?"

"Joseph — Joey — Harte," Hackett said.

"That's right, Joseph Harte," Major de Valera chimed in, as if he felt he was required by duty to provide corroboration.

Hackett had produced a packet of Gold Flake and was offering it round. He struck a match. He was still looking at the humped form on the ground. "Joseph Harte," he repeated musingly. "We checked up on him. There's a few charges to his name — trespassing, poaching, petty burglary, nothing serious."

Lascelles, catching something in his tone, gave him a sharp look. "Should we be interested in him?" he asked. "I mean, should we dig deeper?"

"I would have said no, except —" He broke off, and turned to Sergeant Brody. "Show us that thing." The sergeant lodged the cigarette at one corner of his mouth and unbuttoned the breast pocket of his tunic and brought out with care a folded square of rain-drenched paper and handed it to Hackett, who looked to Lascelles and said, "Except for this." He passed the scrap of paper to the Englishman. "He had it on him. The sergeant here found it."

Lascelles glanced at the faces around him with an uneasy frown. It was plain he would have preferred not to know whatever it was the paper was about to inform him of, but he had no choice except to unfold it carefully — it was so wet it was in danger of disintegrating — and lay it out flat on his palm. He gazed at it for a moment. "My God," he said, under his breath.

Strafford, tilting his head, peered at the blurred photograph.

"You recognise those folks, I take it?" Hackett said to Lascelles.

Lascelles grimaced, as if in pain, and lifted his eyes from the photograph. "It's the Royal bloody Family, of course."

"Aye," Hackett agreed. "And the two girls marked with circles around them are the royal bloody princesses."

CHAPTER
TWENTY-FIVE

They sat, the four of them, in Lascelles's car, still parked by the roadside — Lascelles and Inspector Hackett in front, Strafford and Major de Valera in the back seat — and discussed what was to be done. Hackett led off by saying that the two girls should be got away from Clonmillis at once, since clearly they were under imminent threat, as the presence of the photograph in Joey Harte's pocket had indicated. If Joey Harte knew who the girls were, then surely others did, too.

Lascelles was lighting yet another cigarette; the hand that held the match was not entirely steady. "That's all very well," he said, in a vexed tone, "but where are we to move them to?"

Fine cracks, Strafford could see, had begun to show in the Englishman's so far carefully maintained mask of insouciance.

"Wasn't there talk of them being sent to Canada?" Hackett said.

Lascelles gave him a quizzical look, surprised, it seemed, that the policeman should be in possession of such a piece of supposedly confidential information. Yes, Strafford thought, he's rattled.

"Canada is out of the question," Lascelles said shortly. "The sea lanes have become more dangerous even than England's industrial ports and cities." He brooded for a moment, worrying at his cigarette. "We'll have to bring in more protection. There's a new outfit, set up recently on the prime minister's direct orders — the Commando Force. Strictly hush-hush for now, by the way. A tough lot. They carry out special operations, mostly behind enemy lines. I'm sure we could get a unit brought over on the quiet, set them up here —"

He was interrupted by a loud clearing of the throat from the back seat. Major de Valera's greyish brow had taken on a pinkish glow.

"There already is a military force in place here, Mr Lascelles," he said, his curiously thin, piping voice rising to a yet higher, thinner register. Strafford, seated at his side, studied him with interest. He had seen how shocked de Valera had been by the newspaper photograph with the pencilled circles around the heads of the princesses — vulnerable heads, responsibility for the safety of which had been put into his hands. Could it really be that no one had informed him of the identity of the two young persons he and his men had been sent down here to watch over?

Typical of his father, the country's leader, to keep his son in the dark. Strafford's own playfully eccentric father, whom it pleased on occasion to speak in the rolling cadences of a Regency wit, liked to say of Éamon de Valera that his right hand languished in permanent ignorance of what the left one might be engaged in.

"I know that, of course," Lascelles hastened to say. "You and your men are doing a fine job, witness last night's prompt action." He knew well whose son he was addressing, and had no intention of being the cause of a diplomatic incident. "However —"

"However," the major cut in heavily, "there is no question of bringing in a squad of irregulars. For heaven's sake, man, you're talking about British soldiers being stationed on Irish soil! No question, no question. We remember the Black and Tans, Mr Lascelles, all too well. I'm told a young fellow on the estate here lost his mother to those murdering thugs. Besides, you seem to forget that Ireland is a neutral power."

Lascelles looked quickly from Hackett to Strafford. "What fellow are you talking about?" he asked, a sharpness, a shrillness, almost, coming into his voice. "Was someone's mother shot?"

"Name of Denton," Strafford said. "Chap with the shotgun — you'll have seen him about. Black and Tans gunned down his mother on her doorstep here, during the War of Independence."

Lascelles nodded, reassured. "Ah. Long ago, then."

"Twenty years," Strafford answered. "Denton was an infant at the time. It's said the mother was holding him in her arms when she was shot, but that may just be local legend. The house is over that way." He waved an arm. "Denton lives there still, I'm told."

Lascelles was rapidly losing interest in the subject. "Very sad," he murmured, then raised his voice again. "But that's all ancient history, surely."

"History is never ancient over here, Mr Lascelles," Hackett said, with a phlegmy chuckle. He glanced at Strafford. "Isn't that so, Detective?"

It amused Strafford's boss to tease him, the Protestant, about such matters, but he had no intention of being drawn into a mock-political discussion just now.

"Perhaps the girls could be sent up to Dublin," he said. "Lodge them in a safe house, until the threat has passed?"

"What leads you to think the threat will pass?" Lascelles enquired coldly. Now he had abandoned all pretence of nonchalance; he was a man with a problem, one that could blow up in his face and leave him permanently scarred. "Besides, there may be a watch on the house here already. What's to stop them setting up roadblocks?" He turned to the major. "Could you call in some heavy vehicles to make up a convoy?"

By now the major's look was one of barely controlled wrath. "My task, and the task of my men," he said, with narrowed eyes and tightened mouth, "is to mount a guard on the perimeters of the Home Farm here and keep out intruders. For all we knew, that fellow last night could have been armed, and backed up by others like him. The IRA is still active in these parts."

"Gentlemen, gentlemen." Inspector Hackett held up a restraining hand. "Let's keep calm, now. We'll achieve nothing by going at each other's throats." He took off his hat, looked into the crown, then put it on again. He had a wide mouth and a boxer's squashed nose and shrewd little gleaming dark eyes.

Lascelles wound down the window beside him and tossed the butt of his cigarette out on to the road. Strafford was glad of the brief inflow of fresh air. The trace of perfume he had caught earlier was long gone, and the interior of the car reeked of tobacco and damp overcoats and stale sweat.

"Well, whatever we're to do," Lascelles said, turning sulky, "we'd do well to keep in mind the weight of responsibility that rests on our shoulders."

Major de Valera sniffed and folded his arms, looking steadily out of the window at his side.

Lascelles turned the key in the ignition, saying that it was time to get back to the house.

"I'll leave you, so, gentlemen," Inspector Hackett said, opening the passenger door.

Lascelles stared at him. "Where are you going?" he demanded.

"Back to Dublin, and my work," Hackett said, stepping out of the car.

"But —"

"Listen, Mr Lascelles," Hackett said quietly, turning back and leaning down into the doorway, with one hand resting on the roof of the car, "your government requested a favour of our government, and our government was happy to oblige. So far we've kept those two young ones safe, and we'll continue to do that, as long as it's in our power. When I get back to town I'll telephone the minister —"

"I'll be telephoning him myself," Lascelles snapped.

"— I'll telephone the minister," Hackett went on, refusing to be provoked, "and see if we can provide the major here with reinforcements. It's all we can do, if you won't take the girls away."

Major de Valera, who had also got out of the car, gave the hem of his uniform jacket an angry tug, and adjusted his spectacles. "I think," he said, addressing Hackett, "that would be a matter for the defence forces. There's no need to bother the minister — I'll speak to my commanding officer myself."

"Oh, right, so," Inspector Hackett said easily, looking at him over the roof of the car. Then he leaned in again to address Lascelles. "Good luck to you now, sir," he said, touching one finger to the brim of his hat in an ironical salute. "No doubt I'll be hearing from you." He looked to Strafford. "Detective, are you taking a lift back to the Hall? Might I have a quick word, before you go?"

Strafford climbed out of the car, and Hackett put a hand under his elbow and steered him a little way off to the side. Strafford was conscious that the major, still standing by the motor, was watching them with an attentive eye, though he was probably too far away to hear what they would say.

Inspector Hackett took out his packet of cigarettes and lit one. He lifted a foot disgustedly, showing a black hobnailed boot smeared with mud. "Look at me," he said, "I'm destroyed." There was mud too on the hems of his trousers. "Listen, my lad," he said quietly, "you have a care, here. As I said to His Nibs just now, the smart-aleck from the embassy, it was his government that asked us to take in this pair. All the same, if they do come to harm, we'll be the ones that will get it in the neck — you and me, I mean, not young de Valera over there, or the swells up at the Big House. Do you hear what I'm saying? You don't want to find yourself on the beat again, and I don't want to end up a desk sergeant in Ballydehob."

Strafford nodded. The major, who had been watching them, now turned aside and, stooping, made his way off into the wood.

"What do you want me to do?" Strafford asked; his headache was very bad.

"Do nothing, unless you have to," the inspector answered. He gave the barest nod in the direction of the car, where Lascelles could be seen, a dim figure behind the windscreen. "Let him handle it, him and the girl, what's-her-name."

"Celia Nashe," Strafford said.

Hackett peered at him for a second with narrowed eyes. "Aye, Nashe, that's it," he said slowly. "How are you getting on with her?"

There was a faint insinuation in his tone that Strafford decided to ignore. "We get on all right," he said. "She's perfectly civil."

Hackett chuckled. "Is that so?" he said, and gave a nasty little laugh. "Anyway, that's the way to keep it, nice and civil. Go along with you now and join Mr Lascelles in his fine car. But listen" — he gripped the young man's elbow again — "keep me informed, at all times. Don't leave me in the dark, like you did last night."

"Right, sir," Strafford said.

258

Hackett peered at him closely again. "Are you all right? You look like death warmed over."

"I have a cold, I think," Strafford replied. "It's nothing."

He turned and walked away, his head down and his hands sunk in the pockets of his trench coat.

He climbed into the car again, again into the back seat, even though the front one was empty, and let his head recline on the leather headrest. He closed his eyes on to throbbing darkness. He was weak and dizzy, and wondered how he was to get through the rest of this day, feeling as seedy he did.

"Jesus Christ, these people," Lascelles in the front seat muttered, watching through the windscreen as Inspector Hackett got into the squad car and slammed the door. "How do you put up with these people?"

Strafford said nothing. He hadn't the energy to point out that he was probably himself one of what Lascelles considered to be "these people".

The Englishman pressed his foot hard on the accelerator and spun the steering wheel and swung the big car this way and that in a violent three-point turn. Strafford, tossed from side to side, opened his eyes and straightened in the seat; he must keep hold, he told himself, otherwise he might lose consciousness altogether — it seemed to him not at all unlikely. Lascelles was looking at him in the driving mirror — how sinister people's eyes always seemed in that little glass rectangle, Strafford thought, like the eyes of a gaoler peeping in at a slot in the door of a cell — and gave an angry laugh and said: "What do you think about all this?"

"About the shooting, you mean?"

"Of course the shooting! What else?"

"I thought you meant the question of what should be done with the girls."

"It's the same thing."

Strafford looked out of the window beside him at the world moving rapidly past. The sun, still low, flashed through the hedges, dazzling his eyes. "I can't think Joey Harte could represent a serious threat," he said, and added, "Especially not now."

"Oh, you can't, can't you?" Lascelles said, in a sort of snarl. He trod harder on the pedal, and swung the car around a sharp bend, the tyres squealing. Having let his anger off the leash he was a different man. This, Strafford reflected, was the real Lascelles, vindictive and menacing, determined not to be the person on whom the blame fell.

"One thing you can do," the Englishman snarled, "is go and have a chat with that fellow Denton."

"Oh, yes?" Strafford said, from the back seat. "Chat to him about what?"

"About who it was he spilled the beans to," Lascelles snapped back, between clenched teeth.

"You think he tipped off Harte about the girls?"

Lascelles gave an angry laugh. "Our chaps shot his ma, didn't they? Even if it was twenty years ago. One thing I do know about the Irish, they never forgive a wrong, or forget."

"All right," Strafford said mildly, "I'll talk to him."

260

"Yes, you do that."

Lascelles was glaring at him in the mirror again; Strafford wished he would keep his eyes on the road. The clock was showing sixty, and there were some frightening bends. To his surprise, he felt invigorated suddenly — fear must have got his adrenalin going. Nothing like the death of another to quicken one's own sense of being alive. Or was it just the fever, boiling in his blood?

Billy Denton had gone out just after dawn to finish the fencing job that had been interrupted the day he heard the girl crying in the wood and had to carry her back to the Hall. He wanted to get the rest of the work done today, not because there was any great urgency, but he had a passion for neatness and hated to leave any task unfinished once he had started it. Soon rain came on, in fine, cobwebby drifts of greyish moisture that was hardly more than a light mist. He paid no heed; he was used to getting wet.

Unseen rooks cawed raucously in the high trees, seeming to mock him, their unrelenting nemesis.

After an hour he had made good progress, and the job was almost done. His hands were bleeding where the wire had nicked him. This, too, he ignored; the skin on the backs of his hands and all along his forearms bore many scars from forgotten small woundings.

Gradually the feeling came over him of being under scrutiny, and when he stopped in his task and straightened up and turned, he saw Pike standing some way off among the trees, watching him.

261

How long had he been there?

Billy was wary of Pike, always had been; despised him, too. He bent to his work again, but he knew he would get no peace.

"Aren't you the right Sir Galahad, now?" the old man said, coming up behind him, laughing softly. "I suppose they greeted you as a mighty fellow, when you appeared that day at the Big House with the young one in your arms." Billy only kept on working. The rooks were making a great racket, as if they knew Pike had appeared on the scene and were issuing a general warning of his presence. "Have you not got your gun with you? Them fuckers" — he meant the rooks — "could do with a few blasts of buckshot to shut them up."

Billy sighed, and stopped working and straightened again. He had a wire-cutter in his right hand; the hooked blades, the shape of birds' beaks, gleamed in the silvery rain-light.

"Have you nothing to tend to yourself?" he asked. "As you can see, I'm busy."

Pike chuckled.

"Ah, you're always busy. The duke" — he pronounced it "dook", which never failed to amuse him, as if it were a fine joke — "must think you're a treasure. He'll be taking out adoption papers on you yet." He laughed again, wheezily. "My boy Billy."

Billy gave him a level look. "You've no cause to make fun of me, Pike," he said, sounding more bored than angry.

262

"Who's making fun?" Pike exclaimed, raising his eyebrows and opening wide his good eye. "I'm only saying you're well got, up there at the Hall."

Billy shook his head almost in anguish, like an animal tormented by flies. "Will you for Christ's sake leave me alone to do my work?" he pleaded.

It was Pike who had put about the rumour, years before, that Billy was the duke's bastard son; no one believed him, but it had given people a laugh, and sometimes even still he would be greeted in the street as "Your Grace", followed by a guffaw.

"Come on and we'll go up to Gaffney's in the van, and have a pint," Pike urged, putting on the friendly act, as Billy saw, with contempt.

"I told you already," he muttered, "I've work to do."

"Have you a smoke?"

"No, I haven't."

Then Pike said, in a mild voice, as if he were uttering a pleasantry: "You're a cross-grained bollocks, do you know that?"

Billy had turned his attention to the fence again. The back of his neck had gone red. Pike stood and looked down at him, his one eye half shut, moving his jaw in a rotating movement, chewing on nothing.

The wire-cutter, as Billy plied it, made a sharp, clean, clicking sound.

"Mind you don't lop a finger off," Pike said. "What would you do without all your digits?" He turned and strolled away, over the wet grass. Both men were aware that neither one of them had mentioned the killing of Joey Harte, news of which had already flashed from farmstead to farmstead and had even reached the town, along with the milkmen and the first post.

CHAPTER
TWENTY-SIX

It was still early when a telephone call was received at the Hall from the office of the minister, Dan Hegarty. Strafford heard of it after he and Lascelles had arrived back at the house and Lascelles had gone off to park the Bentley.

Hynes the butler had delayed answering the call for as long as he dared, in the hope that whoever was on the line would lose heart and ring off, but eventually he had to give in. He approached the apparatus at a defensive crouch, like a gladiator armed with a spear and a net, for he regarded the thing — a machine that talked! — with an abiding primitive dread. He picked up the earpiece and listened, and heard himself requested to inform His Grace the Duke that the minister, Mr Hegarty, would arrive at Clonmillis Hall on the following morning, by government car.

Was this Mr Hegarty speaking? Hynes enquired.

No, it was not: it was his private secretary.

At first the old man could hardly understand what was being said to him — he had never heard of any Mr Hegarty, and could not think why a person should imagine he might simply ring up out of the blue and announce the imminent arrival of some other person, whom seemingly he represented.

He was heading for what the duke liked to call his office, a hidey-hole accessible only through a hardly noticeable low door under the main stairs, but just then Strafford entered the front hall. Hynes had taken something of a shine to the young man who, apart from being polite and exceptionally well-spoken, had slipped him five shillings at the end of his first week here. The butler veered aside now and accosted the detective as he was balancing on one foot on the mat beside the coat stand, pulling off with an effort one of the too-tight wellington boots he had borrowed earlier.

"The minister is coming here?" Strafford said in surprise, with the boot in his hand. "Did he say what for?"

Hynes treated this as a piece of drollery. He could not conceive of anyone seriously imagining that a government official, especially a minister's private secretary, would elaborate on his master's intentions to anyone, and certainly not to a servant; unlike Mrs O'Hanlon, Hynes had no illusions as to his status in the household.

"Oh, no, Mr Stafford, sir, he didn't say." Hynes, like so many others, could not quite credit Strafford's name, and always got it wrong. Strafford had long ago given up correcting him. "Anyway, it wasn't himself that rang."

"So he's coming down," Strafford said, grinning. "Bloody hell." He was, he realised, rather tickled by the prospect of seeing how Dan the Man would deal with

266

the intricate social niceties of Clonmillis Hall, not to mention the killing of a civilian by defence forces' fire. "And he's arriving tomorrow, you say?"

"That he is, sir. After breakfast. Or so the person on the telephone said."

"The person?"

"His secretary is what he said he was." The old man obviously considered a male secretary a highly unlikely, not to say risible, proposition. "He's being driven down."

"Does the duke know this?"

"I was just on the way to tell him, sir."

"Yes, well, I think you had better do so straight away."

Hynes sketched a sort of salute — Strafford suspected the old boy took him for a soldier in mufti, only claiming to be a detective — and shuffled away down the hall.

Strafford got the second boot off, and stood luxuriantly flexing his cramped toes and digging them into the pleasantly prickly ticking of the mat.

That was how Lascelles found him. The Englishman had put the car away in the stable yard, thinking it best to keep it out of sight — "Don't want it riddled with bullet holes, in the event of a siege," he had said to Strafford, with a death's-head grin, before driving away towards the rear of the house.

Now he took the news of Hegarty's intended visit with a baffled frown. "Why's he coming here?" he demanded.

"Well, he would have heard of Harte being shot. Indeed, you informed him of it yourself, last night, didn't you?"

"Yes, but what business is it of his?" A thought struck him. "I wonder if he'll expect to stay?"

The two men looked at each other in silence for a moment, then laughed at the same time.

Celia Nashe appeared at the top of the staircase, her look clearly indicating that she considered the men's show of levity hardly appropriate, in the circumstances.

"The bloody minister is coming down," Lascelles called up to her. "Can you believe it?"

She began to descend the staircase. "What minister?"

"Hegarty," Strafford said. "External affairs."

"Oh, I see." She seemed surprised, as if it had not occurred to her that Ireland would go in for such things as government ministers. "That's all we need," she added grimly. She turned to Lascelles. "I've told the girls they're confined to the house until further notice."

Lascelles smiled wryly.

"How was that received?"

"How do you think?"

Celia Nashe looked discomfited and cross. It was clear Lascelles had no intention of letting her forget that it was she who had insisted on a relaxation of control on the girls' freedom of movement about the estate.

"What reason did you give them for keeping them in?" Strafford asked.

The young woman coloured. "I said there'd been a gas escape from the cow barn. I mentioned urea." She

268

bit her lip. "It was the only thing I could think of on the spur of the moment."

Strafford nodded, keeping a straight face.

"Good, good," Lascelles murmured absently — he had not really been listening. He had taken off his coat, and now he hung it on the coat stand, and neatly flicked his hat end over end to land neatly on a hook beside it. "I don't know which to be, amused or terrified," he said. "It's turning into a sort of Irish farce — old Shaw would have great fun with it. Paddy gets potted in the pine wood while the toffs prepare for the government inspector's visit."

He walked away from them abruptly, whistling and patting the pockets of his jacket in search of his cigarette case. He had regained much of his sangfroid.

"Well," Celia asked, turning to Strafford, "what developments have there been?"

He could have laughed at the stiffness with which she spoke: when in doubt become a robot. But he didn't laugh, and instead told her of the newspaper photograph found in Harte's pocket. She took it, he had to admit, with admirable calmness.

"The girls' identity was a secret that was never going to be kept," she said.

"I'm to go down and talk to young Denton," Strafford said. "The thinking is, he's probably the informer."

"The informer?"

"The one who told Joey Harte the real identity of the girls — the one who gave him the newspaper photograph. You know his mother was shot by the British?"

"Yes, I did." She paused. "Do you think it was him who broke the secret?"

"I don't know. Do you?"

She said she would come with him. He put on the ill-fitting wellingtons again — they were still horribly warm and damp inside — while she went upstairs to fetch her walking boots, the ones she had not had the chance to wear in the far-off, much regretted and, as it now seemed, never to be attained Highlands of bonny Scotland.

They went out together at the front door and set off in the direction of the wood.

"Did you bring a gun?" Strafford asked, deliberately offhand; he was pretty sure she hadn't noticed him catch a glimpse of the pistol in her underwear drawer.

"Did you?"

"Ours is an unarmed police force."

"So is ours."

"But you're not a policeman."

As they were crossing the lawn the mass of rain-clouds that had been roiling about all morning parted suddenly, and a weak sun struggled out and shed upon the grass a splash of pale yellow radiance.

Mary spotted them from the landing window in her wing of the house and stood and watched until they were out of sight. She had been keeping an eye on the two of them from the very start, when they had all first arrived at the Hall, convinced that sooner or later they

270

would fall in love. Now, seeing them disappear together into the wood, she was gratified to think that she had been right.

She liked it when people fell in love: it always made things more interesting, especially if there was likely to be a third person on the scene to stir the brew. Mr Lascelles would fill that part nicely.

She knew about these things from long study of the scores of servants among whom she and her family lived their lives, like whales gliding about among ever-present shoals of minnows.

There had been that occasion at Buck House one afternoon when, bored and in search of something to do, she had walked into one of the bedrooms — the Palace had fifty-two of them, one for each week of the year — and discovered her mother's senior lady-in-waiting, the Duchess of Bristol, in bed with a footman. She had told no one what she had seen, but the duchess, who was well acquainted with Mary and her capacity to keep a secret, made a quick departure anyway, offering only the flimsiest of explanations for her going, and settled in her husband's house in the South of France until she judged it was safe to creep back to England, which was not until years later.

As for the footman, whose name was Fred, he was to prove for Mary a rich source of treats of all kinds, including boxes of chocolates from Fortnum & Mason — pilfered by him, of course, from the regular deliveries of goodies to the Palace — and a tame white rat, one of a litter reared by Fred's younger brother, which she kept in a cardboard box under her bed for a week and fed on titbits of baked ham and fruit cake until it escaped, and she never saw it again. She supposed the Palace cats had got it.

She speculated as to what it was exactly Miss Nashe and the detective would get up to in the woods. There would be kissing, and hugging, and sighing, all that — but after that, what? She had seen farm animals engaged in copulation, but couldn't believe that such gross, clumsy and comical grapplings could be anything like what human beings did together in bed; if it was, then she would certainly never let anyone do it to her.

In a corner of the windowsill the dried-up corpse of a wasp was ensnared in the torn remains of a spider's web. She detached the miniature mummy from the silk threads, which, though greyed with dust, were sticky, and lifted it carefully between a finger and thumb and held it close to her eyes and studied it. Nature was so strange, she thought, so wasteful of beautiful things. She had only to give the wasp the lightest squeeze between a finger and thumb and it crumbled into a puff of straw-coloured powder. She wiped her fingers on her dress and went back into the bedroom.

Her sister was sitting up in bed, with her nose stuck in a book, as usual.

"I've just seen Miss Nasty and the 'tec sneaking off together into the wood."

Mary had by now managed to forget the night she had slipped into Celia Nashe's bed in need of warmth and comfort, and her subsequent resolution to stop calling Miss Nashe by the nickname she had devised for her.

272

"You shouldn't spy on people," her sister said, without lifting her eyes from the page.

She had her knees raised under the bedclothes with the book propped against them. Her sprained ankle was quite recovered, although occasionally, when she remembered, she would put on just the hint of a limp, to remind everybody of the sufferings she had gone through and the lingering aftermath of the injury she was still bravely bearing up to.

"I suppose they must be in love," Mary said now.

"Oh, for goodness' sake, don't be absurd."

"What's absurd about it? People are always falling in love, especially when they're stuck in a place like this with nothing else to do."

She sat down on the side of her own bed and began picking at a hangnail on the middle finger of her left hand. "I miss Crawfie," she said. Crawfie was the family's name for Miss Crawford, the girls' regular governess, who had been none too pleased when she heard she was not to be sent to Ireland to look after them. "I wish she was here."

"Were, not was."

"What?"

"You're supposed to say, 'I wish she were here', which is correct grammar."

Mary narrowed her eyes. "I hate you," she said.

She tugged on the resistant pale scrap of skin at the side of her finger, and a tiny sting of pain shot all the way back along her hand. Pain was interesting. She knew very well she wouldn't be able to bear much of it — imagine being tortured! Fred, her tame footman, had told her how the Gestapo pulled people's fingernails out when they were torturing them to make them betray secrets. Imagine that! She shivered.

"I wish you wouldn't fidget so," her sister said.

"How long do you think we'll have to stay indoors?" Ellen tightened her lips and pretended to concentrate on her book. "I don't believe that stuff about a gas leak in the cow sheds, do you?" Mary said.

"No, of course not."

There was silence for a while; then Mary remarked calmly, "Miss Nasty has a gun." She was peering so closely at the hangnail that her fingertip was nearly touching her eyeball. She thought of Pike taking out his glass eye and letting it plop into his palm; there had been a thin film of shiny slime all over it, as if it had been submerged in waterglass. "She keeps it in a drawer in her room, with her stockings and things. It's a pistol, in a leather holster. I saw her putting it away the day we —"

"Will you please be *quiet!*" Ellen slammed shut her book, and was lying back against the pillows with her eyes turned upwards, doing her martyr act. "Why must you insist on telling such lies? Don't you understand? I'm not in the least interested in your fantastic notions!"

Mary smiled. It was so easy, really, to get her sister going. "I'm not lying," she said, in her mildest, most reasonable tone, which was much more annoying, she knew, than shouting back. "I'll show you, if you like."

"Oh, yes, of course, you'll show me," Ellen said, opening her book again.

274

Mary sat quite still and regarded her sister for some moments, then stood up and walked slowly out of the room, head high, back straight and arms held stiffly at her sides. Ellen, despite herself, looked after her, frowning. What a ridiculous child she was! What was she trying to look like, one of the Life Guards on sentry duty?

In a moment Mary was back, carrying in her hands a leather holster attached to a peculiarly shaped leather belt, which, after a moment, Ellen decided must be a shoulder strap.

"See?" Mary said, approaching her sister's bed and clicking open the holster. "Now tell me I'm lying."

CHAPTER
TWENTY-SEVEN

They found it with ease, the gingerbread house standing alone in its leafy hollow. Although it was only a little way in from the main road it might as well have been lost in the deepest depths of the wood, so isolated did it seem. They stopped among slender boles of pine trees on the slope above the glade and surveyed it. The roof was steep, with a tin weathervane in the shape of a two-dimensional cockerel at one corner. At the other, a lazy trail of smoke drifted almost straight up from a chimney pipe with a bend in it.

The windows were blank, no sign of life showing in any of them.

"He was very good with — with Ellen, when the horse threw her," Celia said. "He carried her in his arms all the way to the house."

"Yes, I was there when they came into the yard. Quite the hero, he looked."

"I think even she was touched."

" 'Even'?"

"Well, she's hardly the most demonstrative of young ladies, at the best of times."

"No, I suppose not." He was studying the house. "There doesn't seem to be anyone at home. Shall we have a closer look?"

"Mind he doesn't take a pot-shot at us with that gun of his, which he never seems to leave out of his hands."

They scrambled down the slope, wading through deep drifts of damp and slimy leaves. Strafford approached one of the windows and made blinkers of his hands and put his face close to the glass and tried to see inside. Dim outlines of a table and some chairs, a wood stove, a kitchen sideboard. Bachelor quarters. He thought of his own flat in Dublin; it was in Clare Street, above the offices of a firm of chartered surveyors. These past days he had begun to miss it, though he had never thought he would.

"Do you think he's mixed up in this business? I mean with the fellow being shot, and so on," he asked, his breath clouding the pane in front of him.

"I don't know," Celia said behind him. "I'd find it hard to believe." And then, after a moment, quietly, "Why don't we ask him?"

Strafford turned from the window.

Billy Denton was standing at the edge of the trees, watching them. He wore his threadbare green Norfolk jacket, and a flat cap and leather leggings. Sure enough, Strafford saw, his trusty shotgun was resting in the crook of his left arm. It was a wonder, he thought, the thing hadn't grown into his hand, like Orpheus's lyre.

"Good morning," Strafford said, rather too loudly, making the trees round about seem to tremble a little.

"Morning," Denton answered, tonelessly.

277

He really would be quite good-looking, Celia thought, if only he would allow himself to smile once in a while. She registered a strange sensation, watching him there, a strange sort of downwards trickle along her spine, starting at the waistband of her skirt. Once again he had crept up on her without a sound; she trusted he wouldn't fire his gun this time. She hadn't brought her own weapon with her, thinking she would hardly be likely to need it. Billy Denton certainly wasn't a danger, not to her or the detective, she was sure of it. She believed he was much softer than he liked to pretend.

"We were just wondering if you were in," Strafford said, again raising his voice to call across the space between himself and the young man standing at the edge of the trees.

"I wasn't, but I will be now," Denton answered, without the slightest hint of humour or even of sarcasm. He really was a charmless creature, Strafford thought — which probably meant, of course, that every girl he met thought him a dreamboat. Strafford was perfectly aware that he knew little about girls — next to nothing, really. The image of Isabel Galloway rose before him, like a wood wraith, and immediately vanished.

Denton stepped forward, and crossed the clearing, keeping his head lowered and his eyes fixed on the ground. When he had come level with them, Celia said: "I didn't thank you properly for rescuing Ellen, after she'd come a cropper, that day."

Denton reached into a pocket of his corduroy trousers and brought out an iron key. "It was nothing," he said dismissively. "I'd hardly call it a rescue."

278

"Well, goodness knows how long she'd have been out there, with a sprained ankle and unable to walk, if you hadn't found her."

The young man unlocked the front door of the house and pushed it open and stepped inside.

Celia and Strafford exchanged an uncertain look. Were they to take the open door as an invitation to enter?

Strafford led the way.

The narrow room in which they found themselves had a neglected and shabby air. It smelt of wood smoke and food gone sour and countless brewings-up of strong brown tea. The furnishings, to Celia's eye, were pathetically meagre. How could he live here all alone, she wondered, this odd, aloof young man who, despite everything, despite the shotgun and the cold shoulder kept firmly in place, seemed hardly more than a boy in need of a mother?

Denton took off his cap and set his gun on the table — on the bare wood it looked uncannily like the severed, dried-out haunch of some spindle-legged animal — and went to the sink under the window and gave his fingers a quick rinse at the tap. Then he turned to his visitors, drying his hands on a tea towel.

"Was there something in particular you were after?" he asked.

A tiny muscle was twitching at one corner of his mouth, making him seem to be sardonically smiling, although Strafford knew it wasn't so.

"You heard a man was shot and killed last night, not far from here?" Celia said.

"Joey Harte, aye," Denton answered. "I heard," He was frowning, and looked off now into a shadowed corner of the room, as if something that only he could see were standing sentinel there. "What happened?"

"There were soldiers," Strafford said. "They challenged him, he didn't stop, they fired. He might have been drunk."

"Soldiers," Denton said quietly, and, for the first time since the three of them had entered the house, looked Strafford straight in the eye; the tic at the side of his mouth was beating faster. "I seen them," he said, "creeping around. What need is there of soldiers here?"

Strafford regarded him carefully, trying to penetrate that twitching mask of a face. It was impossible to know what he might be thinking. Perhaps he wasn't thinking anything. It seemed, at any rate, that the death of Joey Harte meant little to him.

Celia said: "There are threats the Hall will be attacked."

"Threats by who?"

"I don't know," Now it was Celia's turn to look away into the corner. "The duke mentioned it. There's probably nothing to it."

Strafford seemed to see a faint sardonic gleam come into Denton's eyes. The young man knew more than he was letting on. Could it be he knew a great deal more, after all?

"And that's why you're here, is it?" Denton asked.

"Us?" Celia raised her eyebrows.

"You two, and the squaddies we're not supposed to know about — you're all here to protect us, that right?"

280

Now he did smile, if it could be called a smile, and gave a faint little hiccup of laughter. "Tell that to Joey Harte."

Strafford put his hands into the pockets of his unbuttoned trench coat and looked about the room. He had begun to feel odd again, as if he were afloat an inch or two above the floor, swaying slightly in the empty air. The buzzing in his head was like the medleyed clamour of many far-off voices excitedly discussing him. His forehead was horribly hot.

"Lived here a long time, have you?" he asked.

Denton eyed him with his twitchy smile. "All my life," he said.

"Is this where your mother was shot?" Strafford made sure to keep his tone mild and polite; he might have been enquiring about the weather in these parts.

"That's right," Denton said. "In that doorway. Why?"

"Just curious." Strafford paused for no more than an instant. "You would have known Joey Harte, of course?"

"I knew him."

"Friend of yours?"

"Everybody knew him."

"Did he do much poaching on the estate? I mean" — he glanced at the shotgun on the table — "was he a serious annoyance? You'd know about these things."

"Would I?"

"The duke tells us you're sort of his unofficial steward here."

This last seemed genuinely to surprise the young man, and for a second something in his expression

281

altered. It seemed no one, least of all the duke, had ever bothered to hint to him that he might be a valued presence on the estate. Of course, if his position were never to be acknowledged, then he need be paid no more than a pittance, along with, say, a guarantee of a roof over his head. Strafford knew well the ways and wiles of his own people.

"Joey got a few rabbits now and then, sometimes a brace of pheasants," Denton said; his expression had gone blank again, and even the twitching at the side of his mouth had ceased. "I'd hardly say he was a serious nuisance. Not enough, at any rate" — he made a deliberate pause — "to merit shooting."

Strafford smiled agreeably. "So you didn't bother much with him."

"Nobody did. He was harmless."

"Yes, I'm sure. Very sad, what happened to him, all the same."

There was another silence, like a stone set down in a slow river. The three of them stood there, in the middle of the room, Strafford and Celia side by side and Denton facing them. Strafford drummed a tattoo with the fingertips of his left hand on the edge of the table.

"He had," Celia said, "a scrap of newspaper with him — Mr Harte, I mean — when he was shot. It was a photograph, torn out of a newspaper."

"A photograph of what?"

Strafford, annoyed, glanced sidelong at the young woman. He had planned to keep back the photograph until he judged just the right moment to mention it.

"It's of some people," Celia answered, "standing on a balcony."

The young man watched her steadily. "What sort of people?"

"Oh, just — people. A family. You know nothing about it, the photograph?"

"How would I? I haven't seen Joey since — I don't know when. Anyway, why would he be showing me snaps?"

Something had tightened in the atmosphere. Both Strafford and Celia at the same moment looked at the shotgun on the table. Denton seemed amused.

In the stove a burning log settled with a muffled bump.

"Well," Strafford said, slipping his hands into his coat pockets again, "we'll be off."

Denton nodded. "Right." He seemed not at all surprised by the abruptness of Strafford's announcement.

Strafford and Celia crossed to the door, and Strafford drew it open and the young woman stepped past him and out into the clearing. He stopped on the threshold, and turned back to Denton, who had not moved from where he stood by the table. A beam of thin sunlight from the window touched the stock of the shotgun, making the wood look like the bright, tawny surface of a trout stream.

Strafford eyed the worn lino on the floor at his feet. "Was it the regular army or the Black and Tans that shot your mother?"

Once again Denton showed no surprise. "Who says it was either?" he asked.

"Oh, pretty well everyone I've spoken to. Are they wrong?"

Denton looked to the window and the sunlight and the confusion of autumnal shades — pale gold, dark gold, dull green, a buttery yellow — beyond the glare of the glass.

"People round here say more than their prayers," he said. "You can't believe everything you hear."

Strafford nodded, and ducked out through the door. Celia Nashe, gone ahead, had stopped and turned back to look at him questioningly. He said nothing. They set off together up the slope, through the drifts of leaves. His brain felt swollen. Oh, he was not well, he was not well at all. He had a sudden picture of his mean little narrow bed beside the stone wall of the stable; it was, at that moment, an entrancing vision.

CHAPTER
TWENTY-EIGHT

The Boss Clancy put his head round the door of Redmond's to check who might be in ahead of him. It was early evening, just starting to get dark, and the sole customer was the widow Biddy Jenkins, sitting in a corner in her moth-eaten black coat and battered cloche hat. A glass of sweet sherry, not the first of the day and not to be the last, stood on a small circular table in front of her.

Redmond himself was perched awkwardly on a high chair behind the bar, dozing, his big pink head slumped against a framed mirror advertising Sweet Afton cigarettes in scrolled gilt lettering. The Boss consulted his wristwatch for the fourth or fifth time in as many minutes. A quarter of an hour and they'd be here. He judged they would be on time; they knew what discipline was, those fellows.

Biddy was looking at him fondly out of a tipsy eye. She was probably too far gone even to know who he was. He made a sign to her, putting a finger to his lips, and indicated the sleeping man behind the bar. Then he passed along the corridor as quietly as he could — his left shoe had a creak in the sole — and climbed the narrow stairs and let himself into his office.

He took off his overcoat. It was cold. He had sent one of the messenger boys from the shop on his bike to ask Redmond to ask his missus to get the fire going — the paraffin stove would make an awful smell — but either the publican had forgotten or the wife hadn't bothered; she was a disobliging bitch, was Sadie Redmond.

He hitched the knees of his trousers and hunkered down at the grate and threw in a few wadded balls of newspaper and a handful of sticks and struck a match. The smell of burning newsprint always reminded him of afternoons when he was a child, and he and his sister used to sit in front of the fire in the kitchen at the back of the house in Rose Street when their mother was out — as she was most of the time — the two of them smoking rolled-up tubes of paper torn from the *Irish Catholic*, pretending they were cigarettes. Strange to think of her, his sister, widowed already and working with the books in the County Hall.

He stacked three sods of turf in a tripod over the flames and stood up, brushing his hands. He checked his watch again, and just as he did so he heard a brief, low whistle outside. That was the agreed signal. He went to the window and drew back a corner of the curtain and peered down into the laneway.

They were there, two of them, standing side by side with their hands in their pockets, looking up at him.

He should have lighted his pipe. He always felt more in charge of things when he had a pipe going. But there wasn't time. Those two below weren't the kind to be kept waiting. He went down the stairs to the back door, and hesitated a second before drawing the bolt. He was nervous, he couldn't deny it.

They gave him no greeting, only stepped inside and waited for him to lead the way. One of them, middle-aged, medium height, wore a seaman's short black woollen coat with brass buttons and a knitted woollen hat pulled low down to the tips of his ears. He was the one in command, Clancy saw that straight away. The other one, younger, was compact and muscular, with broad shoulders and bowed legs. He wore a zipped-up short leather jacket with an elasticated waist, in the side pockets of which his hands rested lightly, his elbows jutting out at an angle; his stance, chin tucked in and feet well apart, gave him the look of a boxer. He was bare-headed, and bald.

They climbed the stairs, Clancy going ahead and the two following close on his heels. They made no effort to be quiet, and Clancy cast an anxious glance over the banister rail in the direction of the public bar. But what was he worrying about? What matter if the sound of the two of them clomping behind him up the stairs wakened Redmond? The publican was careful to keep his nose out of whatever business it was that went on in the upstairs room. As for Biddy Jenkins, if she heard the noise she would probably imagine it was the angels of the Lord coming to carry her away to Paradise.

On the turn at the top of the stairs, where a bare bulb cast a spectral glow across the landing, Clancy got a clearer look at his visitors. He was shocked to see the state of the older one's face. His features from midway up were unremarkable, but below that there was only a frozen mask of pitted, dead-white flesh. The right cheek was nerveless and deeply scarred, and the lips on that side were wrenched upwards in a sort of fixed and desperate grin — Clancy was reminded of a struggling fish being hauled up out of the sea with a hook embedded deep in its jaw.

The most shocking thing of all, though, was the man's nose, which was pared back so sharply at the sides that there seemed to be no flesh left at all, only a sharpened blade of cartilage pierced by two stark black holes that were his nostrils. What had happened to him, to cause such damage? Had he been in a fire, or waited a second too long before a bomb went off?

Oh, yes, they had seen action, these two, in particular the older one; they were renowned, among those in the know, for the things they had been through, for the things they had done.

Clancy opened the door to the office, and noticed how the two behind him instinctively held back for a second before stepping across the threshold. How would it be to live knowing that any room you walked into might have a squad of men with guns already there, waiting for you?

The one with the damaged face pulled off his woollen hat and looked around slowly, taking everything in: the table with Clancy's papers on it, the fire in the grate still struggling to take hold, the curtained window, the framed photograph on the wall of Pádraig Pearse, 1916 leader, patriot and martyr. It was a famous portrait, taken in profile to hide a bad squint, the uniformed hero's pert little face tilted at a proud angle.

"Will you have a pint or something?" Clancy said. "I can go down to the bar."

The older man said nothing, as if he had not heard, while the bald one in the leather jacket gave a short laugh, making the offer of a drink seem too absurd to be considered. A star of light from the sixty-watt bulb in the ceiling gleamed on his bald skull, the skin of which was taut and polished, like the rounded back of a boxing glove.

"I'm Jones," the older one said, in a heavy Belfast accent, "and he's Smith."

Clancy frowned. "But they told me —"

The man looked at him. "It don't matter what they told you. I'm telling you: I'm Jones, he's Smith. Have you got that?"

"Right. Right. I've got it."

Jones, so-called, unbuttoned his sailor's coat, and threw his cap on to the table and pulled out Clancy's chair and sat on it with his knees splayed. He wore what looked like army-issue olive-grey trousers, a ribbed polo-necked black pullover and heavy black boots with thick rubber soles. That ruined face with its little pale beak of a nose gave him uncannily the look of a bird; not a hawk, no, nor even a jackdaw, but something equally lethal and quick, with relentless, beady eyes. God help any scrap of furry, warm-blooded life he might chance on, Clancy thought.

Smith meanwhile made a sauntering tour of the room, looking around with smiling contempt, still with his hands hitched high in his pockets. He stopped in front of the portrait of Pearse and lifted the tip of his nose at the same angle as Pearse held his, humming a snatch of the national anthem under his breath.

It occurred to Clancy to wonder, for a terrifying moment, if he might have been betrayed, and these two weren't who they were supposed to be at all. He had only ever heard tell of the ones he had been waiting for, and had no idea what they were supposed to look like. This older one had the unmistakable air of a soldier about him, maybe of an officer, even. Had things gone wrong, had there been a leak? Had the Brits got wind of what was afoot and eliminated the two who were supposed to come down and sent this pair instead, to trap him, and take him off somewhere, over the Border, and put a bullet in his brain?

He told himself to stop panicking and calm down. Many a volunteer had been instructed to enlist with the British Army and lie low, for years in some cases, training as soldiers and learning tactics to be used later in the campaign against the very army they had been members of. That could be the case with these two.

"So, tell us," Jones said, leaning back on the chair, "is it them?"

Clancy felt frighteningly exposed, standing in the middle of the room with his arms hanging limp and not knowing what to do with his hands. It was as if he were the one who had just arrived, while this so-called Jones fellow sat at his ease in front of the table with the papers on it, looking like he belonged there. "We're fairly sure, yes."

Jones's eyes narrowed.

"'Fairly'?"

"No, we're sure, we're sure," Clancy said stumblingly. He swallowed, and when he spoke again his voice sounded breathless and weak. "We're sure."

He really wished he had got his pipe going before they arrived; now, somehow, it was too late. The bald one, Smith, would have great fun watching him as he fumbled with crumbly tobacco and matches that resisted striking, not to mention the little nickel-plated tamper that was every pipe-man's main tool — that would give the bastard a great laugh.

The fact was, the pipe didn't really suit him, no matter how hard he worked at getting used to it. The doctor had ordered him to lay off the smokes — he had a heart murmur, inherited from his father and his father's father — and so he had taken up the pipe instead. Now he depended on the bloody thing far more than he ever had on the cigarettes.

Part of the attraction of the pipe, of course, was that you never had to be idle, but could always pick it up and start fiddling with it — if you needed time to think, you could spend a full minute or more just getting it lit, while looking thoughtful and wise. All the same, he often had the suspicion that it made him look a bloody fool.

Jones reached into the pocket of his coat and brought out a packet of Gallaher's and lit one. "Right, then, you're sure it's them," he said. "That's good," He didn't sound as if he thought it was either good or otherwise. "So our journey south to your lovely Republic will not have been in vain — eh, Jimmy?"

Smith was still posing in front of the framed photograph, turning his head from side to side, trying to see his reflection in the glass.

"That's right, Jimmy," he said, putting a finger to the tip of his nose and pushing it up a fraction, to make it look like Pearse's.

Clancy looked from one to the other with a puzzled frown.

"Aye, we're both Jimmy," the one seated at the table said. "He's Jimmy Smith and I'm Jimmy Jones."

The one called Smith, turning from the photograph, laughed and shook his bald head. "What were the chances, eh?"

Clancy knew he was being mocked. He knew also that he was, by now, very much in fear of these two, the one with the bird-mask for a face, and the sinisterly jaunty welterweight with the smooth, polished skull. They were nothing like what he had expected. They had more the air of Chicago gangsters than soldiers of the rearguard dedicated to carrying on the fight for freedom, the fight that had been abandoned twenty years before by turncoats, pen-pushers and priests.

But then, he reflected, in an effort to calm his fears, they were from across the Border, where things were done differently. Hard men, up there. All the same, he hoped they wouldn't hang around for long. Get the job done, and off with them. Somehow, he didn't think it was going to be as simple as that; no, not as simple as that at all.

292

Christ, what had he got himself into?

Jones flicked ash from his cigarette on to the floor. "So tell us," he said, "what about this unfortunate poor fucker that got himself shot by the Free State warriors?"

"Joey Harte," Clancy said. "What about him?"

"That's right, what about him? It's what I'm asking you."

"He was no one. Ran a few errands around the place, that's all."

"'A few errands'!" Jones exclaimed, widening his eyes. He turned to Smith. "Will you listen to that! He has fellows to run errands for him." He looked at Clancy again, his crooked mouth twitching in the icy semblance of a smile. "So that's why you call yourself the Boss." He took a draw on his cigarette, which was no easy thing, given the mangled state of his mouth. Clancy ran the tip of his tongue along his lower lip; his own mouth had gone dry.

The fear, the real fear, he had to admit it, had seized hold of him the moment he opened the back door and saw the two of them standing outside in the lane.

He shouldn't have requested Head Office to send them down. What need had he of hard men from Belfast? Couldn't he have carried out the thing himself? He and the Squad could have gone up to the Hall one dark night and — and what? That was as far as he could see it, him and the Squad padding silently up the drive, wearing balaclava helmets they didn't possess — how could you come by a balaclava helmet? Ask someone to knit it for you? — and carrying imaginary guns. What

293

would happen when they got to the door? And where would de Valera and his men have been, and what doing, while he was laying siege to the place?

Twenty years ago, when he was a volunteer with the South Tipperary brigade, he had taken part in night-time raids on half a dozen Big Houses in the vicinity, and helped to burn down three or four of them. But that was then, and this was now, and besides, it was never him who got to set a light to the petrol that had been poured out from the can along the parquet hallways, under the family portraits. He wouldn't be thanked today if Clonmillis Hall were to go up in flames. Old Edenmore, unrepentant Unionist and West Brit though he was, employed a score and more of farm labourers, along with the household staff. The proprietor of Clancy & Co., Hardware and Timber Merchants, would know all about it if he was the one responsible for putting that lot on the dole.

No, the fact was becoming clearer by the second, and he had to face it: he shouldn't have started any of this in the first place.

So what if a couple of young ones were sent over here for safekeeping, even if they were the King of England's daughters, as he was sure they were? He could have turned a blind eye, could have kept his mouth shut and walked away, but no, oh, no, he couldn't resist the chance to show off to the town and play the big fellow. The thing had fallen into his lap, so neat, irresistible and easy, and what did he do but hand it over to Head Office in Belfast, so they'd have to give him his due and recognise at last his true value to the

294

Cause. And now look at him, presented with these two jokers.

Someone, he realised, was saying something to him.

"Hey, Bossman, wakey wakey."

"What?"

It was Jones, still seated at the table, still looking at him with his half-dead face and his mocking eyes. "I asked you a question."

"I'm sorry, I — I was just —"

Jones turned to Smith and shook his head in sad disgust. Then he turned back to Clancy and spoke in a loud voice, slowly, as if he were addressing a dim-witted child or an idiot.

"I said, how far is it from here to this place, this what-do-you-call-it Hall?"

"Not far. Ten miles."

"And you say there's soldiers guarding it?"

"Only a handful."

"What have they, in the way of arms?"

The Boss shrugged. "Rifles. An armoured car."

"And that's the lot? By Christ, they pulled out all the stops, didn't they? An armoured car, no less."

Jones looked at Smith and they both laughed. Smith had tired of trying to be funny in front of the photograph of Pearse, and had come to the table and was sitting on it now, sitting with his backside on Clancy's papers, in fact, and swinging his legs, his hands still in the pockets of his tough-guy's shiny leather jacket.

"I believe there's a tommy-gun of some sort mounted on the armoured car," Clancy said.

Smith took his hands out of his pockets and waggled his palms in the air in a parody of terror. "Ooh, I'm frightened, Sergeant Major!" he said, putting a quiver into his voice.

"A handful of squaddies, a few rifles and a rusty machine gun," Jones said, smiling and shaking his head. "Overpowering odds!" After each sentence spoken he had to lift a knuckle and wipe away the little blob of white stuff, like cuckoo-spit, that had gathered at the frozen, upturned corner of his mouth. Now he lobbed the butt of his cigarette into the fireplace and took another one from the packet and put a match to it. "Who's in command?" he asked. Clancy didn't understand. Jones clicked his tongue and looked towards the ceiling in mock despair. "Who's the commanding officer, you fucking dope?"

Clancy was about to tell him, but stopped himself. Wait a minute. The less he revealed, the less he could be charged with, if things went wrong and they got caught. And he had a feeling in the pit of his stomach that things were more likely to go wrong than otherwise.

"Don't know," he said. "They're not from round here. They were sent down special from Dublin — from Collins Barracks," he added, to make it sound more convincing, though in fact he didn't know where it was they had been dispatched from.

The one thing he wasn't going to tell this pair, if they didn't know it, as seemingly they didn't, was that the officer in charge of guarding the King's two daughters was Major Vivion de Valera, the taoiseach's son. There was such a thing as treason; he supposed it was a capital offence over here, the same as he knew it was in England. He had no intention of dying with an Irish hangman's rope around his neck and ending up in a quicklime grave somewhere out in the plains of Kildare.

"Right," Jones said briskly, rising to his feet. "Let's get on with it."

"What are you going to do?" Clancy asked, unable to mask his alarm.

Jones looked at him, lifting an eyebrow. "What do you mean, what are we going to do? We'll go out there with our tommy-guns and mow down the Free Staters guarding the place, then break into the house and slit the gizzards of anyone we lay our hands on, royalty or otherwise."

A moment of silence passed — Clancy's eyes seemed to start out of his head — and then Smith, still perched on the edge of the table, gave a whinny of laughter. "Look at him," he said, to the man standing by the chair. "I think he's after shitting himself." He regarded Clancy with disgust. "What the fuck is wrong with you? What do you think we came down here for? To call on Their Royal Highnesses and kiss their hands?"

"All right, let's go," Jones said brusquely. He turned to Clancy. "Get your coat. And stop your shaking — there'll be no gunplay, unless there has to be. We like a quiet life, don't we, Jimmy?"

Smith laughed.

They moved towards the door, then Jones stopped. "Oh, and listen," he said to Clancy. "There's a couple of milk churns in the boot. Get them filled with petrol, will you?"

"Petrol?" Clancy asked, with a hint of alarm, and for a second seemed to see, from twenty years ago, flames dancing along wooden floors in lofty hallways, and open front doorways rolling out clouds of smoke that smelt of the centuries.

Jones heaved an exaggeratedly weary sigh. "That's right, petrol. The stuff that makes cars go."

"You have a car?"

"Well, we didn't walk."

"Where is it?"

Clancy had a vision of a group of townsfolk gathered outside the pub, examining the unfamiliar vehicle with the deepest interest; there weren't many motor-cars in Clonmillis, and cars from elsewhere rarely stopped there.

"It's down in the lane, back along a wee way," Jones said. "And don't worry, it's a Free State job. We picked it up in Dundalk."

"You picked it up?"

"Well, we didn't fucking buy it, now did we? Or did you think we were going to drive in our own car down from Belfast, firing off shots in the air and singing 'A Nation Once Again'?"

Clancy took his overcoat and his hat from the stand in the corner. He put a hand to the outside of the right pocket, and felt the reassuring outline of his pipe. He wondered when he would next get a chance to smoke it.

298

CHAPTER
TWENTY-NINE

The girls, on Celia Nashe's orders, had been told nothing of the night's events, but early the previous morning Mary had been woken by the headlights of the Bentley coming round the side of the house, and a little while later she had heard people moving about downstairs, and the distant sound of voices.

She wasn't alarmed, only curious.

What could it be that had brought Mr Lascelles back, especially as he had seemed so glad to get away the first time? And why had Miss Nashe looked so peculiar all day, with little fans of wrinkles at the pinched corners of her mouth? And what was wrong with Strafford the detective, who was much paler than usual, though she wouldn't have thought that would be possible, and whose eyes were runny? At first she supposed he, too, might be in love and unhappy, but then she realised he just had a cold or flu or something.

What was up?

Nothing ever happened in this dump, and now suddenly something obviously had happened, and no one would tell her about it.

She speculated wildly as to what it might be. Maybe the Germans had invaded Ireland, and she and her sister would have to be moved on again. If that was the case, where would they end up this time? Someone had said, ages ago, that they might be sent to Canada — she hadn't been supposed to hear of it, but she had, for she was a practised listener at keyholes and outside bedroom doors, and on landings above alcoves where there were telephones on little tables and people speaking into them in low, secretive tones.

All she knew about Canada was that her father was recognised as the king there, as he was in so many places around the world, and that it snowed for most of the year, and that there were bears and wolves and lots of other kinds of wild animals. Also there was a town, or maybe it was a city, the name of which, Calgary, had stuck in her head, for some reason. She had looked it up in the *Encyclopaedia Britannica* in the library at Windsor, but she only remembered that it stood — why did people always speak of cities as standing? — at the meeting of two rivers, called the Bow and the Elbow. That had made her chuckle.

It would be just the way of things if that was where they were to be sent. *Dear Mummy and Daddy. We've just come back from a boating trip on the Bow, and tomorrow we shall be going up the Elbow.*

Now it was night again and she was in bed. She liked her own smell, under the blankets. It was a bit like the smell of custard, though she couldn't think why. Custard, and something biscuity as well. Washing facilities at the Hall were primitive, a circumstance she took full advantage of, and rarely bathed.

Maggie's eyes had been red-rimmed all day, and she had dragged herself around like a fat little pig with a sickness. Pike had told Mary there was a disease that pigs got, something to do with their skin, that was called "greasy pig". She had learned a lot about porkers since she had got to know Pike.

But why had Maggie been crying? Maybe somebody in her family had died. No, she didn't think that was it. The maid had the look that always came into Fred the footman's eyes whenever there was mention of Mopsy, otherwise the Duchess of Bristol, the lady-in-waiting Mary had caught him in bed with, that time, and who had fled to France. Was there someone Maggie had loved like that, like Fred, and who, like Mopsy, had been sent away — or who had died, even?

But why would there be such a fuss over something that had happened to someone who was special to one of the servants? Nobody cared what servants got up to, so long as they kept the results of their doings to themselves.

Oh, but wouldn't it be marvellous, if they were all, even the servants, all of them in love with the wrong people, the way it was said to happen on country-house weekends?

The question of love and its pains inevitably turned her thoughts to Billy Denton. She had done everything in her power to make him take notice of her, but he kept ignoring her — he seemed, in fact, hardly aware that she existed. She wished she had been the one who was thrown by a horse and carried back to the Hall in

Billy's arms. But, no, it had happened to her prissy sister, who didn't know how lucky she was.

She felt sad, suddenly. She would have to give up thinking about Billy Denton. She couldn't stop being in love with him, but she knew there was no hope of his loving her back. How could he, even if he wanted to? She was ten. She hated being ten. When she was twenty she would find a ten-year-old and be really nice to her, and take her out on excursions, and treat her as if she was a grown-up. It would be the least she could do, and it would compensate, even by a little bit, for having felt so fed up when she was young.

Billy must be sad too, sometimes at least, since his mother had been shot. But he had only been a baby when it happened, and he probably wouldn't even remember what she looked like. All the same, maybe a tragedy like that stayed with you all your life.

She wondered if tonight's Blitz would have started yet, at home. It didn't matter what her sister said, she knew very well that if a bomb fell on the Palace it would probably kill everyone inside, if the bomb was big enough. She used to think the Palace would withstand any kind of bombardment, but since coming here she had heard on the nightly news — she would come down from her bedroom and listen on the landing to the wireless set that stood on its trolley in the dining room — of factories and shipyard buildings that were every bit as big as the Palace being flattened and all the people working in them being killed.

She squeezed her eyes shut and tried to think about something else.

302

Billy Denton: yes. She would keep thinking about Billy, even if he didn't love her and never would.

She thought about his hair, and the way little curls of it fell over his forehead. It wasn't like the 'tec's hair — his was lank and floppy, especially at the front, where it was like a bird's broken wing. Though she had to admit he was handsome too, in his way. Or, no, not handsome, that wasn't the word — so what was the word? Nice-looking? That would have to do, though it sounded too soppy. And then he was so skinny! If he took you in his arms his pointy bones would stick into you, like the corners of coat-hangers.

That afternoon she had seen Billy Denton and Pike talking together about something and seeming very agitated. They were out by the piggery. Billy was angry-looking, and Pike kept jabbing him in the chest with a forefinger as blunt as a sausage.

Now she heard a sound nearby and stood motionless, listening. Cautious footsteps in the corridor, faint whispers, then a door opened and there were whispers, and then the door was quietly, oh, ever so quietly, closed again. She listened harder, straining into the dark. She thought of getting up and going out to see what there might be to see, but instead she waited, attentive as a cat. There was silence for a time, then what sounded like a muffled cry, though not a cry of pain.

Someone had gone with Miss Nashe into her room. Well, well.

It wasn't late. She sat up and looked at the illuminated face of her wristwatch: a quarter past ten,

303

and already beddy-byes time for someone — two someones, in fact. Well, well, well.

Her sister was asleep, lying on her side and facing the wall, which was how she always slept. Mary slipped out of bed and crept across the room, the chilly nap of the carpet tickling her toes. At the door she stopped and turned and stood sentinel for a moment, watching her sister's form in the bed; it did not stir.

She opened the door. There had been a squeak in one of the hinges but she had smuggled a pat of butter from the breakfast table in her hankie and smeared some of it on that hinge; she needed to be able to come and go without being heard.

She put her ear to the door of Celia Nashe's room. Not a sound. Who could it be in there with her? Surely not — oh, no! — surely not Billy Denton. The possibility of it came to her with a jolt, like an electric shock. Mary had seen the way Miss Nashe had looked at Billy the day when he fired off the shotgun behind her in the wood, and it wasn't only fright that had made her cheeks go pink, that was clear. If it was him, in there with her, she would never forgive him — never. And as for Miss Nasty —

She turned back and moved a little way along the corridor. A faint glow came from a ceiling lamp burning at the bottom of the stairs. She stopped, and knelt on one knee and, with the greatest care, so as not to make a sound, lifted free a length of the skirting board and reached in behind it and brought out a bundle wrapped in one of her vests. Then she hurried back into the room and shut the door and climbed into bed again, and unwrapped the bundle, stuffing the vest under her pillow.

She slipped Miss Nashe's pistol from its holster, which she pushed down into hiding under the mattress, and lay down, cradling the weapon against her tummy. The metal struck cold even through her pyjamas, but it would soon warm up.

Oh, of course she knew she shouldn't have kept the gun — she had pretended to her sister, after showing it to her, that she had put it back in the drawer under Miss Nashe's things, while in fact she had hidden it in the space behind the skirting board.

She had discovered the hiding-place one day when Miss Nashe had sent her to her room for deliberately knocking a jug of water over a watercolour picture her sister was painting. Passing along the corridor, she had kicked the skirting board in fury, and it had fallen open, just like something in one of those books her sister read, by Robert Louis Stevenson, or that other writer, whose name she had forgotten, who wrote about that stupid boarding school for girls in the Swiss Alps.

She kept a number of her treasures in this space in the wall, in the dark among the cobwebs and the mortar dust. There was a spent shell casing from Billy Denton's shotgun, and a ten-shilling note that had fallen out of the duke's jacket pocket by accident in the dining room after dinner one night, and a so-far-unopened packet of five Wild Woodbine cigarettes that Pike had exchanged for a Swan fountain pen she had filched from her sister — but the gun, of course, was the pride of her collection.

What would happen when Miss Nashe looked in her drawer, as she was bound to do sooner or later, and found that the pistol was missing? The look on her face would be something to see.

Why were knickers also called drawers? It struck her as especially odd since they were kept in drawers. Some things just made no sense.

She was on the very brink of sleep when she began to hear it, a faint, repeated sound from somewhere outside the room but not far away. At first she didn't recognise it, although she knew she had heard it before. It was a soft, rhythmic thumping, as if someone were beating the dust out of a rug with a carpet-beater.

She sat up, wide awake now. The thumping sound was getting faster, and there were more stifled cries, too. She got out of bed, and stood a moment on tiptoe: from her sister's steady breathing she knew she was sleeping deeply. Good.

After padding to the door she eased it open, and crept along the corridor to Celia Nashe's room. Yes, this was where the sounds were coming from. She put her ear to the door. What was going on? Were people fighting in there, hitting each other with their fists? Then suddenly she remembered. It wasn't a fight at all — oh, no. The sounds were just like the ones she had heard that afternoon when she listened outside the bedroom at the Palace before pushing open the door and discovering the naked duchess and Fred the footman in bed together.

All at once the thumping stopped. Had she been heard? She was sure she hadn't made a sound. She stepped back, ready to bolt, but too late. The door was wrenched open, and Celia Nashe was suddenly there. She was wearing a slip and, as the lamplight behind her revealed, nothing else.

"You!" she said, in a furious, hoarse whisper. "You little — ! What are you doing here?"

Mary turned and ran, but not before she had glimpsed, in the room behind Miss Nashe, by the light of the bedside lamp, Mr Lascelles with his back to her, half sitting up in bed, peering at her over his shoulder with a shocked look, the sheet falling away from the top half of his naked torso.

CHAPTER
THIRTY

On his return from viewing Joey Harte's corpse, Strafford had gone to the main house and cajoled Mrs O'Hanlon into having the boiler stoked so that he might take a bath — the water when he stepped into it was almost hot — and had spent the rest of the afternoon in bed, burning up with fever. Spasmodic shivers swarmed across his back, and there were times when he couldn't keep his teeth from chattering. He had piled every cover he could find on to the bed, including his coat and his jacket, and a tablecloth, and even a rug from the floor, but still he couldn't get warm.

At intervals he drifted off into something that was neither sleep nor waking, but a nightmarish zone between the two in which he was subjected to lurid, violent dreams. In one of these, particularly memorable, Mrs O'Hanlon, wearing an enormous pair of lederhosen and wielding an alpenstock, galloped wildly through the house on the back of a cow, a grotesque, mad maenad. He had a continuous thirst, and would drag himself out to the kitchen and drink mugfuls of water from the tap there, standing with the floor rug wrapped around his shoulders and gazing out of the window at that infuriatingly anonymous and ever-present blue hill in the far distance.

The afternoon waned, the light turned grey, and then it was dusk. With the darkness his fever worsened, then suddenly began to abate. He got up again, and tried to make tea at the stove, but lost heart and contented himself with another mugful of slightly brackish water from the tap. He crawled back under the covers, and at last sleep came, real sleep, drawing him away into blissful oblivion.

It was so light a tap upon the door that he was surprised it had wakened him. He lay for some moments with his eyes closed; the lids were hot and felt as if they had been boiled. There was another knock. He got up from the metal bed, which groaned protestingly, and crept rather than walked out to the living room, again with the smelly old floor rug, the warmest covering he had, draped over his shoulders.

He opened the rickety door, his front door, and felt on his burning cheeks the damp breath of the darkness outside.

For a moment he didn't recognise the little plump young woman standing in the doorway, wearing a man's old raincoat and a faded blue headscarf. "Since you didn't come to dinner, sir, I brought you this," she said.

It was Maggie the maid. She was carrying a tray covered with a cloth.

"What is it?" he asked, blinking.

"A bit of dinner, sir. It's nearly gone cold, but you should eat it anyway. I could see earlier that you weren't well."

He bade her come in, and stood back to let her pass. He noted her red-rimmed eyes, swollen from weeping, so it seemed. She set down the tray on a spindle-legged card-table under the window. "Thank you, Maggie," he said. "It was kind of you to think of me."

She was looking at the floor rug draped over his shoulders, the legs of his pyjamas, his bare feet. "What is it that ails you, sir?"

"Nothing — just a fever. I think I've caught the flu."

"Oh, and I woke you up!"

"No, no, don't worry. I was worse earlier."

"The dinner will do you good."

"I'm sure it will, Maggie, I'm sure it will." He stood gazing at her helplessly, his brain aswirl with a kind of hot fog. "And you, are you all right?"

"I'm grand."

He was about to ask why she had been crying, but then thought he knew the reason.

She drew back the cloth from the tray, revealing a thick white plate piled with boiled potatoes, beige strips of what he guessed must be parsnip, and three layered slices of thickly cut corned beef. "There now," she said, and sniffed, and stood back, wiping her nose on a knuckle.

He sat down on the straight-backed chair. The smell of the food assailed him, making his stomach heave. And yet he was hungry. He would wait a little, and then make himself eat; perhaps he'd be able to manage some of the potatoes.

"It's late," he said vaguely, but Maggie made no move to go.

"I wanted to ask you, sir," she said softly, "what happened to Joey Harte?"

"Was he — was he something to you?" he asked, not knowing how else to frame the question, to which, anyway, he was sure he knew the answer.

"I used to — I used to see him, like," she said, and drew a fluttery breath that at the end turned into a small, dry sob. "That's to say, we were in the way of being engaged to marry. Not that anyone knew, save him and me." She paused. "What happened to him, that he got shot?"

Strafford was finding it hard to concentrate, despite the significance of all that the poor creature was asking of him. How account for Harte's senseless death?

"He was in the wood, where he shouldn't have been. A challenge was issued, and he tried to run away."

"But why would they shoot him?"

"It was a mistake. Sentries get nervous and do the wrong thing."

From far off came the plaintive lowing of what sounded like a cow in labour. Immediately Strafford saw in his mind's eye, the lamp-lit byre, the heaped straw, the farmer on one knee, and the cow's eye flashing in fear and pain, and for a moment he was comforted by the archaic homeliness of the pictured scene.

"You should eat your dinner, sir," the maid said. "Any warmth left will be gone out of it."

"I'm sorry," he said.

Maggie nodded, standing before him in her headscarf and the old grey coat — Strafford wondered if it might have belonged to Joey Harte — with her hands clasped before her and her gaze lowered. She might have been a figure out of Millais; he felt a pang of pity. And yet he wished she would go.

"He had something with him," he said, "a photograph, torn from a newspaper. Do you know anything about that?"

"And how would I?" she said, suddenly defensive.

"He might have shown it to you. He might have — he might have asked you about it. About the people in it, in the photograph."

She raised her eyes and looked at him, her mouth drawn tight. After a moment she said: "He wouldn't need to ask me about them. He'd have known, himself."

"What would he have known, Maggie?" Strafford asked gently, looking up at her and trying to smile.

"Who they were."

Her face was still closed against him. Something had come into her look, something cold, vindictive, knowing. It was almost, for a moment, as if she hated him, or hated, at least, all that he represented, the hard, imperious, unforgiving world and those who were in charge of it.

"I'll go now, sir," she said, pulling the coat close around herself and turning away. "Eat your dinner. You'll be the better for it."

312

"Maggie." She stopped, with her back to him, her head lowered. "Does everyone know?"

"Does everyone know what?"

"Who the people are, the people in the photograph. Who the two girls are, whose heads someone drew circles around, with a pencil."

When she spoke, her voice was so low he could hardly catch the words. "There's a fellow in the town, name of Clancy. He has the hardware store, the big one. You might want to talk to him."

"Did Joey know him?"

"As I say, sir, you might want to talk to him, to Mr Clancy." She went to the door, drew it open. "And you'd want to warn them soldiers, too, to keep a sharp eye out." He began to rise from the chair. "Sit down, sir," she said, in a weary, worn-out voice. "Sit down, and have your dinner. It'll be gone stone cold."

He had pushed the plate aside and was on his feet now, with the rug over his shoulders, and was making for the field telephone.

From within the open doorway, Maggie said, "He wasn't much, poor Joey, but he was mine."

But Strafford was cranking the handle of the telephone, and didn't hear her.

CHAPTER
THIRTY-ONE

Clancy by now had given up all pretence that it had been anything but folly to call in that pair from Belfast. He was frightened and close to panic. As soon as Jones and Smith, so-called, had marched behind him into the upstairs room above Redmond's pub, his whole life had begun to fall asunder in front of his eyes. All that stuff about commanding a squad and itching for the next round of the revolution — had it ever been anything but a way of spicing up his life and looking important, to himself and to the town?

Why couldn't he have been content with running Clancy & Co., one of the foremost business concerns in the county, and being recognised as a mainstay of commerce and employment for the entire area? Oh, no: he'd had to get involved in the Cause, and brag about driving the Brits into the sea and liberating our people in the North and turning Ireland into a sovereign thirty-two-county state — a nation once again!

And, anyway, who were "the Brits"? A ragbag of Scots-Irish Protestant settlers crowded together up there behind the borders of their precious six counties, marching up and down waving Union Jacks, and banging their Lambeg drums and tootling on their penny whistles and bellowing about King and Country, when everybody knew, including themselves, in their hearts, that neither the country nor the King they pledged their loyalty to cared a hoot for them or their glorious inheritance.

Yes, he should have minded his own business and said to Hell with the lot of them. He should have married, settled down, had a couple of sons to carry on the business after he was gone. As it was, what would he leave behind him? A shop, a house, a car, and a widowed sister, who worked in a library and had hardly a civil word to throw his way just because he knew nothing about books. He didn't even keep a dog that would greet him when he came home from work of an evening. And now here were these two, come down from Belfast to maybe get him killed.

They weren't as bright as they thought they were, Soldier Jones and Boxer Smith. Had they seriously expected it would be possible to transport two milk churns full of petrol in the boot of a Ford car, with worn-out shock absorbers, that they'd pinched that afternoon from outside a barber's shop in Dundalk?

It had taken him a good five minutes to explain to them that, first of all, there wouldn't be room enough in the bloody car to stand the churns upright, and even if there was, the fuel would spill, from being sloshed around, since the lids couldn't be sealed tight enough to be petrol-proof; and furthermore, if metal knocked against metal and made a spark, the petrol would catch and the car would be blown sky-high and the three of them along with it.

In the end he had made them dump the churns and drive round to the rear of Clancy & Co. and park behind the loading bay and keep quiet and not let themselves be seen. He unlocked the garage where the delivery van was kept and got three five-gallon cans with screw-on lids and filled them with Esso from the pump in the corner of the yard. Then they had gone back to Redmond's and passed the rest of the evening in the upstairs office playing cards and smoking cigarettes. He hadn't dared light his pipe, knowing he'd be laughed at, and instead went down to the bar and bought a packet of twenty Player's Navy Cut, and by the end of that long night he knew the pipe was a thing of the past and that he was back on the fags. To Hell with the doctors — he didn't care.

In the early hours of the morning, they were out on the Clonmillis road again, with the lights dimmed, heading off to make mayhem.

He must have been mad, he told himself, to get into this thing. Under his suit jacket the armpits of his shirt were soaked with sweat.

He had tried first to get into the back seat but Jones had ordered him into the front. Behind him now, bald-headed Smith sat creaking in his leather jacket and whistling faintly through his teeth. His presence made the hairs stand up on the back of Clancy's neck where it bulged over his shirt collar.

It almost made him laugh to think that he was off on a mission at last — the kind of thing that for years he had dreamed about engaging in — dressed in a shirt and tie, a blue suit and a camel-hair overcoat, and a

316

pair of slip-on shoes with buckles on the insteps. Oh, yes: a warrior arrayed for the battle.

"So tell me," he said, clearing his throat with an effort, "what's the plan?"

"The plan?" Jones said, and jiggled his fingers on the rim of the steering wheel, drumming out a martial rhythm. "What makes you think we have a plan? We're just taking a bit of a sightseeing drive out into the country."

Aye, in the pitch dark of night, Clancy thought. "Strictly speaking," he said, his voice gone thick, "I'm the one in charge of this operation."

"Hear that, Jimmy?" Jones said over his shoulder. "The commandant here thinks he has a right to know our intentions."

Smith leaned forward until his mouth was at Clancy's ear. "You've fuck-all right to know anything, Comrade," he said, "so keep your fucking mouth shut and concentrate on not getting us lost."

Smith sat back, and they drove on in silence for a mile or so. There was a strong smell of petrol from the jerry cans in the boot. When they'd set out on the road, Jones had started to light a cigarette, until Clancy pointed out that the car they were driving in was to all intents and purposes a primed explosive device. Jones had given him a nasty stare, but put away his lighter, all the same.

"I'll have to know what you have in mind," Clancy said doggedly. "Otherwise let me out here on the road, and continue on your own."

317

Jones sighed, like a father compelled to deal with a demanding child.

"First, we're going to get a bit of a fire going, to divert the Free Staters, and while they're busy, standing around scratching their heads and wondering who lit the bonfire, we'll have a look in the house and see what's what."

"Are you going to take them, the two children?"

"If they're who you say they are, then it'd be a pity not to, wouldn't it?"

"What will you do with them, really?" Clancy asked, in a faint voice.

"There's a wee cottage up north, in Donegal, hidden away at the bottom of a glen, that'll be just the place for them, while we negotiate terms for their safe return to the bosom of their family."

It was a reasonable plan, Clancy had to concede, but Jones had spoken in such a playful tone that Clancy didn't know whether to believe him or not.

"How will you get them there?" he asked, licking his parched lips. "Not in this jalopy, surely."

"Oh, no." Jones had slowed and put the headlights on to full, and now he peered into the trees at the side of the road. "Would you say this would be the place to start up the conflagration?"

"I have to tell you something," Clancy said, with a breathless sensation, as if he were about to fall headlong from a high place.

Jones, struck by the tone in which Clancy had spoken, steered the car to the side of the road and

318

stopped, and turned in his seat to look at him. "Oh, yes?" he said softly.

Clancy licked his lips again.

"It's de Valera's son who's in charge of the soldiers."

For a moment no one spoke. The engine was still running; one of the spark plugs was misfiring, Clancy noted. Amazing the things that came into your head at times like this. Although when had he ever before known a time that was anything like this?

"What are you saying?" Jones asked quietly. Clancy could feel Smith move close up behind him, until he was practically breathing into his ear. Jones spoke again. "You mean young Dev — what's his name, Marion?"

"Vivion," Clancy said.

Jones leaned back in his seat. "Are you telling me that the long streak of misery who runs the show down here sent his own son to guard the children of the British King?"

Clancy nodded. Pledge or not, he could have done with a glass of something fortifying, at this moment.

"Fucking hell," Smith whispered.

The idling engine made a syncopated rattling.

"Well, then," Jones said, "we'll have not only a brace of turkeys for the coming Christmas, but Rudolph the Red-nosed Reindeer as well." He opened the door beside him and began to get out of the car. "Let's get these fucking Yule-logs blazing."

One of the duties Major de Valera had taken upon himself was the monitoring of traffic passing by the camouflaged sentry box beside the Clonmillis road. There was a gateway in the dry-stone wall a little way along that was wide enough for the armoured car to squeeze through; it could then descend a short bit of lane and park in a hollow there among the trees, where it couldn't be seen from the road. Satisfied that his post was sufficiently well camouflaged, and the armoured car out of sight from the road, he retired to the sentry box and settled down to his watchman's duty.

He was well aware that the records he kept — he wrote down, in a sixpenny school jotter, with an indelible pencil, the licence number of every vehicle that went past — could not be considered in any way comprehensive. After all, he could only be at the sentry box for a certain number of hours of the day or the night, and for the rest of the time no tally was kept. When he wasn't here, a flying squad of IRA gunmen — or a file of German tanks, for that matter — could have rolled past without anyone being the wiser.

He could have set up a rota system to ensure the road was watched on a twenty-four-hour basis, but he didn't trust any of his men to give their full attention to the task, or even to stay awake. The truth was that the detachment assigned to him, a dozen strong, could hardly be described as a crack squad.

For one thing, all of them, apart from Sergeant Brody, were Dubliners, and knew nothing about conditions in the countryside; some of them, he suspected, were afraid to be by themselves in the wood, especially after nightfall. True, the sergeant was dependable, but he was slow, and slowness was, in the major's view, the worst trait in a soldier. In the early days of the operation he had tested their alertness on a couple of occasions when they were on sentry duty. He had blacked up his face — he'd had to use boot polish, which was the devil to get off afterwards — and wreathed his helmet with strands of ivy, and crept up on them on his belly through the undergrowth, to test if they were on the alert and not dreaming about their girlfriends back in the city.

The initiative had not proved a success. None of the sentries had seen or even heard him before he got close enough to them so that, had he been the enemy, he could have risen up behind them and slit their throats with the greatest ease. Afterwards he had gathered them together and made them stand to attention, if that was what to call it — they really were a slovenly bunch — while he paced up and down before them and delivered a scathing dressing-down. He could see they weren't bothered much, for all his severity.

All this was worrying, and made the burden of duty weigh all the more heavily on his shoulders. As it was, his father had scant regard for him as a soldier; if he were to fail here, if intruders got into the Hall and the people staying there were harmed, he would never be allowed to live it down.

He knew very well that he wasn't cut out to be a soldier, not really. His father knew it too, but that didn't prevent the father from expecting nothing but the highest performance from his son, wherever he was deployed, and in whatever duty he was assigned to.

How would it be if the son of the taoiseach of the day, who had also been one of the foremost leaders of the Rising, were to bungle something as simple as a stint of guard duty?

Thank God he had only three more days to get through, before a fresh detachment would arrive and he would be allowed to return to barracks at the Curragh Camp, where his duties — mainly guarding IRA internees — would be comparatively light and, most happily of all, someone else would be in overall command.

There wasn't really room enough for two in the sentry box. The private on duty tonight was a stout, ruddy-faced fellow smelling of Brylcreem and sour socks. It was bad enough to be squeezed into this confined space — not much larger, it struck him, than an upright coffin — with one of the thinner of his men, but with this fat one pressed against him it was almost suffocating. Every ten minutes or so the fellow would ask permission to nip out into the wood for a smoke. These brief intervals afforded the major a welcome relief, and he was able to stretch his legs and flex his stiffened arms. However, when the soldier returned, he filled the confined space with the stench of tobacco.

It was strange, to be in uniform and on sentry-go, with the country at peace and war being waged across on the continent. It gave him the sense, though he tried to suppress it, of taking part, in a minor role, in one of those French or Viennese operettas his mother used to take him to at the Theatre Royal or the Antient Concert Rooms. He had never seen action in the field, and probably never would, unless the Germans defeated Britain and crossed the Irish Sea.

But would there be fighting, even in that eventuality? It was said, by the would-be wits, that the question the Irish had to keep asking themselves was, Who is it we're neutral against?

For his part, he rather admired Germany. He had no time for Hitler, that hysterical, noisy little martinet, but the German people themselves were a fine, clean-limbed race. Foolish of the British not to have come to an accommodation with them. An Anglo-German Europe would be a great world power and an unbreachable buffer between an overweening United States and Stalin's godless Russia.

He had attempted to talk to his father about these things, but his father had shown no interest in his opinions. Well, his father was the leader of the country, and had many grave matters to deal with. The fact was, he didn't talk much to anyone other than those whom he considered his peers. And he never spoke about his own days as a combatant and leader in three successive and bitter campaigns: the Rising, the War of Independence, and the Civil War. The major often dwelt wistfully on all the things his father could tell him about those times.

It was not easy to be the son of a great man, to have a father who considered himself the Father of the Country.

Nothing had passed by for ten minutes or more, but now he heard a vehicle approaching, and lifted his binoculars and applied them to the eye-level slit cut into the door of the sentry box. He could hear his companion-in-arms — his companion-in-arms! — breathing behind him; it was most distracting.

The vehicle was a civilian motor-car, an old, bull-nosed Morris Oxford, licence number ZF 574. He recognised it, for he had seen it twice before, the first time earlier that evening, then again about twenty minutes ago. There were two men in the front, and possibly a third in the back, though the latter might have been only a shadow. Odd: it was going in the same direction as last time. Which must mean it had driven all the way around the estate and come back again. Why? And was he imagining it, or did it slow down as it passed the spot where he was in hiding? They couldn't have identified the sentry box for what it was, could they, not in the dark, surely?

But what if someone, that shadowy figure in the back seat, perhaps, already knew the position of the hiding place, and was pointing it out, a second time, to the two men in the front? That would account for the car slowing down. They could have been having a closer look to see if the sentry box was occupied.

Could a secret be kept, any kind of secret, in a place like this? Already the town was in an uproar over the shooting of this fellow Harte. What if it was known whose son was in command of the guard detail? There were many people in this country who still loathed his father, the people who kept their guns from the old days buried in oilskins in their back gardens or under the thatched roofs of their houses.

The twin rubies of the car's rear lights were dwindling along the road.

He must not let his imagination run away with him.

But what if — ? Ambushes used to be commonplace, when the old wars were on. Some said his father had given the direct order to the sniper who, in 1922, during the Civil War, from his lookout place on a hill above Beal na Blath in County Cork, had shot Michael Collins, his father's sometime friend turned enemy. Many there were who still itched to avenge that murder.

The major put away his binoculars and settled down for another wait. ZF 574 did not appear again. An hour passed. The soldier behind him sighed frequently. When he asked to be allowed out to smoke another cigarette the major refused.

Then Sergeant Brody arrived with a dispatch from the house. The major stepped out of the sentry box to meet him.

"Yes, Sergeant, what is it?"

"The detective, sir, Stafford —"

"Strafford."

The sergeant frowned. "Sir?"

"His name is Strafford, with an *r*. But never mind, carry on — what about him?"

"He phoned up, sir. He said to tell you it's known who the girls are."

"Yes — and?"

"That's all, sir. 'It's known who the girls are,' was what he said. And that we're to keep a sharp watch out."

325

The major snorted. "What does the fellow think we're doing here, if not keeping a sharp watch out?" He smacked a fist into a palm, then remembered who and where he was. "All right, Sergeant. Carry on."

Sergeant Brody saluted, in his infuriatingly sloppy fashion, and blundered off through the trees.

"Keep a watch out, indeed," the major muttered. He turned back to the sentry box, and stopped. *Father*, he thought, permitting himself a moment of unresisted, heartfelt misery, *Father, oh, Father, that this chalice might pass from me!*

He couldn't have said exactly how long a time had passed, except that it had to have been some hours, before he clambered once more out of the coffin-like shelter, to take a deep breath of the night's damp air in which he could savour the absence of his fellow watcher's meaty odour and tobacco breath, and saw the redness in the sky far off above the trees.

CHAPTER
THIRTY-TWO

Celia Nashe was furious with herself, and frightened. How could she have been such a fool as to allow Richard Lascelles into her room on this of all nights, after a day in which a man had been shot, and word had come that her two charges were under serious threat? And who was it who had seen Lascelles in her bed but one of the very pair whom she had been set to protect! She could lose her job — she could lose everything. The child would tell. Not tonight, maybe, and not tomorrow, either, but at some point, when it suited her.

Could she be bribed? It was a shocking thought, and Celia was shocked at herself for thinking it. What would the child be likely to want — what would she accept? What could one offer a daughter of the House of Windsor in return for her silence?

Celia sat down on the side of the bed — Lascelles had fled the room, of course, half dressed and mumbling excuses — and bowed her head and pressed her fingers to her eyelids as hard as she could bear.

Fool! Fool!

Strafford had eaten no more than half a potato when weariness overcame him again and, hardly aware of what he was doing, he slumped forward slowly, until his head was resting on the table beside the plate, and fell fast asleep.

A long time later he woke with a grunt of alarm, not knowing where he was or what had happened to him. His nether lip was stuck with dried saliva to the table top. The fever had abated a little, and now he was chilled to the bone. What had woken him was the rug slipping from his shoulders and dropping on to the floor behind his chair; it was as if he had shed his own pelt, in one slithering go.

He rose and made his way to the outhouse where, still shivering, he dropped to his knees in front of the lavatory bowl and was sick into it. What came up was the remains of the potato he had eaten, drawing behind it a quivering string of bilious slime. After that he felt somewhat better, though he was still cold.

In the bedroom, buttoning himself hurriedly into his clothes with trembling fingers, he looked up to the window and saw a corona-shaped glow the colour of red-hot iron above the far trees. It was not the light of dawn, but a fire, a fire in the wood.

He must call, he must issue an alert. Turning the handle at the side of the phone made him think of old Kate the maid, in the kitchen at Roslea, preparing a chicken for the pot and twisting off a leg, the sinews as they severed making just the same grinding sound.

The bell at the other end, way off across the fields, rang and rang. He stood by the table, waiting, his eye fixed on the plate of uneaten food beside the phone. Where were de Valera and his hapless band of warriors? Even if they were on patrol, someone should have been left at the camouflaged covert where the field telephone was housed.

Strange, but what was to stay with him from that moment was not the impatient sound of the unanswered telephone bell, or the raspy feel of the high collar of his sweater against the tender skin of his throat, or even the hollow, panicky sensation in his breast. No, what he carried away with him most vividly was the look of the suggestively sinister, whitish glaze of congealed fat on the slices of corned beef on the plate, and the strips of parsnip, four of them, neatly arrayed, like four pulpy fingers severed at the knuckle.

The bell went on ringing. Then he understood: like him, the major and his men had seen the trees on fire, and had rushed off, all of them, to investigate. He was, for now, on his own.

The rest of it happened in what seemed to him one extended and uninterrupted fever-driven dash.

He sprinted across the stable yard, passing by Lascelles's car, and burst into the house by the back door. Maggie was in the kitchen, putting on a kettle to boil, and turned to him in fright. She must have gone to bed after she had left him, and now had got up again, well before first light, to start on the day's chores.

"What's happened?" she asked in fright. "What's wrong?"

"There's a fire in the wood."

"What?"

"A fire."

She stood there with the lid of the kettle in her hand and her tiny mouth open in the shape of a perfect O. He pushed past her and took the stairs three at a time — where did he get the strength, sick as he was? — and almost collided at the top with Mrs O'Hanlon. She, too, was shocked, not so much by seeing him as by him seeing her, for she was in her nightgown, with her hair in curlers.

"Where's the duke?" he demanded.

"The duke?" the woman repeated. "Why, he'll still be in bed, at this hour."

He silenced her with a gesture. "Listen to me. Go to him. Tell him I'm taking the girls away. After that, he's to lock the house, close the shutters — seal the place, as best he can."

"But —?"

"Do as I say."

She took a step backwards, wide-eyed: she had never seen him like this — half mad, it seemed, with bloodshot, starting eyes, and face as white as a bedsheet.

He dodged past her and ran on, the flaps of his trench coat flying behind him.

Outside Celia Nashe's room he paused to catch his breath. His throat was parched, his forehead throbbed. When the young woman came to the door, a silk wrap

330

pulled tight around her, he saw at once that she had expected not him but someone else. Lascelles, he thought. Lascelles, of course. She was about to speak, but he held up a hand and cut her off.

"We've got to get them away," he said, and stood breathing. Her eyes went blank; she didn't know what he was talking about. "The children," he said, "the girls, we have to move them. Men will be coming. They've set fire to the wood."

"What men?"

"I don't know. IRA, I suppose. I don't know."

He turned from her before she could say more, and ran to the girls' bedroom.

Mary, standing by the window, said, "The wood is on fire."

"Yes. I know."

Ellen, in bed, sat up quickly. She had been asleep. The night-light cast an unearthly glow, as if the room were filled with a delicate, pale-blue mist.

Celia Nashe appeared in the doorway, in her corduroy trousers and woollen sweater. She had tied back her hair, which gave to her face a naked look.

"Did you take it?" She'd fixed on Strafford. He was urging the girls to hurry and get dressed. She strode forward and grasped him by the shoulder. "Did you take the gun?"

"I don't know what you're talking about," he said, speaking past her, and hurried out of the room. A moment later he was back. Ellen, stepping into her slip, hopped back under the bedclothes to shield herself from his eyes. He spoke to Celia Nashe. "Which is Lascelles's room?"

They stood in the hallway, Strafford and Celia Nashe and the girls, waiting for Lascelles to bring the car round from the stable yard. The girls wore their coats and hats, and looked incongruously prim and formal, with the handles of their pink leather handbags over their wrists. Ellen was very pale.

Mary turned on Celia Nashe. "I told you," she said, in a thin, hard voice. "I warned you."

Celia frowned. "What did you warn me about?"

"I told you about the sky being on fire."

"But that was a dream," Celia said, almost plaintively. "How could you have known?"

"I just did, that's all."

Lascelles came in at the front door, and at the same moment the duke, in dressing-gown and slippers, appeared on the upper landing. He looked dazed and old and tired. Strafford went to the foot of the stairs. "Have you a gun?" he asked. The old man, uncomprehending, goggled at him. "A gun," Strafford said again, more loudly. "Is there one in the house? A shotgun, a service revolver, anything?"

Lascelles rattled the car keys. "Come on," he said curtly, "there's no time to go searching for blunderbusses."

They went down the front steps in a flurry and got into the car, Celia in the back with the girls, and Strafford in the passenger seat. Doors slammed, the engine gave a deep-throated roar, the rear wheels threw up twin sprays of gravel.

The duke had descended the stairs and stood now in the lighted front doorway, lost and afraid. He was thinking of the war, of whizz-bangs and wire, of gas, and dead men. As the car drew away, Strafford saw Mrs O'Hanlon come up behind the old man and put a hand on his shoulder. He hoped she would remember what he had told her, about sealing the house. Not that it mattered. If whoever was coming wanted to get in, a locked door and a bolted shutter would not bar the way.

He told himself he should have gone back to his quarters and tried the field telephone again. De Valera and his men might by now have realised that the burning wood was a diversion.

Lascelles was in a fury. What the hell was going on? he demanded. Strafford gave no reply. The Englishman, he knew, would be lining up the scapegoats in his mind.

The car sprang forward. Cartwheels of stars spun crazily behind the stark black branches of the trees on either side of the road.

Strafford sat hunched in the seat with his eyes closed, swaying from side to side with the movement of the speeding car. He thought it possible he would pass out. The pounding in his head was very loud, and he could feel the blood swarming under the surface of his skin, a hot red tide. He would not have thought it possible to be so sick and still be conscious.

"Are you going to tell me what's going on," Lascelles snarled, "or are you just going to sit there like a corpse?"

"The wood is on fire," Strafford said. "Someone set it alight." He lowered his voice, so as not to be heard in the back seat. "They know the girls are here, and who they are."

"Who does?" Lascelles barked. "What the bloody hell are you talking about?"

"Probably the fellow in the town, the one you mentioned."

"What's-his-name, Clancy? There was no suggestion he was a serious threat, just a local blowhard."

Lascelles struck the steering wheel with the palms of both hands. The car streaked forward, the beams of its headlights probing the darkness.

They had rounded a long, shallow curve in the road when they saw the Ford stopped at an angle in front of them, blocking their way. Lascelles jammed his foot on the brake pedal and the Bentley slewed sharply to the right, its tyres screaming, and crashed against the hedge and came to a juddering halt with two wheels sunk in the ditch; the engine died, giving a kind of gulp.

Strafford turned to look into the back seat. Celia Nashe had been thrown violently sideways, banging her head against the door frame, and the two girls had toppled over and were piled against her. No one had made a sound, and in the silence they could all hear the ticking of the expired engine.

Lascelles was slumped against the door, apparently unconscious. He looked strangely composed, as if he had been arranged there, with his chin on his chest and

334

his eyes lightly closed. Strafford wondered if he might be dead, but decided he was not — no such luck.

The Bentley's headlights were still on full, and now into their glare two men stepped out from behind the Ford. One was short, broad-shouldered and bald; the other wore a seaman's coat and a woollen hat pulled down to his ears. They were both armed, the one in the hat carrying a sawn-off shotgun, the other a semi-automatic pistol with a wooden stock.

At sight of the second one, Mary in the back seat drew in her breath sharply. Strafford turned to her. "It's him," she said, pointing along the road. "The man with the bird's head."

"It's all right," Strafford said. "He won't hurt you, I promise." He was far less convinced than he sounded.

Now a third man appeared, climbing out of the passenger seat of the Ford, a portly fellow in, of all things, a belted camel-hair overcoat and a black felt trilby with a turned-up brim.

The man in the woollen hat walked forward to the Bentley and rapped the barrel of his pistol on the window at the passenger's side. "Out," he said, gesturing with the gun.

Strafford was about to open the door when he felt something touch his left elbow. It was a small warm hand, holding a metal something. He glanced over his shoulder and saw the glint of Mary's eyes close behind him. He took the pistol from her and dropped it swiftly into the pocket of his trench coat. Then he swung wide the door and stepped on to the road. The man with the gun ordered him to throw down his weapon.

"I'm not armed," Strafford lied.

Afraid though he was, at the same time he could not but gaze in fascination at the man's scorched, scarred face, the twisted mouth and the little beak of a nose; he did look like a bird.

"What the fuck are you staring at?" he snapped.

Celia Nashe opened the back door of the car and stepped out.

"We're security officers," she said, in a crisp, calm voice. "Put your gun away."

The man looked at her and laughed. "The cavalry, are you?" he said. "Well, say hello to us, because we're the redskins." He leaned down to peer into the interior of the car, and saw Lascelles reclining against the driver's door. "Hey, you! You asleep, or dead, or what?" Lascelles gave no response. The man laughed again. He put his head in at the door and peered into the back seat. "Ah, there you are," he said, "my two fine ladies. Come on out of there now, come on. Let the dog see the rabbits, eh?"

The girls emerged slowly, Mary first, followed by her sister, and stood close side by side on the road, in their coats and hats.

"Right, then," the man with the shotgun said. "All present and correct." Celia began to say something but he swung the barrel of the gun and pointed it at her midriff. "Will you shut the fuck up, Mrs Security Officer? Will you do us all that favour?" He hefted the gun, showing it to her. "Unless you want me to cut you in half with this thing."

He held the weapon relaxedly, the first and second fingers of his left hand resting lightly on the trigger; Celia thought of Corporal Lucas, at the firing range outside Guildford, teaching her how to shoot.

Strafford was watching her, and experienced, all at once, a strange, anguished tenderness. He had an urge to reach out and touch her, to lay his hand against her cheek, in the hollow between her shoulder blades, on the back of her neck where her hair was tied in a black elastic band. Instead, turning slightly aside, out of the direct beam of the headlights, he dipped a hand into his coat pocket and curled his fingers around the butt of the pistol that Mary had passed to him. With his thumb he slipped off the safety catch, amazed that he could remember how to do it. His heart was beating floppily like a paddle in his chest, and there was a strange sort of thickening at the root of his tongue, which he supposed must be the effect of fear. He was shivering a little, too, but that, he was sure, was from the fever.

Yet how calm he was!

Everything was retreating before him, retreating and growing small and sharply defined, as in the barrel of a turned-around telescope, while at the same time he seemed to be looking down on the theatrically lighted scene from somewhere at the level of the treetops. Such composure he felt, such strange serenity! The fluttering of blood in his veins was stilled. For a moment he wondered if he had been shot, without noticing it, and was dying, or even dead already. He viewed the prospect with equanimity, almost amused; if this was the end, how trivial a thing it was, after all.

Then Billy Denton stepped out of the darkness of the wood, with his shotgun, and at the same moment, the twin beams of a vehicle's headlamps appeared over the brow of the road in the distance beyond the Ford, and Strafford recognised the sound of the armoured car.

Here's the cavalry, he told himself, arriving too late.

Someone moved, someone said something, he thought it was Celia Nashe, and at once, astonishingly, the shooting began.

CHAPTER
THIRTY-THREE

They left two of the bodies on the road, a stretch of which had been cordoned off by Major de Valera's men, and carried the third up to the house.

All was confusion, and at the same time a funereal silence reigned. In the morning room, whiskey was brought out and administered to the men, while the women drank tea, except for Mrs O'Hanlon, who, at the duke's insistence, permitted herself a small glass of sweet sherry. It was all very decorous and strange, and Strafford was reminded of the evening of his mother's wake, when numerous relatives, most of whom he had thought were dead, gathered in the drawing room at Roslea, wearing tweeds and clearing their throats.

It was Maggie who made the tea, and swan-necked Florence who served it. Strafford, seated by the fire in his trench coat, watched the latter, struck again by her fragile beauty. Perhaps he should have — ? But no, no: he had his private code of behaviour. Yet Florence was a beauty, and he would remember her, and recall her, with wistful melancholy. Going out at the door, she smiled at him, and her smile was somehow a confirmation of what he already knew, that he was no longer what he had been, that he was someone else, a

339

stranger it would take him a long time to become used to, and whose acquaintance he might not entirely welcome.

The duke was dressed now, in a shooting jacket and plus-fours and fawn-coloured worsted stockings. He drank three whiskeys in rapid succession, and then sat down suddenly on an upright chair and looked about him with an expression of dazed dismay.

Lascelles, as soon as he got to the house, had hurried off somewhere, with a look at once urgent and furtive. Strafford wondered if he might have soiled himself — when he had followed the Englishman in at the front door he'd thought he caught a lingering faecal whiff. He also had the suspicion, which he could not shake, that the fellow had not been knocked out when the car plunged into the hedge, but had feigned unconsciousness, as the better part of valour. If so, he thought, it was hardly cricket, now was it, old boy?

The events on the road had been a confusion of livid flashes and curiously flat, muffled bangs, not unlike, Strafford thought, the damp Guy Fawkes Nights of his childhood, which used to be celebrated, or at least marked, by the family and a few friends in a fallow field down behind the tennis courts in the garden.

Billy Denton had shot the man called Jones — his name, in fact, was Seamus Molloy, though he had been nicknamed Birdy, because of his beak-like nose — and Strafford, aiming Celia Nashe's neat little pistol at the bald young man, had by some means managed, to his consternation, to hit the man in the camel-hair coat instead. The bullet caught him along the line of his left cheek and tore off his left ear, a wound that he would, after many weeks on the critical list, manage somehow to survive. De Valera's men had thought he was dead, and only when the meat wagon arrived to pick up the two bodies from the roadway was it discovered that he was still breathing. This was, it turned out, Thomas Clancy, of Clancy & Co., known as the Boss; after that night he was to be for evermore, for the town, plain Tom Clancy.

Celia Nashe sustained a wound that should have killed her.

The bald young man, seeing his companion sent sprawling backwards with a blossom of blood bursting open in his chest — Billy Denton had fired a single barrel, but one had been enough — had got off a panicky rattle of shots from his automatic pistol before turning and fleeing into the wood. One of his bullets caught Celia in her left side, penetrating the spleen and lodging perilously close to the spine — the doctors who treated her and eventually removed the bullet expressed amazement that she should have survived such an insult to her system.

Strafford had knelt on the roadway and cradled the young woman in his arms, murmuring nonsense to her in an urgent undertone; she gave no sign of hearing. Her eyes were open, and she gazed up into the darkness with an expression of blank amazement. A bubble formed between her parted lips, swelled and swelled, and burst — Strafford was convinced he had heard the tiny pop it made.

Lascelles emerged at last from the wounded Bentley, stumbling about and blinking exaggeratedly — at least, his carrying-on had seemed exaggerated to Strafford, who admittedly was biased.

Major de Valera had led his men in a chase after Smith, but in vain. The fellow's real name was Vinnie Considine, and in fact he *had* been a boxer, and had even won a title when he was in his teens. Later, behind the stables, a fire had broken out, which the brigade from Clonmillis was even yet engaged in quelling. The blaze, it was assumed, had been Smith's last vengeful gesture, before he made his way, by clandestine routes, back to Belfast. There he would be arrested, though later released, since he came up with an alibi for the night in question that even the RUC had been unable to break.

"Dear Lord," the duke said, peering unsteadily into his whiskey glass, "how dreadful that such things should happen here."

Celia Nashe had been laid out on a sofa in the downstairs drawing room, wrapped in blankets; by now she was deeply unconscious. Mary, who had managed to get a peep at her before being bundled away, was struck by how peaceful she looked, her face pale and fragile and somehow distant-seeming, like the face of a statue on top of a tomb. Mary felt guilty for having been so awful to her, dubbing her Miss Nasty and making everything so difficult for her, not to mention stealing her gun.

She and her sister were put to bed with aspirins and warm milk and hot-water bottles. Although her sister, who was in shock, had gone willingly enough, Mary had protested loud and long. She had wished to stay close to Strafford. He was her real true love, as she had realised the moment she had slipped the warm pistol into his hand in the car. Obviously Billy Denton was a better shot, but in general he wasn't a patch on Strafford — how could she have taken so long to see that? Well, everyone said love was blind, but thank goodness her sight had cleared before it was too late.

One of Celia Nashe's walking boots had come off when she was being carried into the house, and later in the day it was still in the hall, where it had been forgotten about by the adults. Mary, having got out of bed against Mrs O'Hanlon's protests and crept downstairs, had retrieved it, and had gone down to the kitchen, when no one was about, and put it in the range to burn. She didn't know why she did this; she felt somehow it would help Miss Nashe to recover, though she knew how stupid such a notion was.

The shoe had a rubber sole, and produced an awful smell that was to linger for many days, long after Their Royal Highnesses had departed.

When Strafford and Lascelles arrived at the Hall carrying Celia between them, it was Mrs O'Hanlon who had the presence of mind to telephone for Dr Taggart.

The doctor, who had attended to the ailments of the household for as long as anyone could remember, was a fiercely irascible, brown-faced, bewhiskered little man in a tight tweed suit and chestnut-coloured brogues. He was, for Strafford, the very image of Stevenson's Mr Hyde.

He doffed his tweed ulster and his black hat in the hall and stamped into the room where Celia lay. He saw at once the seriousness of her condition, and shouted at Mrs O'Hanlon for not having called an ambulance straight away. "God damn it, woman, what were you thinking of?"

Mrs O'Hanlon deplored the doctor's language — he was an inveterate swearer — but on this occasion forbore to protest. She was already on the verge of tears. Such a morning!

The ambulance had been dispatched from Tipperary town; it would be some time in coming.

Dr Taggart accepted a glass of whiskey and the last slice of Mrs O'Hanlon's sister's plum cake. He stood in the morning room, glass in one hand and the plum cake on a plate in the other, berating anyone who came within hectoring distance; he had already pronounced the household a "parcel of numbskulls". He had fought in the same company as the duke in the last war, and had been decorated for saving, under heavy fire, the lives of numerous of his fellow soldiers.

The duke asked him for his opinion of Celia Nashe's condition.

"Not a hope, man!" the doctor yelled — his own hearing had been impaired by shell-fire at Passchendaele, and he assumed everyone around him to be similarly afflicted. "Her innards are in a frightful mess, that's

344

plain. She'll be dead before the bloody ambulance arrives."

He was, as so often, wrong.

Lascelles had reappeared, and put in a call to the embassy, and one to London, on the special phone in Celia Nashe's room. Then he had left the house, in his bowler and his British Warm and a pair of borrowed wellingtons, muttering something about needing to "have a look at the poor old motor", and wasn't seen again until dinnertime.

Strafford, too, had slipped away, oppressed by the atmosphere in the morning room, which was slightly furtive, as if evidence of a guilty secret had come to light; afterwards the duke always spoke of it as "the room where the girl nearly died".

Everyone was on edge, afraid there might be more IRA men in the vicinity, and that they might make a direct attack on the Hall. Major de Valera had sent urgently for reinforcements, and by noon a lorry carrying a squad of soldiers had come rumbling and rattling up the drive.

Depressed yet restless, Strafford had wandered about for a while, then had gone into the library and shut the door behind him. Now he sat in his armchair by the fireplace, gazing into the cold embers in the grate, his long bony legs extended before him and his hands sunk in the pockets of his trench coat, which he had still not taken off — he noticed now the smears of Celia Nashe's blood all down the front of it. The blaze in the stable yard had mostly destroyed his quarters, and he had no bed to go to, and he was once more feeling markedly unwell.

Eventually he fell asleep in the chair, and dreamed of being in a green Alpine valley, surrounded by tall peaks and snowy crags and the sweet singing of many small, unseen birds.

Next day he would gather up his stack of borrowed books and return them to the county library. He had hoped to see Miss Broaders, to say a word to her about this and that, but she was away visiting her brother in hospital, who, as it happened, was in a room in the same ward as Celia Nashe. He gave the books into the care of the sub-librarian, who regarded him with an eager light in her eye but had not the nerve to ask for an account of the night's happenings.

He had held one book back, for a keepsake, hiding it rather guiltily under his coat. Years later, when he was moving from his flat in Clare Street, he was to come across the volume again, fallen down behind one of the shelves. He read the title and smiled: *Eustacia Goes to the Chalet School*.

In the morning, after breakfast, a large black motor-car appeared on the drive. Maggie it was who saw it first, and ran to alert Mrs O'Hanlon. Who could it be? Then they remembered: the minister, Mr Hegarty, was due to pay a visit. He was greeted at the front door by His Grace the Duke, who, the minister was surprised to see, was wearing pyjamas under his shooting jacket. The two men gazed at each other helplessly, each of them, in his own way and for his own reasons, lost for words.

The telephones had been going for hours: how was it Dan the Man knew nothing yet of all that had taken place last night? There had been deaths! He was the minister! His brow turned purple. Whatever the reason for his being kept in the dark, someone would be made to pay.

No, he wouldn't come in, despite the duke's insistence, no, thank you, no. He would have to get back to Dublin. He hurried down the steps on his incongruously dainty little feet. Before disappearing into the car again he paused and, leaning a hand on the open door, lifted up one foot to inspect the sole of his shoe, as if he thought he might have trodden in something nasty and tenacious, and extremely difficult to dislodge.

The fire brigade had managed to save all the horses in the stable yard, except one. Prince it was that perished. By the time this news came to the house, the girls were dressed and ready for departure, waiting for Lascelles to take them, under escort, to Baldonnel Aerodrome. There they would board an unmarked Royal Air Force transport plane and be flown without delay to Brize Norton, and thence to an undisclosed location in Scotland. It was decided not to tell Ellen about Prince having been burned to death. Things were bad enough as they were.

Billy Denton came up to survey the damage to the stables. He looked in at the door of Prince's stall. What remained of the animal lay on the ground. One of the

347

creature's eyes, which somehow remained intact, gazed at the young man with bright indifference.

He heard a slow step behind him. It was Pike. He, too, looked in over the charred and blistered half-door.

"Is that the young one's horse?" he asked.

"That's him," Billy said. "What's left of him." He drew a breath. "It was you, wasn't it?" he said.

"Was what me?"

"You think I don't know you, what you are, and who you're in with?" Billy said, turning to him. "You burned this place — you didn't even have the guts to tackle the house itself, you had to burn the stables and destroy this poor animal instead."

Pike spat juicily on the ground. "I hear the Boss Clancy got plugged," he said, in a conversational tone. "Was it you fired the shot?"

"What if it was?"

"It's only, I'd be surprised if it was you," Pike said. "Siding with the crowd that cruelly murdered your poor ma."

Billy was silent for a moment. "I know who shot my mother," he said then, "and it wasn't the Brits. It was your crowd."

"Oh, you know that, do you?"

"Yes, I know it. I always did."

Pike lifted a hand and rubbed his chin, making a sandpapery sound. "Ah, she was a wild one, your poor ma. Aye, wild. She'd go with anything in an army uniform —"

"Shut up or I'll shut you up," Billy said quietly.

348

"The way you did Birdy Molloy? We know well it was you that done for him."

Billy put his hands to the old man's chest and pushed him violently. Then turned and walked away.

"Ah, Billy," Pike called after him, laughing. "Ah, Billy boy, come back."

But Billy went on.

That night Billy got the stove going and after his dinner of tinned beans and mashed potatoes he cleared his plate and cutlery away and got out his photograph album and went slowly through the pages, pausing for a long time at the single image of his mother that was the only memento of her he had. All around him was silent, until suddenly he heard a thump at the door. It wasn't a knock: something had been thrown against it. He stood up slowly, reaching for his shotgun.

Outside in the night there was no one to be seen. He stepped across the threshold, peering into the surrounding darkness. His feet encountered something soft just beyond the threshold. He bent to see what it was. A rook, with its neck wrung.

He felt a sharp sting and a sort of thud in the centre of his forehead, and an instant later heard the shot; after that he saw and heard no more. He didn't feel himself fall.

Pike, in the darkness under the trees, slung the strap of the trusty old Mauser over his shoulder and turned away, making off up the slope, between the slim trunks of the pines, the moon lighting his way. He found the climb hard going, with his bad back. All the same, he was pleased with himself. He had always been a crack shot, and was gratified to know his aim was as true as ever.

In time Celia Nashe recovered, and left the Service. She had no choice. "Sorry, my dear," Manling said. "We had quite begun to think of you as one of the boys." At that moment she came as near to striking him as she had ever done.

Years later, on one of his rare visits to London, Strafford encountered her in the Strand. They had caught each other's eye before he had time to dodge away into the crowd. They went to a Lyons Corner House and ordered a pot of tea, and ate warm scones. They were painfully shy of each other. Dr Taggart had been right about Celia's "innards", for they had never fully recovered from the wounding; also she walked with a marked limp. She had become a schoolteacher. She felt that she was contributing in a small way to the recovery of the nation after the horrors of the war. That was how she said it: *the recovery of the nation after the horrors of the war.* She had not changed.

"Of course," she said, "it's a far cry from the kind of work I did back then, but it's something." She balanced her cigarette on the lip of a china ashtray.

How strange life is, Strafford thought, not, by any means, for the first time.

The ballroom was goldenly aglow under a row of sparkling chandeliers, the countless crystal shards reflecting fragments of the circling dancers. The air was heavy with the mingled aromas of perfumed flesh, of the men's pomades, of rich food and sweet champagne.

She was in the arms of her prince, who was tall and blond and by far the best-looking man in the room. Round and round they swirled, as if on the rim of a great gilded wheel.

Voices, glances, colours, movement.

She was dizzy with happiness.

The prince leaned down and spoke a word into her ear.

The music started up again. She seemed to recognise the tune, seemed to remember it.

"What is it called?" she asked. "Do you know?"

"Eh?" Philip looked towards the orchestra. "It's 'The Merry Widow Waltz', isn't it?"

It was. And at once she saw another ballroom, not at all like this one. A gramophone on the floor, and pressed against her a faded ball-gown smelling of camphor; autumn light beyond the windows, and rain, and far wet trees. A vanished world.

For a second something seemed to catch in her throat.

At a table on a balcony above the ballroom her sister sat, in a pink satin sheath that had cost a fortune, eating a raspberry water-ice and smoking a cigarette in a long ebony holder. Her latest beau sat opposite her, with an elbow on the table and a finger to his cheek. He had smooth hair and nice teeth and a dashing little pencil moustache. He was called Gerald, and worked as a salesman at a car dealer's in Berkeley Square. He was amusing and a smashing dancer, but a bit of a rake; the family disapproved wildly, of course. By now they had probably put MI5 on to him, to try to dig up some choice piece of dirt. She didn't care.

He was going to take her to Ascot next week. That would be fun. She would wear an outrageous hat, and hang on her car dealer's arm the entire afternoon, just to show them.

She looked down on her sister, waltzing with her oh-so-adorable husband. The family loved *him*, of course, even if he was a greasy Greek. She hummed along to the music.

Daah da-da dah, daah da-da dah, dah — dah — dah.

Of course she wouldn't marry Gerald, but he would do for now. He helped to take her mind off things she would rather forget.

Other titles published by Ulverscroft:

THE BLACK-EYED BLONDE

Benjamin Black

It is the early 1950s, Marlowe is as restless and lonely as ever, and business is a little slow. Then a new client is shown in: young, beautiful and expensively dressed, she wants Marlowe to find her former lover, a man named Nico Peterson. Marlowe sets off on his search, but almost immediately discovers that Peterson's disappearance is merely the first in a series of bewildering events. Soon he is tangling with one of Bay City's richest families and developing a singular appreciation for how far they will go to protect their fortune . . .

HOLY ORDERS

Benjamin Black

When a body is found in the canal, pathologist Quirke and his detective friend Inspector Hackett must find the truth behind this brutal murder. But in a world where police are not trusted and secrets often remain buried there is little hope of bringing the perpetrator to justice. Quirke and Hackett's investigation will lead them into the dark heart of the organisation that really runs this troubled city: the Church. Meanwhile Quirke's daughter Phoebe realises she is being followed; and when Quirke's terrible childhood in a priest-run orphanage returns to haunt him, he will face his greatest trial yet . . .